DEADLY SILENCE

Detective Laura Warburton Series
Book Three

JAY DARKMOORE

'And here you are living despite it all.'
- Rupi Kaur

Thank you to my amazing girlfriend, the real *Laura,* who told me to keep following my dreams when I was ready to throw the computer out the window.
Also, to the expert I asked for advice on this topic who told me to 'Google it.'
Thanks for nothing.

Take your experience to the next level and join the Darkmoore community, and receive the exclusive free novella 'Gaslight,' upon sign up.
It's much more than another boring newsletter.
It's an experience.

Scan below

DEADLY SILENCE

DIARY

The perfect love story makes the perfect murder.

Chapter One
Clara
December
Home
Fourteen Days Before Alex's Murder

I lay in the bed wishing that I could die.

It's coming back to me. The longer the day goes on. So fragmented. So sharp to touch. Your love. Your control. It's strangling me. I dare not say a word to anyone about it. I stare at the white chipped walls as I lay here, barely alive in this hospital bed. The buzzing in my ears of my heart monitor, and the feeling of nausea in my stomach from doctors pumping it dry like an arid well...I know you are on your way to take me back to that terrible prison we call a *home*.

What have I done to deserve this? All I did was love you. You were so charming. So caring. Everything I wanted when we first met. It was summer. I will remember it forever. The memory burned into my mind like a branding iron. Your smile. Your charm. The way you looked at me that day in the park when I was out for a run. We bumped into each other. Something so simple. So... innocent. But the most trivial of acts often have the greatest consequences, don't they?

The way you smiled. So much said in that smile alone. You nodded, and went to move away, but I didn't want you to go. Something about your eyes drew me in like a moth to a flame. I wish I would have known then how much you would have burned me. But I couldn't help it. I smiled back and went to continue my run when you called out to me. That's all it took, like a hook in a fish's mouth. You reeled me in. I ask myself even now, why didn't I just keep running? And the answer, Alex? Because I felt wanted. Wanted in a world where I had been given nothing. Do you know what that's like? For someone to want to get to know you, who finds you interesting.

Your small talk was well sculpted, extracting as much information as possible without giving much away of yourself. Your flirting, so sharp it cut right through me. The compliments you uttered, like poetry, noticing things I hadn't even noticed about myself. You knew exactly what to say and how to say it, and you pulled me in right there and then. I told you when we slept together that evening that I didn't do this with strangers I meet in parks.

"Looks like we'll have to make it official, then," you said, your big arms wrapping me tight. Little did I know that hold would only grow stronger, like a viper slowly crushing a mouse. I was completely taken aback by the proposal for us to be together. But I believed in fate, and I was filled with post-orgasmic euphoria, like heroin in my veins. I was hooked on you right there and then.

Exactly what you were counting on.

But how you hurt me, Alex. How you broke me day after day. It's not always physical. I know that, and so do you. Bruises heal. Broken skin mends. But the mental torture. That cuts deeper than wounds can recover. Things you complimented me on, my insecurities, are now your weapon of choice. You starve me. You lock me in the house. You use my body then spit on me when you're done.

The first time I tried to escape, I was hungry, and there was no food in the house. In desperation, I went to beg a neighbour for something to eat. You had locked the cupboards. You decided what and when I ate like I was a dog.

I would have never left the house without your permission before, but I was desperate. There's only so much water you can drink to fill yourself up before the shakes and the drop in blood sugar gets too much to bear.

I went outside and felt like the whole world was watching me. Like someone was going to tell you. Like someone was going to come and find me outside my prison. The wind brushed against my face and the sun kissed my skin, making me feel as if I were stealing this moment from the rest of the world. Like it was not mine.

The front gate was locked, and I didn't have a key, so I had to stand there and wait for someone to pass the gate before asking them to help me. After around ten minutes, maybe longer, I saw a young mother walking with her child in a pram. She eyed me, and I smiled at her, my stomach screaming for some substance.

The mother had a small packet of biscuits at the top of the pram, and they caught my eye. Baby food. That was what I had been reduced to. I stood there, watching her silently pass. I went to speak, but I had lost the ability. There was no point in talking when no one listened to you.

The woman stopped and looked at me. She studied my frame, taken aback by my dishevelled state. I could have brushed my hair or at least tied it up in a bun. First impressions mean everything. Her mouth didn't move, but her eyes said everything they needed to.

"Are you okay?" She said, after a momentary pause. I shifted in my stance. I was freezing. So cold. I had lost so much weight, and my clothes barely fit me anymore, like hanging a vest on a coat hanger and letting it blow and ruffle in the wind. Faced with the contact of another human being, of being able to ask for help, or being able to tell someone what was happening made my throat dry up. I stood there, this young woman staring at me like I was something out of a horror movie, her child sleeping quietly in the pram with a Winnie the Pooh blanket over the top of it.

If I asked for help, you would find out. If I said nothing, then I would be stuck here. I fought mentally about what to do. So many choices, and all of them were going to get me killed.

Without thinking, I snapped my hand out from between the bars of the gate, and grabbed the packet of biscuits, and ran as hard as I could back into the house. My feet slapped against the pavement like a drumbeat, drowning out the woman screaming through the gate.

I slammed the door behind me, and my heart thrummed in my ears. I clutched the pack of biscuits fiercely in my hand. Tentatively, I peered through the window. The woman was standing there, another person from the street joining her.

Why weren't they going away? They needed to move before you came home. Oh god, what had I done? I could have gone out and passed the biscuits back, but that would be worse, wouldn't it? I could eat them, but what did I do with the packet? You would find it and see that I had been bad. Not only sneaking food but stealing from a child and a mother who could have helped me. I was so stupid. So desperate. I moved to the back of the house, and I threw them into the backyard and into a hedge. I couldn't eat them now. They were tainted. My body screamed and ached at the relinquished biscuits. I collapsed onto the floor and watched the clock on the wall tick away like I was awaiting the electric chair. Ticking clocks were never to my liking, yet I couldn't take the batteries out as you said the sound soothed you when you were working in the kitchen. Time seemed to stop, then you came home.

My body became electrified. Then, another worry punched me in my stomach. I hadn't done my list of chores for the day. The list was endless, and to make sure that I did it, you would hide small coins around the house to ensure that I had all of them. I had counted six so far today. But I hadn't been as thorough as usual because I was so tired. The first thing you were going to do was walk through the door and find those coins. Paired with the shouting mother outside and what I had done, I knew you were going to be so upset. More upset than I had ever seen you before.

I heard the door handle turn, and you stepped inside the house. It was like the Devil himself had entered the vicarage, and I felt my skin catch fire. I pulled myself up off the floor and started cleaning the kitchen counter, in a vain attempt to show you I had been good. That I had been a good wife.

You grabbed my hair and pulled my head back, slamming it into the kitchen cupboard. A flash of white exploded in my vision, and I crumpled to the ground. A hard kick to my ribs. A fist to my face. I tried to yell out, to make you stop, but your boot slammed into my stomach and knocked the wind out of me.

I don't remember much after that. I heard the door close a few minutes later when you were done with me, I lay there completely still until the sun died and the night set in, like if I moved, you would come back and hurt me again.

I don't know how long you were gone. Minutes. Hours. I couldn't tell. But when you returned, you peeled me off the floor, your breath stinking of alcohol. You turned the lights on, and put me on a chair, soothing my swollen face with an ice pack.

"I'm sorry," you whispered in the dull kitchen light. "I'm sorry. I don't know what came over me." You gripped my trembling hand lovingly. "I just want us to be good. To be amazing. Happy." Your eyes turned hard, and the grip on my hand got tighter. "But I can't do it alone. You must put the effort in. You must want us to be as incredible as I know we can be. No more mistakes. No more going out of the house. I don't think it's good for you." You took out your phone, connected it to the Alexa, and began to play a song about *Lavender*. I had heard it so many times. You played it every second of every day. I wanted to cry. I wanted to cry so hard, but I wouldn't give you the satisfaction of seeing me hurt. "I'm going to lock the doors from now on," you said. "I'll also be taking the keys. You know how hard I work? How much effort I put in to let us live somewhere like this? In this nice place with nice people? All you have to do is keep it clean and not upset the neighbours. If the neighbours turn against us, then we might have to leave, and everything I have done for us will be for nothing, and that will be because of you." Your face showed no sign of emotion. But your eyes. Oh, how your eyes told the true story. I have seen you shaking hands with others around you, smiling, laughing, and drinking. I had joined you. Your arm around me, keeping up appearances. Then your eyes would change. I could never describe it to someone that hadn't seen it. It was like a switch went on inside. When I saw that look, I knew something bad was going to happen. And you were looking at me with those eyes now, and behind them held only one emotion.

Fury.

"This will never happen again" you hissed. "I won't ask you to clean the house again tonight. If you can pick up where you left off tomorrow." You took out the penny coins you had collected from your hiding places. Two coins in your palm. You dropped them on the table, and their clattering filled the room until they suddenly fell silent. Only your breath split the quiet. "Don't let this happen again," you said firmly, your arms wrapping around me in a loving embrace. You kissed me on my head and released your grip on my hand.

The next day, I didn't know if you had locked the doors. I didn't even try the door handles. You had smoothed things over with the lady I stole the food from. You didn't mention about the biscuits for some reason. Maybe you found it too absurd, a grown woman stealing from a child. But you told the neighbour I was unstable and wasn't well. Also, that I had been hospitalised for trying to kill myself and that you had to keep the knives and other sharp objects locked away. With that, the lady went about her day, and I was just a story to gossip with her friends over. The poor, crazy lady at the big house on the street that steals food from passing prams. I would have laughed if I had had the energy.

The next day, I tried to escape again. I went to the kitchen cupboard and opened it up. I took out everything I could find – Drain cleaner. Bleach. Washing up tablets. You name it. I couldn't take it anymore. I hadn't eaten in three days. My neighbours thought I was crazy. I couldn't run. I couldn't fight. I had no control over my life, and this was the only way I could take that control back.

I poured the contents of every bottle I could find from under the sink into a glass. The cocktail of chemical goodness stared at me, swirling in a fragrant mixture that turned a septic yellow, like drinking aromatic pus. This was it; I was going to do it. I was going to be free. I took the glass, and with all my might, I forced the toxic cocktail down my gullet.

I have never felt pain like it, each gulp like swallowing acid. My throat itched from the crumbled washing tablets. The bleach burned the moment it touched my lips, and the fumes burned my eyes. I could feel blisters forming all the way down my throat.

I dropped the glass about halfway, shattering it onto the floor. I stumbled, the chemicals dissolving my insides. You weren't due home for several hours. I should have written you a note, telling you how much I hate you, how much you were was going to pay for what you had done to me. I wish I could have done it outside publicly with an audience, and tell them all, every mother fucking one of them that stared at me whenever I left the house and got into the car, that I was a victim. That this was my way of taking control back.

It hurt. God, I can still remember how much it hurt. It was like someone was taking a chainsaw to my insides. My stomach began to tear itself apart, and I buckled over, clinging to the table as my body rejected the substances, and a mixture of blood, scorched flesh, bile, and chemicals ejected from my mouth. I couldn't feel the burning on the way out. Either the adrenaline was blocking the pain, or I had burned away the nerve endings. I crumpled to the floor, my world dying away, and a sanguine smile crept along my face. Somehow, I ended up outside covered in leaves and brambles, collapsed on the ground. And the next thing I know is I am lying here in this bed, and I can hear your voice in the distance.

Chapter Two

Clara
The Hospital
Twelve Hours Before Alex's Murder

Everything was black. I heard them operating. Cutting. Suctioning. It came in waves and then I would fall back into nothingness. I heard your voice. Heard them telling you I was on the brink of death, and I heard you cry. Oh, how you wept and sobbed by my bedside while others were watching. Night after night, I heard you bleeding your heart out, and then I heard your sinister whispers when the lights went out.

Day after day, the staff saw to me, until I was more alive than dead. The first time I opened my eyes fully, the room was blurry. White and greys. Blinking lights and buzzing machines. My first sensation wasn't relief, but dread. Dread not that I survived, but that I could recognise the sound of your shoes clicking on the floor of the hospital ward. My skin begins to crawl as I hear your voice and your footsteps grow closer to me. Nurses moving to and fro between the sick and the dying, clinking spent syringes. Changing drips of patients who groaned and moaned. I lay there for hours. They came. They changed my clothes. My drips. My bedding. Yet I stayed silent. I dared not speak, Alex. I dared not speak because I was afraid of what would come out of my mouth. You can't unhear something, and you can't unsay something.

I focused on the window by the side of my bed. Tall buildings and busy highways. The vast hills in the distance stretched into the encroaching dawn which morphed the dark sky into something resembling candy floss being set on fire. Like a dark shroud devouring me, you stood by my bedside with a nurse.

"Hey," you said. I could feel my body tensing up. I stared at the wall. Every fibre of me wanted to shoot up and run as fast as I could out of the ward. You had found me. I knew it wouldn't take long. I just hoped I could have a little more time with my thoughts before you came to take me away.

Why did I do it? Why did I leave the house?

You spoke eloquently. Friendly. Even lovingly. Your charm so vicious and disarming. I could feel myself tensing up, but I hid it. I had learned how to do that. To show no emotion. To be stoic. Still. Well-mannered and well-behaved. I could smell the perfume emanating from you. Floral. You have been with someone again. I am not mad about it. Not for me. I wish you would vanish into the air and never come back. No. I am sorry for the poor creature you are working your way into, like a virus that infects the host. You are a parasite, Alex. A dirty parasite that leeches off women and drinks them dry until you discard them and throw them to the wayside like a piece of rubbish.

The weight of the bed depressed as you sat down. Your hand running through my hair, playing with it in your fingers. You always said how much you loved my hair. How much you liked the way I wore it. You always let me take care of it. It was for you, I know. It made me more pretty to look at. Allowed me to cling onto something of my old self.

"How has she been?" You said to the nurse. The nurse replied in kind. My vitals were steady, and that I had come out of the induced coma well. I was touch and go for a little while. My third suicide attempt this month. Another failure, and I knew you were revelling in it. "She's been struggling a lot recently," you said, like I wasn't even here, just an inanimate object in the corner. "I'll take her home, and I will follow up with the mental health worker tomorrow." Mental health worker. I don't have one, Alex. You don't believe in them. You told me I should toughen up and get a grip on my emotions, whilst simultaneously breaking me and beating me to a pulp. I close my eyes tightly, forcing back the tears. I want someone to stop you. Third suicide attempt this month. I haven't ever tried to hurt myself before meeting you. Surely the notes will tell them that. I can feel myself screaming behind my sealed lips, screaming for someone, anyone, to save me. To take me away. To throw me on a plane to the middle of nowhere where you couldn't find me. But the nurse continued talking, soothing you, telling you about my care plan in the hospital. Then, my ears prick up, and as she says the words, you stop stroking my hair, and I feel your grip on my skull tighten. Not enough for anyone to notice. But enough for me to know that I should stay deadly silent.

"I would like her to speak to a mental health worker here, while she is in the hospital," the nurse says. "This was a narrow escape, Mr. Weaver. I want Clara to speak to someone in private."

In private? Was this my chance to say something? Was I being offered a lifeline? Your grip tightened.

"That won't be necessary," you say. "She's not well. I will take her home. We have home carers and cleaners that come in and look after her daily. I will work from home the next few days. Not let her out of my sight." I can hear that you're smiling while you're speaking, using that charm you have perfected, but unlike everyone around us, I can hear the slight hint of malice in your voice. Not intended for the nurse. No. That would be silly, and you aren't an idiot. All the things that you are, an idiot isn't one of them. It's what makes your cruelty so vicious. I hear the nurse shifting in her stance.

Please. Oh god, please don't believe him. I clench the bedsheets tighter, staring at that wall, willing it to crumble and fall around me.

"No," the nurse reiterates, standing her ground. "I will get the consultant. Clara needs to speak to someone in private." I can feel the heat radiating from you. You don't like being told no. Hated being out of control. You control every aspect of my life, from when I eat, sleep, and drink. To when I can shower, to how hard I must scrub the floors of the kitchen until the chemicals make me feel sick and filter into my raw hands. You control business. Money. An empire. Taking over from your dead, silent partner Hugo Black. And yet you can't control this nurse who you see as a worm under your boot. And that is driving you insane.

"Look," you said, posturing yourself up. "I know what you're doing. You're looking after her. You're doing your job. It's what makes the NHS so amazing. Not like the private hospitals we usually go to. Yes, they have better facilities. Better staff. Better training, in fact," you lick your lips. I can hear that tongue sliding along your stubble. "But," you continued, "You care, and that's something money can't buy. I mean, how old are you? How long have you been doing nursing?" The nurse takes in a sharp breath, gripping her clipboard tighter.

"*That* doesn't matter," she said. "I am in charge, and what I say goes." You laugh. A little laugh. A warning sign. The bed releases its pressure as you stand up. I dare not look, but I know you're towering over the nurse by an easy nine inches.

"I'm going to take her home right now," you say, a lick of venom in your words. "If you want to call the police, then fine. But I have spotted several things wrong on this ward while I have been here." Your tone turned hard. "Do you know who I am? I could wrap this ward in so much red tape that your patients will be outside in the street by the time I am done with it." You stop talking. It feels like the air from the room has been sucked out. I can't breathe. My heart is beating out of my chest like a violent drum. Finally, the nurse speaks.

"She's been in a coma for nearly two weeks," the nurse said meekly, her will being crushed under your might.

"I'm taking her home." A silence so charged you could spark a wire from it. Then, dread consumed me as the nurse surrendered.

"I will get her discharge papers." My world implodes around me. You have done it again. Pushed and bullied your way into getting what you want. The power of your profession radiates off you. I feel like there is a blanket of chains wrapped around me that I can't take off. I had a chance. A chance to escape. A chance to finally talk and let that locked box behind my lips spill out for the world to see. This time, it would be different. They would believe me. They would *have to* believe me. But would I have said anything if given the chance, knowing you were only a few feet away? Would I have dared speak and divulge what had happened, and sit in the waiting room for the police to get here, watch you be taken away in handcuffs for you to just walk out and find me again, shaking hands with your solicitor who got you off without any reprimand or charge? It was a fool's game. I was trapped, and my latest escape attempt had only wrapped me tighter in the chains I didn't think could constrict any further.

The nurse reached over the bed and touched my hand. A loving touch. A caring touch. Something I hadn't felt in a long time. I tried to hold it back, but a stray tear fell from my face and dotted onto the bed. My body betraying me. I had let the secret out, and the nurse had seen it. I knew it. In my attempt to tighten myself up, roll myself into a ball so tight that I couldn't give anything else away, I felt the warmth spread from my legs and soak into the bed. The smell was potent. Dehydration and chemicals mixed together. Like a little girl who couldn't hold it in, I pissed myself, soaking my legs. The nurse recoiled, and I knew you were going to make me pay for the betrayal.

"Baby," you said, that hand running through my hair again. Soft and caring. A ploy. A master of disguise. "You had an accident. Maybe you should stay here a little longer." This was my time. If I wanted to get away from here without being punished, I *had* to tell the nurse that I was okay. That I *wanted* to go back home. But again, nothing passed my lips. A silent scream rampaging my psyche until it was all I could hear, like a loud drone in my mind.

"I'll be right back with some clothes and her discharge notes," the nurse said, before disappearing. In her absence, the room seemed to grow smaller. The sun could die in the sky right now and I wouldn't notice. The only thing in the world now was you. You and only you, like a rat trapped by a rottweiler in the corner. The jaws of death inches from its face, growling and snarling for flesh.

"I love your hair," you said. You ran your fingers through it gently. What game was this? I waited for the sharp tones to come splitting through the air in a malicious whisper, but instead you stroked my head and soothed me. I fought back the tears as fiercely as I could, feeling the dampness beneath me grow. The stench of my betrayal filling the space between me and the Devil, like drawing blood in the ocean and waiting for the shark fins to appear. "When we get home, I'll run you a bath and cook you something. Would you like that? I'll take the rest of the day off and we can sit and watch a movie together. Just like we used to. We haven't done that in so long. How does that sound?" This was killing me. You're killing me, Alex. You're making me feel things that I don't want to feel. Things I have told myself that aren't real. You're playing, manipulating. But I wanted it. I wanted to feel your touch, a loving touch, the touch I remember so badly. I want us to be happy like we were at the start. Before all this. I wanted it.

The nurse came back a few minutes later. She wasn't alone.

"This is him," she said. The security guard was standing tall, a black stab vest and a body camera with a flickering red light on top. "C'mon," the nurse said. "The police are on their way."

The police? Oh god, no. What have you done...

I don't know what I was expecting. You wouldn't fight or threaten. That wouldn't work now. But you wouldn't leave me alone with these people. The doctor standing behind the security guard. The second nurse that had appeared with the rest of the rabble. You wouldn't dare leave me alone, less I speak, would you? You stood up, straightened your clothing, and agreed to go. But before you left, you leant in and kissed my forehead.

"See you later," you whispered, and I knew that if I said anything, if I dared give away what was behind my lips, if I broke the silence of your control, then you would make sure I would never open my eyes again. I knew then. When I leave this building, you are going to kill me.

I don't know what happened next. I was standing, being checked over by a doctor. Being probed. I forgot the number of times they asked me *how did I get this bruise? Is this a burn? When was the last time you ate?* Meanwhile, Alex was being held somewhere. I don't know where, but I knew he would be getting angrier and angrier by the minute. They took me into another room to speak to someone. A consultant. A nurse. I don't know. Everything was a blur, and all I could think about was how much I wanted to talk but dared not. Kind faces. Soothing words. Experts in this, advocates of that. Safeguarding. Referrals. All these people that could help. Wanted to help. Wanted to believe what I was going to say. But I couldn't. I couldn't say a word. And he knew it. Alex. Alex knew that no matter what happened, he would walk away free.

"I just need to go grab someone," the doctor said. I don't know his name. My mind focused on the beating of my heart. The body map of my bruising on the clipboard. My mental health history. My suicide attempts. Notes. Weight. Height. Blood type. Complications. You name it. It was all there. My entire life rendered into data on a piece of paper. The doctor left me alone in a silent room. The walls were a lime green. A pin board of every type of charity you can think of with little pull ties that people had taken with the number attached of those who can help. Some tabs were missing, which made my misery amplify. But then, underneath that swirling abyss of despair, a flicker of hope began to emerge, like a candle in a hurricane that refused to extinguish. I felt that this was it. This is what I needed to happen. I was petrified, but I dared to dream that these people could help me. Maybe I could finally open up…

The fire alarm ripped through the silence, and my fingers gripped the blue couch under me tightly like I was sitting on a roller coaster about to fly down a huge dip. I heard screaming outside. The pushing of weight. And then the door flung open, bouncing off the wall. You stood there enraged, your eyes like pits of fire. You didn't say anything, only charged in like a bull and grabbed me and pulled me by the arm and forced me into a wheelchair. Nurses and doctors tried to help, but there were so many people in the corridors. A flood of people evacuating the hospital with the sounding of the alarm. You had done it, Alex. I nearly got away from you, and you managed to get me out of there in full view of everyone. You pushed me along the car park quickly, the wheelchair squeaking, screaming, like it knew what was going to happen when I got home. I wanted to scream, to run, to lash out. But your hold on me was too powerful. Too strong, and I let you take me away.

"We'll be okay, Clara," you said as we got closer to your car. I could see it in your eyes. There was no love for me there, and as I saw the sun rise high into the sky, I knew that this would be the last sunrise I would ever see.

Chapter Three
Laura

Laura stood over the man who had been cut down from his hallway cupboard, the washing line still wrapped around his neck.

"What do we know, Sergeant?" Francis said. Laura eyed him.

"Well," she said. "He isn't getting up dancing anytime soon." Francis let out a small, morbid laugh. Dry excrement and bodily fluids covered the carpet beneath their feet. Laura guessed the guy had been hanging there for around five weeks, as the calendar in the kitchen was still showing mid-October. Not to mention the decomposition levels. His fingers had gone completely black, and most of his eyes had been eaten away. Nature liked to take those first. There were no maggots though, thankfully. They had eaten their fill. "We have a name?" Laura said, turning to Francis.

"Ryan Gerrard," Francis said, looking through his notes. "No trace PNC. Neighbours never heard from him. Kept himself to himself. Phone an old brick thing. Probably barely got used. From the calls and message logs, he had the local GP surgery in his contacts and that's it." Laura eyed the dead man that had been laid out on the carpet. The responding officers muttered that Gerrard had missed his last three appointments, as reported by the mental health worker concerned about his safety. One was normal. Two was worrisome. But three meant he had probably topped himself. Turned out this time, they were right.

"Family?" Laura said, getting to her feet. Francis

shook his head.

"None that we can find. Nothing in the system. Guy is a ghost."

"Complete recluse?" She stood and stretched herself out. "Maybe do some checks with the hospital. See if we can find anything on the next of kin for him." Francis nodded, making some notes. He stood eyeing the body, filling out the paperwork for the undertakers who were on their way. Laura wandered into the rest of the small flat.

"Francis," Laura called from the living room.

"Yeah?" Francis said, the pen stopping scratching on the pad of paper, the silence around them closing in.

"I think I have cracked the case." Francis moved to her. Laura was standing in front of the window, a sheet of black outside. Dawn was beginning to break over the distant horizon.

The deceased man's flat was on the first floor, and from his window, they could see a row of terrace houses across a grass verge with pop-up football nets. Laura pointed to the darkness.

"What do you see?" Francis eyed the window and shrugged.

"Nothing." Laura smiled.

"Well, it's obvious," she said. She pointed to the pair of binoculars on the windowsill, then reached behind the television cabinet that was tucked into the wall, which, instead of housing a TV, had an old-style radio player that Laura figured would be worth a bit of money if it hadn't been completely devoured by dust and rot. "We have a lone man living on his own with no friends or family. We have a pair of binoculars facing a small estate, and a radio that would have been playing." Laura looked out into the darkness with the binoculars. "So, I think what happened is that on those long, lonely nights, he'd turn on the radio, sit here with the lights off, and stare out into the estate with his binoculars at some young woman's window." She scanned the darkness, and just as she predicted, there was a house across the way, the back window facing them, and a 'SOLD' sign was visible. She smiled and peeled the binoculars away. "Yeah, just as I thought," she said. "He's been eyeing up some pretty young thing that lives in the houses along the way. She moved away, and he couldn't handle it. He could have stuck something on the television to satisfy his craving for the flesh, but he doesn't have one, does he? Not even a smart phone for porn. So, what does he do? No hot girl next door. No Porn Hub to wank over. So, he strings himself up." Francis looked at Laura, perplexed.

"He hung himself because he was horny and alone?" Francis said, his face stoic. Laura shrugged.

"People have done weirder things for weirder reasons." They shared a pause, and then both began laughing.

"Nice to know you haven't lost your sense of humour," Francis said. "It's good to have you back." Laura put some nicotine gum in her mouth.

"What else am I going to do? Fucking write for a living? I haven't lost my mind just yet." She smiled a wry grin, then surveyed the dead man's flat. Blank walls. No paint. No wallpaper. No pictures. The carpet on the floor was a worn-out pale blue, and the kitchen was bare, with a single tartan dishtowel strewn over the draining board. A man who had literally nothing in his life was robbed of the only bit of pleasure he had. She wondered how many people each day do something innocuous, such as hold a door open for someone, say good morning, let someone out in traffic, or even send a text to a friend that they should go for coffee in a few days makes the world of difference. Someone on the edge who is shown kindness by someone they will never ever see again. "Right then," Laura said. "Let's leave this lot to it," she said, eyeing up the response officers that were filling out more paperwork. She moved to a uniformed Sergeant. "No suspicious circumstances. Hung himself because he was robbed of a hard on. Have a good night."

Laura and Francis stepped out into the dawn. Laura placed another fresh nicotine gum into her mouth. It burned her tongue as she chewed it, and tasted like rat shit, but she hadn't picked up a cigarette in nearly twelve months. She hadn't had a drink in thirteen months and four days. Not like she was counting.

"You haven't lost your flare, have you?" Francis said, the wind ruffling the lapel of his trench coat. Laura figured he had been watching too much Sherlock Holmes since her departure and subsequent return to front-line duty.

"It's all I have," she said with a smile. A couple of kids ran past kicking a football. Parents probably had no idea, or care, about where they were.

"What's happened?" One of the kids shouted, holding up their mobile phone, no doubt recording live on social media.

"Shark attack," Laura responded. The kid eyed her, puzzled, before vanishing off with his friend who was toking on a vape. "God, when did I get so old?" she asked, shaking her head.

"You're only thirty-five."

"Thirty-Six."

"Still, you're not dead yet."

"Not yet," Laura said. They approached the car and slipped in. Laura in the passenger seat. Francis in the drivers. Laura grabbed the radio from her jacket. "DS Warburton to control."

"Go ahead."

"We're leaving the death on Leigh Street. Suicide. Duty undertaker is en route. Response will hold the scene. No idea who the next of kin is if that can be tasked out for enquiries."

"I thought you said we were going to the hospital?" Francis said, leaning in.

"Cancel that control my oppo has just remembered we have it covered. I must be getting old." She placed the radio back in her jacket and scowled at Francis. He shook his head and laughed. "Just get us to the hospital," she said. "We've got a long day ahead of us. We've only just started the shift and we've seen a dead body. Only downhill from here."

"You never know," he said, putting the car into reverse and pulling out of the driveway. "This might be straightforward." Laura shook her head and chewed the gum some more.

"I bet you a coffee it isn't."

The pair drove through the awakening streets under the lazy morning sun. Winter had gripped the country by the balls, and the nights were growing longer by the day. It was early December. Christmas lights had been erected, and there was always some shit on the radio.

"Any thoughts about Christmas?" Francis said. Laura shook her head.

"I'll probably work. My therapist said to avoid a lot of social gatherings as I'm still at high risk of relapse."

"Twelve months on?"

"Thirteen months, one week and four days," she said with a smile, looking out the window.

"Well," Francis said, "I think it's great how well you're doing. Whatever makes it easier."

"I appreciate that," Laura said. "So yeah. Probably be working. The grind never stops." Francis nodded.

"It doesn't indeed." They continued on and Laura checked her emails while Francis navigated the streets. "How was rehab, anyway?" He said. Laura's face remained like stone. Images filling her mind of being up all night, screaming into her pillow while her bones ached, and she lost her bodyweight in sweat.

"Like a holiday," she said, "but louder." They drove closer to the city centre, planning to grab a McDonald's breakfast before going to the hospital to complete the paperwork for the hanging. Then it would be death message, and probably a coroners file. Then coroner's court. Property tasks. The works. *People have no idea how much of a pain in the arse taking their own lives is,* Laura thought, as she watched the myriad of Christmas lights pass them.

They sat in the line of standing traffic for a few minutes, Laura's patience growing thin. "What's the hold-up?" She spoke. The sea of brake lights taunted her and promised her a long day ahead at the office, assuming she ever got out of the car and felt the touch of tarmac on her feet again. She checked the Google Maps. The journey that should be a fifteen-minute drive showed solid red all the way, looking to take over an hour. Time she didn't want to waste breathing in Francis' farts. Francis tried to look past the other cars ahead. The morning fog descended over them. Laura only noticed it then. They were approaching a bridge. A very big bridge. Her skin began to prickle. Something was wrong.

"For fuck's sake," she whispered, pinching the bridge of her nose.

"You say something?" Francis said, still craning his neck past the traffic in front of him. Someone in front got out of their car and began waving their hands at other drivers. Laura didn't know what they were hollering at, but the sinking feeling in her stomach told her it wasn't good.

The fog moved in quickly, encasing them in a thick grey blanket that had been pulled over them, suffocating them from the morning sun. Laura eyed the stillness around her, then grabbed her radio. "DS Warburton to force control."

"Go ahead, Laura."

"Is anything happening on the A580? We've got a serious backlog of traffic. We got an RTC or something?"

"Let me check." A few seconds ticked by. "Control to DS Warburton."

"Go ahead."

"Looks like we've got a jumper on the ledge. We've got patrols making." Laura felt the sinking feeling in her stomach grow and swell like she was slowly being lowered into the black abyss of the Challenger Deep. If there was one thing she didn't enjoy, it was talking someone off a bridge. She had done her negotiator training, but she was rusty. They could just sit by and wait for patrols to get there, but she couldn't do it. She would have to take charge. First week back at the MIU and she had been to a suicide and now heading to a jumper. Was it a full moon or something?

When it came to those wanting to take their own lives,

it was a roll of the dice. Nine out of ten times, they just needed someone to talk to. A cry for help. But there were other times when it didn't matter how much you spoke to them; they were leaving that bridge in the form of a swan dive. Men and women were different. Women were more impulsive. More emotional, but less likely to go through with it. A woman on a bridge may have been in a bad place and stepped over the other side as a spontaneous act. Men, however, were more likely to plan their demise and less likely to tell anyone about it. Then there were mood disorders, personality disorders, and those seeking attention, which Laura hated even thinking about. They say if you don't think anyone cares about you, don't pay your mortgage. That's bullshit. If you want attention, stand on a bridge. You will have the attention of the police, fire services, mental health workers, doctors, social workers, care placements, domestic violence specialists, Psychiatrists, secure units, family, friends, and ambulances. You name it. Stand on a bridge, and you're the most famous person in town.

"What's going on?" Francis said, pulling Laura from her thoughts.

"You owe me that fucking coffee, that's what," Laura said, grabbing her body armour from the back seat. He went to speak, but Laura didn't hear him. She was already out the car and marching her way up the road. She eyed the grey in front of her. The brake lights creeping along slowly. The railings and structure of the bridge coming into view, bleeding through the thick soup of the descending fog. Laura collected her thoughts. Officers were on their way, but with the build-up of traffic, the morning rush hour, the weather.

They would be held up, which could be too late. The on-call negotiator could take upwards of an hour to get here. She had to make the call. She had to do something to help whoever was on the wrong side of that bridge having the worst day of their life.

Laura arrived at a crowd of onlookers at the top of the bridge, staring into the grey abyss below. She flashed her badge to the crowd.

"Police officer," Laura announced. "What's happening?" To Laura's surprise, a paramedic was standing in the crowd.

"You got here fast," he said. He looked around quizzically. "Where's the rest of you?" Laura stared at him like a dog was meowing.

"What do you mean?" She said. Only then did she notice the ambulance pulled onto the walkway across the bridge. "She a patient?"

"I don't know," the paramedic said. He was young, maybe twenty-five, with short-cut dark hair and a slim build.

"What do you mean, you *don't know?*" Laura barked.

"A neighbour called us about a woman covered in blood three miles away. We attended, picked her up, and headed to the hospital. She dove out of the ambulance and climbed over the railing when we got stuck in traffic." If throttling in public wasn't so frowned upon, Laura would squeeze the life out of the paramedic for letting this happen.

"Okay," Laura said, teasing the word from her lips because *'you fucking idiot'* wasn't appropriate. "What's her name? Age?" The paramedic's face went vacant.

"I have no idea," he said. "She hasn't spoken a word since we picked her up."

"She's going to jump," she heard one of the crowd

say. "Are you going to do anything?" Laura withdrew from the paramedic, who seemed to have the same number of brain cells as an old leather shoe. She peered over the edge into the spiralling grey. She couldn't see anyone, and her blood ran cold. The fog circling below them. Laura had never lost anyone. Not yet. She had talked eighteen people down from rooftops, bridges, and even got someone to pull the handgun from their temple. Eighteen souls saved by her in her career. Eighteen people who got to wake up another day and make things better.

Laura looked down past the walkway and then down into the safety railings. The sight of thick chains swaying in the air, like mechanical arms clinging to the bridge structure from the grey below. She scanned the blue and chipped paint of the bridgework. Rusted ladders. The sound of the fixtures bending and creaking. Cars creeping past slowly.

Then, as the clouds parted for a second, she saw the figure of a woman standing, holding onto a rung of the ladders. She was dressed lightly, in nothing but a pair of pyjama shorts and a thin top. Her hair was shaved short. Skin as white as snow. Her bare feet on the steel netting under the main body of the bridge. Laura saw it. She was coated in crimson. Laura took out her radio, shouting over the wind.

"DS Warburton to control."

"Go ahead."

"I have eyes on the person on the bridge. IC1 female, around age twenty to twenty-five. Slight build. ETA on patrols?"

"Eight minutes DS Warbu —" She pulled the radio from her ear. Francis appeared by her side, and he looked over the precipice of the bridge and stepped away, putting his hands on his knees.

"I don't do heights," he said, catching his breath. Laura had to think quickly. The traffic wouldn't help the situation. Not with them blaring their horns, recording on their phones, and rubbernecking. Paired with the fog, this was an accident waiting to happen. "What do we know?" Francis said. Laura eyed the empty space with venom.

"Someone is going to get their arse chewed, is what," Laura spat before marching to the paramedic who stood with his hands in his pockets. "Has anyone tried speaking to her yet?" The paramedic shook his head. No one else around her spoke up. "I need all of you back in your cars immediately." The crowd moved as directed, like being carried away by the Pied Piper. Laura addressed the paramedic. "Block the traffic with your ambulance," she barked.

"I can do that?"

"If you don't want me to tell your boss that you let a woman escape from your ambulance, then yes, you'll do what you're fucking told and smile while doing it." The paramedic moved quickly like a bad dog being shouted at by its owner. He jumped into the driver's seat and threw the ambulance in front of crawling traffic trying to cross the bridge. "Francis," she ordered, grabbing his shoulder. "I need you to clear this traffic from the immediate area, then bring your car up to the front and block the road from the other side. I need quiet when I speak to her."

"We should wait for patrols," he said breathlessly, trying not to look over the edge of the bridge, his face turning pale. "The negotiator is on their way," Laura leaned in close.

"We don't have time," Laura said. "She's barely

dressed. She'll freeze and fall anyway."

"But," he stammered. Laura pushed him in the chest and pointed to the line of traffic. Just do it." Francis said nothing further. He raced back to the unmarked car and drove on the wrong side of the road before pulling sharply across it, blocking the creeping traffic. The silence that followed was ominous, just the blowing of the wind through her hair. She listened for the sound of patrol cars in the distance, hoping desperately. But no sirens met her ears. The cloud cleared, and she saw her again, vacantly staring into the void, clinging onto the metal beams. She was covered in blood, her clothing, her arms, and even her feet.

What have you done? Laura thought. She took a breath, gathered her thoughts, and stepped to the edge of the railings.

Chapter Four
Laura

"Hello?" She shouted down to the spiralling grey. "Can you hear me?" The cold cut into Laura's bones. She scanned the grey for movement. Then she saw the pale face of a woman that wished for death staring back up to her. Her face coated in crimson. "Can you hear me?" The woman didn't respond. The clouds parted. She must be freezing. Laura needed to get her off quickly, before she got hypothermia, and she took a tumble off of the edge. "My name is Laura," she said, calling down from the railings. The girl was an easy three metres below her. Maybe more. The wind abated a moment, the ensuing silence unnerving. Not even the birds dare soar this high.

Francis appeared behind her. "What do we have?"

"Young female, picked up by ambulance. Got out the back and then went railing hopping. She's covered head to toe in blood."

"Whose blood?"

"You know as much as me. Go find out more information, I'm working." Laura batted him away. She didn't care if he thought her a bitch; she needed her attention on the woman on the bridge, not the feelings of her colleague. Francis moved away, pulling his radio to his lips. "What's your name?" Laura called down. The girl vanished in the fog again. "I can't see you. Will you do me a favour and come up a little bit?" Nothing moved in that grey. She had a silent one. They were usually the hardest to gauge. Fighting an internal battle in their heads. The ones who screamed and shouted and spoke about ending it all were the easiest to talk down. You knew what they were thinking, and they would enter into dialogue.

Sometimes, they just aren't getting off that bridge. She hoped to God this wasn't her first loss. Her recovery was fragile. If she lost this girl, Laura might lose herself again. She couldn't let that happen. The clouds parted again. "What's your name?" Laura shouted. The girl looked up at Laura. Her eyes were devoid of emotion, like staring at a doll.

"Why don't you come back up here, and we can talk? You being down there makes it hard for me to hear you." The girl continued to stare. A beat of silence went by. "Whatever has happened," Laura said. "We can fix it." She gestured to her hands and arms. "Did you hurt yourself?" Laura shouted. "Do you need a hospital?" The girl looked up at Laura. She stepped closer to the edge, like she was toying with the idea. Laura's knuckles grasped the railings. "Don't!" Laura said, then pulled her emotions back. "Don't move any further." The girl was going to jump. She looked cold and had either hurt herself or someone else. She was standing closer to the edge, not responding. This girl was not stepping over those railings. Laura knew what she had to do. Turning, she saw Francis standing there, speaking into the radio and relaying what was happening. "I need to go over," Laura said quickly. Francis' mouth dropped.

"Don't you dare," he said, jaw dropping.

"She's not coming over," Laura said. "I have no choice." Francis rushed to Laura to grab out at her, but she was already clambering over the railings and moving to the ladder. He called after her, but the wind picked up, and then the clouds eclipsed him from her view.

The girl was a few metres below her by the time she reached the ladders. She was on a metal walkway, maybe a foot thick. Laura's heart jackhammered. The wind bit into her body, fiercely cold, like knives of ice carving into her. She got closer, then with shaking boots, began her descent down to the platform where the girl was standing.

Laura got to the bottom rung of the ladder. The girl a meter away from her. Laura called out to her, for her to move closer to her, to step away from the edge. All around them was a spiralling grey. The sound of sirens in the distance. The clouds smudged with flashing reds and blues. It was like she was in another world. Only her and this woman, who was three inches from annihilation. The blood coated on her arms was thick. She grabbed hold of the ladder as she stretched out as far as she could to grab the woman, Laura's brow bursting with sweat. Her body flushing with heat. Laura knew she had to let go of the ladder, meaning there was nothing stopping her from falling to oblivion. One strong gust of air. One wrong move, and she would find herself rapping on the door of hell. Laura let go of the ladder rung and stepped onto the thin platform. She steadied herself, her hair blasting around her face like angry red worms. Slowly, she moved inch by inch, her fingers an eyelash away from the woman.

Without warning, the girl turned to face Laura. Her face was that of someone who had been destroyed in every way imaginable, and Laura, for a second, saw her own life in those hollow eyes.

"She did it," the girl said before leaning back into the abyss.

Chapter Five
Clara
Home
Two Hours Before Alex's Murder

The hospital melted away, and then soon, the familiar streets of our neighbourhood appear. I felt like I was in a dream. I had been taken. Taken from under the watch of those who were there to care for me. To keep me safe. It wouldn't be long now. You were getting desperate. The hold of your control slipping away. What had I done. My escape. My desperation. I had tipped you over the edge. I was going to die, and they say that a sense of peace falls over you when you accept the coming of death, like a warm blanket that envelops you. But I didn't feel peace. Calm. Relaxation. All I felt was terror, and as I looked at you – your mouth moving. Face red. Your spittle slapping the windscreen, words lost in a cacophony of insults, screaming and manic laughter. I knew the sun I could see in the sky would be the last shred of daylight I would ever see.

High trees that had shed their leaves stood over us like a skeletal entourage at a funeral march. We pulled up to the gated entrance. Our home. My prison. Detached with a front and rear garden. A balcony that overlooked the rest of the estate when I would, at one time, enjoy sipping a glass of wine by the garden table and chairs you had laid out. The distant sound of cars filtering through the silence of the night. But those days standing out on the veranda with a glass of lemonade, had long since been forgotten. My walks on the treadmill replaced by making sure the house was immaculately clean. I had asked you if we could hire a housekeeper, that the work was too much. I don't know why I did this. It was a challenge to the status quo. In reality, I just wanted someone else to talk to. You screamed at me and punched me to the side of the head. It was your place of choice. My hair was thick. Bruises couldn't be seen. You both loved and loathed my hair. It was the one piece of me I took care of. The one thing you couldn't take from me.

At least that's what I led myself to believe.

An abundance of money, affluence, and security. But love. Well, that was something that was severely lacking in those walls. The gates to the front of the house crept open silently as if being pushed open gently by a ghost, their strong steel gliding effortlessly over the paved spiralling driveway. Those mechanical arms welcomed me into nothing but a house of empty smiles and tears.

"We'll be okay," you said. It was the first time you had directly addressed me. You had been ranting, shouting, and screaming at the world. Not directly at me, your eyes never falling that far. But now, as the steel gates closed, locking me again into my prison, your eyes stabbed into me, cutting through me with the savagery of a mad surgeon with a scalpel, I saw something worse than death in them. I saw torment. I saw glee. I saw malice.

You pulled the handbrake tight and unclipped your seatbelt, reaching over the back to me. Your hand found my leg. I dared not recoil. "I can take care of you," you said. "I love you. You are my life." You eyed me up and down, like examining a sick animal you had stumbled across in a field, weighing up whether to leave it to die slowly, or to bash its brains in with the nearest rock. "I know what we need," you said. You stroked my legs. Your fingers fat and rough. "We need some more love in this house. Me and you. We haven't been great. I know you try, but your head is all over the place." You smiled. Your teeth stained like rotting bones. "We should have a baby. I know you want one. Something to focus on. Something to bring us closer together, like we used to. Our baby will grow up strong, healthy, and happy. Because I love you. Because our baby will have an incredible mother and father. He'll go to the best school. The best university and you will want for nothing." You eyed the urine stain on my joggers. The stench was repugnant. Sharp. "You love me, don't you?" I swallowed hard. I smiled. Not too wide, or it would look fake. Not too shallow, or you would know I was lying. I had to make it look just right. I couldn't say a word. Words meant tone. Inflection. Emotion. If I stayed quiet, there were fewer ways to mess up. You studied my smile, and I fought back the tears that wanted to rush through. "There's a good girl," you said. you cracked open the door and moved to the back seat where I was sitting. You pulled open the door slowly and moved over me to unclip my seatbelt.

You put your hands under me and carefully, like lifting out a fragile piece of glass, you helped me out of the car, supporting my elbows as you hauled my weight out. As we walked up the driveway, you were whispering to me.

"It will all be okay, baby. I promise. We can get past this. Just me and you in our wonderful home. Together."

The wooden flooring reflected blurred halos from the back patio doors of the kitchen that had been newly fitted. You had had the old carpets replaced with wooden flooring. You said it was because of the aesthetics. But I knew it was so you could hear me moving about the house.

"I'll go fix you some lunch," you said. You disappeared into the kitchen, leaving me alone in my dread and silence. I didn't know if I was to move, to relax, or simply lie on the floor and wait for further instruction. "Clara," you said, calling from the kitchen. I revived my weary body and walked into the kitchen. you were staring at something, and then my eyes fell on it and my heart picked up its pace. I hadn't left it there, and confusion plucked at my brain. You looked at it, like it was insulting you just being there.

A picture of the two of us. I can't remember where it had been taken. I looked so youthful then. So full of life. We were both smiling, you holding the camera, taking a selfie. Our smiles beaming for the world to see. Perfect. Instagramable. Fake. That photo belonged on the fireplace in the living room at the other end of the house. Why was it in the kitchen? Then I saw the source of you outrage, and my stomach sank. It wasn't the misplaced photo. It was the crack running through it, like the splitting of earth from an earthquake.

"Why have you done that?" You said, your arms on your sides, scalding me like a schoolmaster after returning my homework late. I searched for the words, but everything came up as the wrong answer. If I said I was sorry, you would see that as I wasn't trying hard enough, and you would beat me. If I blamed you, saying you must have done it, you would tell me I was belittling you, and you would beat me. If I told you it was a mistake, then you would see me as not taking things seriously, a slight to your hard work, and you would beat me.

So, I did what I have learned to do. I said nothing, and I let whatever fate had in store for me come, and I would be a simple passenger. I could see the flushing of your cheeks. The deepening of your breath. The tightening of you knuckles.

"Well?" You stabbed, the noise sharp in the rooms silence. I jolted. The sound like a lightning whip across my face. My eyes must have said it all because I could feel them burning. You picked up the photo and placed it in my trembling hands. "I must have put it there by accident," you said, your breath slowing. "Go put it back for me." You leaned in and kissed the crown of my head. I winced. I didn't know what to do. Was I going to get a hug, or a belt across the cheek with the back of your knuckles? I couldn't tell. Couldn't read you. You never took the blame, and the fact that you were doing it now made me even more terrified. This was uncharted territory. Were you genuinely sorry? I couldn't tell anymore. I was so confused. "What would you like?" I thought about my answer. Such a simple thing to respond to, but such a complicated answer was needed. "I know," you said, my silence speaking for me. "Salmon. I will make you a salmon salad. You need a good meal." The comment cut through me. I hated salmon. I smiled anyway. "Perfect," you said. "I think that's the best thing for you. Lots of omega three. Plus, with your recent," you looked at my stained trousers. "Accident, I think we need to be extra careful as to what we are putting in your body. I think that's what I'll make you."

You leant in and wrapped your arms around me. A part of me wanted to embrace you. Wanted to believe that you were sorry. You were just mistaken. That you wanted to love me. But I knew. I knew that this was all part of you game.

I remember one day last year. It was a Wednesday. It was summer. There were flies. So many flies. You screamed at me for making the house untidy. You told me how worthless I was, and only when I crumpled to ground and cried more than I knew possible, did you tell me you were sorry. That you didn't mean what you said. That you were just stressed from work. That I was amazing. Wonderful. The best thing that had ever happened to you. We made love that night. Not just sex but made love. It was a wonderful evening, and you told me everything you loved about me. The next day we went out around town. You bought me flowers. We went to the cinema. A long walk in the park. I remember the wind was warm on my cheek. The smell of summer grass. The sweet smell of roses. Young lovers meandering around us, their hearts filled with warmth, their eyes filled with joy. You slapped me. Without warning. Without reason. You slapped me with the back of your hand and my mouth filled with the taste of copper, like chewing on a metal pipe. You didn't say why, and I didn't question it. But we carried on like nothing had happened.

"I'll run you a bath," you whispered into my ear, your voice pulling me back to the washed-out grey hall I was standing in. The kitchen flooring numbing my feet. "And then I'll go get started on the food. Follow me." You took the picture off me. "I'll sort that later." You moved to the stairs, and I followed you like a lost dog. You told me to stay put at the front door, and you kicked off your shoes and climbed the steps that were layered with a plush cream carpet and vanished into the bathroom.

I stood there, alone in the gloom. The sound of the

tap running and soon, the steam filtering onto the landing like smouldering flames. Why was the picture frame out? Why was it cracked? Had you done it? If you hadn't, why were you accepting blame? I felt ill, like I wanted to throw up. My chest tightened like someone was gripping it in a clenched fist. I felt my legs grow weak, and steadied myself on the banister, before wiping off the fingerprints that lingered like an unseen betrayal. I felt it again. The pressure in my bladder building. I clambered up the stairs. Each step daring to break my will and threatened to force me to relieve myself on the carpet. I made it to the top of the stairs.

I stopped outside the door, daring myself to knock. But then I heard your voice, filtering through the tumbling of water. I leaned in closer.

"You need to stop. Stop messaging me. Stop calling my office. Stop, or I'll make your life hell."

Who were you talking to?

The call ended. I heard you drawing closer to the door. My body exploded with fear. You would know I was eavesdropping. It opened, and you stood looking at me. Your face etched with rage.

"What are you doing?" I put my head down, trying to point to the bathroom. You pushed my hand away. "How long have you been standing there? Were you listening to me?" I shook my head quickly, trying to push past you, but you blocked my path like an immovable boulder. "Can I not have any privacy?" You spat. You lifted your phone up, as if to demonstrate your personal life. You stared at me, your gaze like a flame to a moth, your eyes like knives in my mind. I tried to speak, but the hard ball in my throat wouldn't allow it. I mouthed a response. "Speak up!" You shouted. I jolted. I could feel myself about to break.

"You don't trust me, do you? I was on the phone to work. They need me to go in tonight, but I told them I can't. I told them that my beautiful wife had been in the hospital, and I can't leave her. I told them she is my priority." You waited for a response. None came. "Is that it?" You continued. "Is that all you have to say?" You moved into my face. Your teeth an inch away. "You stupid cunt." The word slammed into my mind. Your chest was rising. your face flushing with red. "We get home, I run you a bath. I am about to make you some delicious, nutritious food, and you have the cheek to stand at the door, listening to me on the phone, and you don't have anything to say about it? Not even an apology, or a *thank you Alex for being so goddamn nice to me*? I thought we had spoken about you showing me a little gratitude and respect?" I pointed to the bathroom. "Is that all you care about!" You screamed, slamming your hand into the bathroom door which rattled loudly. I saw the tub filling up to the brim. It would overflow soon. Your breath hissed through tightly gritted teeth. "You don't give a shit about me, and you don't give a shit about this family. I am the one that works. I am the one that provides, and you drink bleach. Look at you. Dithering. Shaking. Stinking of piss. Why the hell am I even with you? Why do I even bother?" You leaned in closer. The staircase was directly behind me, and I thought for a moment you would lose control and shove me. Then, as if reading my mind, you looked down over my shoulder to the bottom of the stairs. You focused your menacing eyes back on me. "How hard would it be to prove that you didn't slip?"

The sound of water breaking through filled the air. You snapped your head back to the tub. It was brimming, but not a slash touched the bathroom floor.

You turned back to where I stood, my sobs breaking through my tight lips. Your face contorted, and you looked down at the sodden patch on the carpet. The familiar sharp smell of piss found your nostrils.

"Oh baby," you said. You raced and turned the tap off. The ensuing silence was deafening. My eyes clenched shut, my mouth hanging in a desperate, humiliated, silent scream. I felt like an incontinent child that had been discovered by the playground bully.

You pulled me into you. The stench of sweat attacking my nostrils. You stroked my hair and pressed me into your chest. I could hear your heartbeat. It was steady. Calm and controlled. Your lips found the crown of my head.

"I love you," you said softly. "I'm sorry I got angry. You're just so beautiful." You pinched a few strands of my hair and ran it through your fingers. "Come on, let's get you cleaned up."

The bath was so hot I felt like it was going to peel the skin from my flesh, but I welcomed the heat. You were preparing food downstairs. Cutlery being moved around. A chair scraping along the floor. The sound of a song playing on the Alexa. One you always played. Over and over. When you were in a bad mood. It was your go to. *Lavender. Lavander.*

You had scrubbed the carpet without a moment's hesitation, apologising profusely whilst doing it. I was so confused as to what was real anymore. Was the rage real? Or the remorse? Was it all real? Or none at all? When done, you laid out some fresh clothes and put them on the towel rack so they would be warm when I got out and lit a scented candle.

"Take as long as you need," you said, stroking my

naked body and kissing my cheek, before leaving the bathroom. Leaving me to my silence.

I pulled my legs as tightly as I could into my chest, cradling myself like a scared child. You wanted a child. The thought terrified me, but would I be strong enough to say no? Maybe a child was a *good* thing? Maybe you needed something to focus on. Something other than me? The wave of anxiety that came from that thought rattled me to the point I had to grip the side of the tub to stop from vomiting.

A child. To be tied to you through blood and not just through marriage. you would turn the baby against me, and you would raise it in your own image. I would have two oppressors, instead of one. I couldn't bring a baby into this world. A world where love is conditional. A world where pain is currency. The thought made my eyes burn and salty tears mix with the water. I was slowly losing my grip on reality. I could feel myself slipping away into madness. I had to do something.

"Are you nearly done, babe?" your voice was like a siren calling to sailors to jagged rocks on the shore. I shrunk into the tub further, letting the water cover me. The water coming up to my neck and submerging my shoulders. I closed my eyes, and slipped a little lower, the water sitting just below my nose. I could end it right here. I thought of the family I didn't have. The life I could have lived but was stolen from me. The future I wanted but would never see, and I slipped below the lip of the water, welcoming the end.

The door pushed open, and you bounded in with a large bath towel. I pulled myself up to the surface and placed my hands on the side of the tub. The water overflowing and splashing onto the floor.

"How was the bath?" You said, getting me dry. You

towelled down my shoulders, then stopped and picked up my wet hair in clumps in your fingers, like wet vines pulled from a lake. You grabbed the bathrobe from the towel rack and put it around me and took hold of my hand. "Come on," you said. "I have something to show you."

You led me out of the bathroom, and I went to move downstairs, but you tugged at my hand towards the bedroom.

Oh god, I thought, my body nearly convulsing at the sight of our bed through that open door.

"Follow me, silly," you laughed. I felt confused. What were you doing? I moved with you, my mind twisting, racing with the myriad of possibilities of what you were going to do to me. But when I saw it, all other possibilities were rendered obsolete, and I would have begged you to defile my body. You stood by it with a huge smile on your face. Not one of love, but one of malevolence.

I eyed the face creams, the massage oil, the flickering candles that emanated a warm glow, and the smell of lavender and jasmine filled the air. Fresh flowers on the bedside table. Even heard the faint sound of music. But that wasn't what made my fear red line and would have me throwing myself out the window if you didn't still have my wrist locked in your hand. You came up behind me as she stared at it, your hands like sandpaper on my skin. You kissed my hair again. It made sense now.

"I don't want you to leave me," you said, your voice sounding like it was meant to be kind. "I couldn't bear it. I couldn't live with the pain it would cause me." You griped my shoulders and whispered into my ear. "I want to take care of you. I want to make you be the best person you can be." You gestured to the instrument that sat on the bed on a laid-out towel. The flickering flames danced along its metallic teeth. The wire protruding from the bottom like a long, swollen centipede. "Relationships are about sacrifice. We sacrifice parts of ourselves for the other person because we love them. I sacrifice my time to provide for you. Now, it's your turn." You closed the bedroom door and applied the lock. The room began to close in around me. My chest was so tight I could hardly breathe, like the room was on fire, the oxygen being sucked out by hungry flames.

I always loved your hair. I heard your voice in my mind. I went to speak, to make any sort of sound.

"Shh," you whispered. You leaned down and pulled out the electronic hair clippers, the console bulbous and big in your hand. The metal teeth were dull and hungry. "Now sit down."

Chapter Six
Laura

Laura watched the woman slip into the clouds. Forgoing all preservation, Laura leaped after her, thrusting her hand into the spiralling grey, hoping to catch her Laura felt the graze of flesh on her arm and snapped her fingers tightly around it. The handcuffs securing her other wrist to the ladder viciously cut into her skin. Adrenalin coursed through her body, making the excruciating pain feel like it was miles away. She heaved the woman back into her. She was screaming. Crying. Her face ashen. Her body soaking from the mist and her skin so cold that Laura thought she was holding a husk of meat from a butcher's slab. Laura could feel the body shaking as the cold slipped into her bones.

Laura called out loudly, and after what felt like an eternity, officers arrived at the top of the ladder and pulled the jumper up and off the bridge.

"Get her to an ambulance," Laura said, her teeth chattering, as she unlatched herself from the handcuffs and Francis helped her up the bridge.

"You're freezing, Sergeant," he said, quickly followed by, "what the hell had got into you?" Laura massaged her wrist and then her arms. The paramedic from earlier, the one she had torn a new arse hole, came and threw a blanket around her.

"Thanks," Laura said, sitting on the kerb. The bridge was a frenzy of cars, ambulances, and cops. She had created quite a scene with her antics. She couldn't wait to go speak to her superiors at the office and them tell her how smart it was to go climbing over a bridge to pull a jumper off. Oh boy, she was in for such a great day.

"What were you thinking?" Francis said again, his mouth agape with what the hell his Sergeant had done. What *was* she thinking? She knew the score. Do not go onto the bridge. Talk them back over. She had had negotiation training. She had read the books. Been on the courses. Everything she had learned had told her to not do exactly what she had just done, so why did she do it? Excitement? Fear? She didn't know.

"Honestly," she said, quietly. "I wasn't even thinking. I just did what I thought I should do, and that was to get that woman off the bridge." Glancing over at the paramedic who was checking her over, she asked, "Do we even know anything about her? Has she spoken to anyone?"

"Not a word," the paramedic said. "We don't know who she is, where she is from, or why in the world she is covered in blood."

"Does she have any injuries?" Francis said. The paramedic shook her head.

"None that we can see."

"Then it's not her blood," Laura said, cooly. She turned to Francis. "We need to go to the hospital with her. Question her. Get some details. We need to know who she is, why she was trying to jump, and whose blood she has on her." Francis nodded his head. His confusion about Laura's heroism forgone. His mind back to the task at hand.

"That won't be necessary." The voice cut through their chatter and the chaos of directed traffic surrounding them. Laura looked up, and she saw a tall woman standing there in a white shirt and a black pencil skirt. Her pitch black hair tied back in a bun. Her face aged. Her eyes hard. Laura already didn't like her.

"And who the fuck are you?" Laura said, eyeing her with venom. Francis' eyes went wide. He went to speak, but the new woman interjected.

"I am Amy Burnell," she said. "I am your detective chief inspector." The words hit Laura like a truck.

Shit.

"DC Francis will go to the hospital with the other officers," DCI Burnell continued, her voice like fire. "You, Sergeant Warburton, go back to the station and debrief myself and Inspector Jeremy Marriot on why you thought it appropriate to put yourself at risk to climb over those railings." Laura rolled her eyes, trying not to let the sound of her frustration be heard by her new chief inspector, to whom she had just told to fuck off.

"I think I would be better suited to speak to the female on board of the ambulance, ma'am," Laura said. "I think it's only right, considering I got her off of there."

"You will do as commanded, Sergeant." Laura felt herself growing hot. Francis placed his hand on her arm and gave it a light squeeze.

"I'll sort it," Francis said before Laura could throw her fragile career over the bridge. "I need to sort out the next of kin for the suicide, anyway."

"Another suicide?" DCI Burnell said. Francis grimaced.

"It's been quite a morning."

The pair drove in silence. Francis tried to make some small talk, but Laura didn't answer with more than a grunt. She couldn't believe the audacity of the new inspector. How dare she.

"Why the hell am I being thrown into the frying pan, Francis?" Laura barked, seemingly out of nowhere. "That bitch? 'DCI Burnell'" she said mockingly. "Who the hell even is she?"

"I think she's new to the rank. I believe she asked to work on this case specifically," Francis said, his voice low under the splattering of the falling rain on the windscreen. "She's a transferee. Trying to make a name for herself. She's only a stand in though, like Jeremy. I think she wants the full-time position, so she's been cracking the whip." Laura turned her head and stared out into the grey morning. She had cut one man down, dragged another woman off a bridge, and she was in the shit for it.

Her first week back after coming out of the rehab had been gruelling. Delving deep into her past trauma, everything she had locked away. All her pain. Every sordid detail of her life laid out for the world to see. She had had more psychotherapy sessions than she could count. She was nearly thrown out of the centre following an explosive barrage if insults she hurled at the councillor when she suggested that due to Laura's weak boundaries and her need to help people, that she had welcomed these creatures into her life. Craig. Ron. Celine. All of them. That paired with the withdrawal from alcohol, and the meagre dose of Disulfiram she was given daily, she would have been charged with murder if the security hadn't stepped in and dragged her out of the consultation room. Laura spent that night crying, screaming into her pillow. Shouting insults at herself in the mirror, and spiralled into the deepest, darkest pit of despair she had ever found herself in, and boy, there were a few to choose from. All those monsters resurfaced, their teeth bared and ready to gnaw on her bones.

The next day, she had written a letter of apology to the councillor, but she had been assigned a new one. One that didn't take her shit. One that told her to go fuck herself and leave if she gave the slightest bit of backchat. Laura got on with him brilliantly, and her recovery was cemented well under his guidance.

And now, one week back, she had been thrust into the misery of ordinary life again, putting the pieces of humanity back together just like she had done for the last thirteen years of her police career. And now she would be thrown into the wolf's den for doing the right thing. The brave thing. The stupid thing. But the thing that meant that she could go home knowing there was only one body for the coroner instead of two.

God, I need a drink,

Laura felt her breath catch in her throat as she thought of the sweet nectar. She pushed the thought away, Francis rambling away in the distance as they drove back to the precinct. She couldn't ever go back to that life. No matter how much it called to her. How much she wanted it. One drink, one sip, was all it took to drag her back to that dark place filled with nightmares. She was fragile. Laura was offered the chance to do a phased return to work, but she wanted to dive right back into the fire. She just hoped she didn't get too burned in the process.

"Take me to the hospital," she said. Francis turned his neck to her so quickly one might think his neck would snap.

"You have to go back to the station." Laura eyed him, her gaze burning into his flesh.

"She told me, right before she jumped, that *she did it.*

The blood on her clothing, Francis. It's not hers. She's hurt someone, and I am not doing a half assed job of pulling her off the bridge and then getting chewed up over it without finding out why she was there in the first place." She let out a long sigh. "Take me to the hospital. I need to speak to her."

"Look, I'm sorry that you're in this position. But you put yourself in it," Francis barked. "I'm not having you drag me down with you."

"Take me to that fucking hospital!" Laura slammed her hand off the dashboard. "That's an order." Francis gripped the wheel, the blood draining from his knuckles.

"No," he snapped. "You need to calm down, Laura."

"Sergeant Warburton."

"But not inspector anymore, is it?" When he said the words, he felt the cut of guilt carve through him. "Sorry," he said quickly. "I didn't mean that."

"If I wanted your sympathy, I would ask for it," Laura snapped, her body tense. She saw the sign for the general hospital moving closer. "Stop the car." Francis let out a laugh.

"No way." They approached a set of lights. She needed to find out what the hell was going on. Something wasn't sitting right with her. *She did it.* Who was she? The ramblings of a madwoman? Someone else? Why wasn't she speaking? No one had heard an utterance escape the woman's tight lips. Francis pulled up to some traffic lights, and Laura darted out of the passenger seat into the heavy rain. Francis called out to her, but Laura was already running.

DIARY

I woke up this morning to the sound of the bluebirds singing in the tree outside my window. They're beautiful, spritely little things. I saw a squirrel, too. Spritely little thing. His big bushy tail following behind him as he scurried up the tree to retrieve his bounty and nectar. He scared away the birds, however. They made me think of my mother. When we went to the red squirrel sanctuary. I can't remember where it was. Near a beach, I think. I waited by the side of the bushes and shrubbery with a horse chestnut in my hand, hoping that one of the little red squirrels would venture close and pluck the nut from my fingertips. I remember the feeling of the sun on my neck and the sweat on my brow.

Mother was standing behind me, putting my belongings into the car. Dad was towelling off from taking a dip in the sea. Although it looked warm, the water had bitten into his flesh, and that made him glow like he had been badly sunburnt.

That must have been why Mum was so anxious for me to get inside the car. She thought I was going to get red like Dad. But I was insistent on waiting. Daring to not make any sudden movements.

I saw one. His tiny amber head peeking out from behind the bright green leaves and blackberry bundles. My face lit up. I wanted desperately to reach out and touch him, to shriek and tell Mum what I had found. Those giant eyes were like shining marbles. But I remained still. Like a good girl. Stayed so very still.

The creature emerged, standing on his hind legs, and surveyed the area.

"It's okay," I whispered as quietly as I could. "It's okay. I won't hurt you."

The squirrel moved out into the open, barely a foot from my hand. It drew closer, inch by inch, paw by paw. The chestnut glowing like a large ruby in Aladin's cave.

"Baby, watch out!" It was Mum. I snapped my head to look at her, her face ashen, pale, sheer terror. My Dad was rushing to me. I felt his ice-cold hands wrap around me and I was flying through the air. The wings of the hawk slapped against my face as I heard the screams of the squirrel being torn apart.

I may have been just a child. But I learned so much that day.

Never. Be. Vulnerable.

Chapter Seven
Laura

Laura ran through the estates that surrounded the hospital until she finally found herself on the car park. It was only a short run, but she was fighting for each breath. The years of cigarettes still taking its toll on her respiratory system. She felt her phone going off in her pocket. It was Jeremy. Then Francis. Then Jeremy again. A text came through.

Jeremy
ANSWER THE PHONE NOW.

Laura placed the phone back in her pocket. Since her absence, Jeremy had been made the temporary detective inspector of the MIU. From all accounts, he was doing a terrible job, and clearly didn't know what he was doing and was making it up as he went along. There was only so long someone could do that before they dropped the ball. The MIU had changed considerably since she had returned to work a week ago. Catherine had since moved on to the proactive unit, breaking down doors and doing drug busts. Laura never thought she would be into something like that, but she was cleaning up the streets of Wigtown. Since the removal of the Heywoods, there had been a power vacuum, and the small fish were now rising up through the criminal ranks. Murders had gone up. Violent crime and robberies, too. Mostly, the scum of the earth just killed each other, and the cops had two great results – one drug dealer dead, the other in prison, it was high fives all around. Soon, Laura will be in charge of MIU again, and Jeremy will return to his subordinate position. Being a detective was in her blood. Being a leader was even more engrained in her DNA. Which was why as she stood at the foot of the ambulance station, and the woman from the bridge, this *Jane Doe*, was brought out on a gurney, she was risking so much for a woman who hadn't said a single word to her.

They wouldn't do the same investigation as she would. They would send Francis, who was very good at his job, but he was too clean. To bound by the rules. Laura had the authority and experience to go a little renegade. She took a breath, threw another piece of nicotine gum into her mouth and crushed the hard shell until her mouth gave that satisfying burn. Lost in her own determination, she didn't notice Francis flying through the entrance and making his way to her in the unmarked car. He slammed on the brakes and dove out of the driver's side.

"Get in, now!" He barked, his grey hair blowing in the wind. His body flushed red. "You're going to get me sacked!"

"Go back to the unit," Laura said, walking past him like he was a beggar asking for change. "I need to take the lead on this investigation. There is more to it than we think." Francis eyes her with fascination, the words not quite computing right in his mind.

"Sergeant, we need to do as the boss said. Hell, we have the DCI ordering us back. She'll ring your neck when she finds out you're disobeying her." Laura stopped, the wind picking up and blowing through her red hair.

"Not going to happen," Laura said, and she continued to walk. "Save your own skin, but I have a crime to investigate." Francis looked like he had just bitten into a beehive. After a moment, he caught pace with Laura.

"You get me sacked, and I swear to god."

The two of them vanished through the ambulance entrance. Jane Doe was being wheeled through the corridors. They both flashed their warrant cards to the security guard who manned the entrance. He let them through without barely looking up from his book. A black cover with the silhouette of a night shift worker on the front. Laura thought it quite fitting. They followed the paramedics into a ward, and Jane Doe was parked in a bay like a broken car that had driven through a slaughterhouse. Laura was going to grab a nurse, but at the sight of the woman, a nurse with more curves than should be legal erupted into a frenzy.

"Oh, thank Jesus! You brought her back!" Laura stood there and flashed a look of concern to Francis. The nurse moved over to her quickly. "Oh, my word, what the hell have you done?" The nurse studied her and her bloodied garments.

"You know this woman?" Francis asked loudly, his voice barely audible over the rabble of voices, beeping machines, and squeaking trolleys.

"Yes," the nurse said. Laura eyed her name tag. Natalie. "Who are you?" Laura took out her warrant card and held it up for the world to see.

"Detective insp..." she caught herself. "Detective Sergeant Laura Warburton of the Wigtown Major Investigation Unit. This is my colleague, Detective Constable Francis Cline." Natalie glanced at the warrant cards, then went back to Jane Doe, her face awash with pain. "Her name is Clara. Clara Weaver. Oh, I was so worried about her." She ran her hands over her arms and clothing.

"Don't do that," Laura barked from the back.

"Why?" Natalie said, "She's a patient."

"And she is a crime scene." Laura couldn't have sounded more robotic if she had tried. That's the way the job gets you. You see so many terrible things on a daily basis, that you forget what compassion and empathy feels like. It's like part of you dies, and Laura found that since being in the police, part of her soul had been eroded each day like rocks fighting a heavy tide.

"A crime scene?" The nurse said, her eyes washing over the patient with horror. Laura gestured to Francis. "You have scene logs in the car?" He pinched the bridge of his nose.

"We really shouldn't be…"

"Answer the question," Laura snapped. Francis nodded. "Go and get one and start a scene log. I will radio for some uniform to take over once I have some more information." Francis went to move. Laura grabbed him. "I appreciate everything you've done today," she said. "When we get the information we need, we will go." Francis looked like the balloon of worry that was slowly filling his chest was slowly depressing.

"Thank you," he said. "I was beginning to think I was saying goodbye to my pension." With that, he left the ward, leaving Laura standing there, the harsh lighting refracting off the freshly buffered floors. Beds of patients lining the walls with thin blue curtains hanging loosely on the railings. The beeping of heart monitors. The cushioned steps of nurses and doctors with their heads glued to their notes moving around. The sharp scent of disinfectant. Laura hated hospitals, and since being a cop she had never spent more time in them. Laura stood eyeing Clara while the nurse sat by her, whispering to her, wanting so much to touch her and console her. Clara stayed silent, staring at the ceiling like she was a mannequin trying out a new look of bloodied and dishevelled.

Francis returned a moment later and started the scene log. Laura signed it too, and Francis took up a chair and sat by Clara. Clara didn't seem to notice, and Laura thought that the world could erupt in flames, and she wouldn't even feel the heat. Lost in her own mind. A world behind her own eyes. *What was going on in that mind of hers?*

"I need to speak to you," Laura said to Natalie. Natalie grabbed the big green sheet the paramedics had left behind and moved to the computer to start booking Clara in.

"Just a moment, detective," Natalie said, the light from the monitor reflecting from her glasses. "I appreciate you have questions, but my patients come first." Laura put Natalie in her sixties, and she wondered how, after so long in the NHS and putting people back together again, could she still be so compassionate? Laura felt her phone buzzing in her pocket again. It was Jeremy. She let out a long breath that felt so hot she thought it could melt steel.

Outside, Laura stood by the ambulance station. More people being pulled out of the wagons. Some groaning, some silent, some with paramedics laughing with them. Others, with paramedics driving their hands into their sternum, completing CPR.

She stared at the busy entrance. Patients there smoking cigarettes and gathering around each other, each dressed in their pyjamas or their hospital gowns. All huddling together, their wrinkled smiles etched across their face. Their teeth blackened and yellow from years of tobacco use, and yet they still found a community where they belonged. Laura wondered why she smoked when she knew that it would one day kill her, as with 50% of other smokers. And it was because human beings want to be part of something bigger than themselves. Being a smoker was part of an identity, just like being a football fan of a certain team or enjoying going to a show. It was being something that was bigger than just yourself, even if that meant filling your entire bloodstream with over five thousand chemicals.

Smoking was the one thing that she missed the most. She put a piece of nicotine gum in her mouth. She had the addiction without the reward. She was a slave to nicotine, and she couldn't even be part of a group and willfully ignore the fact that it's killing them. The fact that they're standing outside a hospital with cancer ward wristbands on their wrist. The human mind can block out almost anything if it tries hard enough – memory suppression, convincing yourself what you saw you didn't actually see, and even just being so used to something terrible, it loses its shine.

So many things we ignore when we really shouldn't, and then ten years pass by, and we wonder how the hell we got so old and broken.

Her phone buzzed again, and Laura groaned loudly.

"Sir," Laura said.

"Where the hell are you?" Jeremy said. "You left that bridge half an hour ago. I have the DCI here breathing down my neck that you told her to fuck off?"

"I didn't tell her to fuck off," she said. "I asked who the fuck she was." Laura heard Jeremy nearly collapse of a heart attack.

"They didn't teach you people skills in rehab, I see."

Bite me.

"The DCI says you climbed over the railings…" Jeremy continued, his voice mellowing a little. Laura dared to think he was a little impressed. "You haven't lost your nerve, have you?" Laura laughed a little.

"It's good to be back," she said, the scent of the cigarette smoke finding her nose. That sweet smell of burning. The toxic concoction of chemicals that hooked their way into her brain and pulled her in. "So you're going to rip me a new one when I get back?" She said, trying to take her mind off the smoke.

"You know the drill," he said. "New DCI is trying to make an impression to the Superintendent Bill Bennett. Sadly, given what happened before you went away, and now you have been back only a week and you're rocking the boat, your cards are marked."

"I saved her life, Jeremy." Laura said, forgoing the formalities. Jeremy let out a long sigh.

"I know you did, Laura. How is she?"

"She still isn't talking, and she's covered in dried blood. I have Francis in with her trying to find out some information. Check the system for a 'Clara Weaver.' The nurse told me that's her name. Around age twenty-five. No older than thirty. Given she was on the bridge, check for missing persons reports, and check for mental health calls of females of that age. White. Shaved head."

"I thought I was in charge, here?" He laughed. Laura's mouth crooked into a grin.

"Do it … Sir."

"Wait, did you say shaved head?" He said. Laura gave a noise of confirmation. "Why does she have a shaved head?"

"It's not just shaved; it's got long parts on it too. Like strands where it's been missed. I don't think she did it to herself."

"What are you implying?"

"I'm *saying* that whoever cut her hair, she didn't want it to happen. And now we have a woman who tried to kill herself, covered in blood, who isn't speaking."

"You think there's a body somewhere?"

"Blood has to come from somewhere," Laura said. "I'll find out her address from the nurse and then go from there. But something else is bugging me." An ambulance pulled into the Accident and Emergency Bay. Paramedics diving out and dragging another patient into the hospital. "She said something to me before she jumped, and I grabbed her. She said, '*she did it.*'" Laura could hear the cogs turning in Jeremy's mind.

"Maybe she's psychotic or something? Maybe she's trying to cast the blame on someone else, or she had a split, you know, like we see in the movies?"

For such an experienced detective, Jeremy, Laura thought. *You do come out with some dumb shit.*

"Maybe," Laura conceded. "I'll finish up here, and then come back to serve DCI Burnell my arse on a plate." Laura ended the call, and she lay back against the wall for a moment. Just one, sweet moment of peace. She had been thrust right into the frying pan again. There were no half measures in this game. The game of murderers. The game of killing. Even with the best will in the world. The strongest resolve. The thickest skin. Things still got to you. There was only so much a person could take. As Laura exhaled a deep breath, breathing in the lingering smoke that filtered from the smoking shelter, she wondered how strong she actually was. Whether she was strong enough to walk through the fire and make it through to the other side without being burned alive over the coming days.

Chapter Eight

Clara
Home
One hour before Alex's Murder

As I stared at my broken reflection in the mirror, I knew my husband Alex was going to kill me. I didn't know how or when, only that it was coming, and there was nothing I could do to stop it. At this point, it was the only way I could ever be free of him.

I stood in just my underwear, eyeing my ribs prominent under my breasts like wet tissue paper draped over machine parts. My legs had grown so thin it was a wonder they didn't snap like dry twigs when he put his hands on me. They were littered with bruises, like white pipe cleaners smudged by inky fingers. The hair on my forearms had grown thick. My eyes sunken back in my head. My reflection in the polished mirror was unrecognisable. I resembled a walking corpse that refused to die. My scalp, once home to long flowing black hair, was now an ash grey, like pencil scribblings on dulled paper.

I ran my hands over my shaved head, the memory of the hair clippers fresh in my mind. I wanted to cry, but I couldn't bring myself to shed a tear. I had filled a lake with my misery in the past, and the well of emotion had run bone dry. I could hear Alex downstairs making me the meal he had promised before he shaved my head.

"I want you to show me how much you love me," his words sliced through my body like a fierce wind naked in an artic downpour. The breath caught in my chest, unable to release. I ran my fingertips over the short spiky hair,

tracing each fine strand like a trimmed hedge. The one thing I had tried to take care of. Alex had taken everything else - my dignity. My freedom. Friends. My hair was the last thing I could call my own. The last thing I could truly care for. And now he had stripped that away, too, and I had been too weak to stop him. My captor. The man who told me he loved me. He took the last part of me away. I'm nothing but the shadow on the monitor of her former life.

There was a knock on the bathroom door. Alex walked in. His face was gleaming, the same look he gave me the day we met. A look I seldom saw anymore. The once bright, beaming smile, which used to warm my body like a hot bath on a cold winter's day, now sent a shiver of fear down my spine.

"Food is ready," he said. I nodded a silent reply. He stared at me, his face like a wax painting. A mask he was so good at wearing. "You look beautiful," he said. The words like nails being driven through my heart. He had taken everything. All that was left was to take my life. "Now come on," he said, marvelling at my skeletal shape. "You need to eat. You're wasting away."

I moved downstairs like I was walking through a dream. Everything seemed a hundred miles away. I felt nothing: not the touch of the expensive carpet under my feet. Not the feel of the black-varnished banister under my palm. Not the slight breeze that was ever present in the house due to the back patio doors not fitting correctly. I felt absent, like the world had eclipsed around me. I was but a passenger on the journey, waiting for the bright lights from an atomic bomb to surface on the horizon and the shockwave to decimate all glass, shredding me in a flurry of blades.

I emerged at the foot of the kitchen. The tiling blaring

back the bright light from the lighting that was fitted into the chalk-white ceiling. Alex was busy preparing food. It had gone evening time, and the night had drawn in. My reflection stared back at me from the glass doors, the black canvas consuming the outside world.

I am a ghost, I thought. *I could vanish into a wisp of wind, and no one would notice.*

Alex pulled out the stool and moved to me. I tried not to recoil at his touch. Forced myself to stay still, like an obedient dog. He took my arm and guided me like a terrified puppy in a new home. I sat down as he tucked my seat under the bar so tightly I could hardly breathe. He plated up the food and put it in front of me. It was as promised. Salmon. Salmon that had been overcooked. The once bright orange flesh was now an ash grey. The juices pooled around the edges, resembling cooled vomit mixed in with a plethora of badly shredded salad. I normally cooked. I was good at it. When your safety depends on appeasing the monster three times your size, you have to be. At first, I had tried new recipes. After numerous episodes of Alex throwing the plate against the wall and shovelling the destroyed food into my mouth, I began sticking to what I knew he liked. Foolishly, I thought if I could surprise him with something new, then he would be kind. Sticking to the rules was working for now. But the rules always change.

"How're you feeling?" Alex said, tucking into the burger and chips. The juicy Angus beef burger oozed fat onto the plate, soaking the thick chips cut from Maris Piper potatoes. They were delivered weekly from the farmer's market. Only organic. Only the best for Alex. The cheese was thick and melted over the meat, and the chips were crispy and coated in sea salt. He had made me salmon. I detested fish, and he knew it. This was another game to him. "You really embarrassed me today," he said. "I can't believe you put yourself in the hospital. What was it this time? Bleach?" His mouth curled into a tight sneer. "I can't believe you. The things you put me through when all I do is provide and provide. This house. The Bentley. You're too busy thinking of yourself. All I ask is that you show a little respect and gratitude for the work I do." He pointed his fork at me. I imagine him sticking it in my hand and covering my mouth while I screamed out. "What would you do without me? You wouldn't last five minutes in the world on your own. I'm just happy you kept your mouth shut in the ward when the doctors started talking to you. They wouldn't believe you anyway, and you know it. You made a rod for your own back after the last time you got sectioned. Do you want to go back into the psych hospital with the other crazies?" I remained silent. Alex rolled his eyes. "I didn't think so." He sliced into the meat again. The tip of the knife carving against the bottom of the plate. He eyed my untouched meal. "And you aren't eating your food. To think that you drank bleach, but you won't eat fresh Norwegian salmon. I bet you didn't even drink it, did you? I bet you just pretended. The nurse didn't seem to give a shit. But that makes sense because *no one* gives a shit about you. Not even you. Look at the state of you! Your clothes don't even fit you anymore. I am the only one that cares about you, Clara. And you can't even eat your fucking food to say thank you for me taking you out of the hospital before they sectioned you again." Alex stuffed more meat into his face. The fat dripping, mush slopping around his fat jaws. His face flushing with red. He was getting angry. As much as he tried to hide it, I could tell. Always.

I glanced at the front door, not letting him see. Could I run for it? Maybe get to a phone? Scream loud enough in the front garden that someone called the police? I pushed the thought out of her mind. The thought of escape was deadly, because it gave me hope, and hope keeps men trapped in their misery. I knew I would never leave Alex outside of a body bag.

The police wouldn't help.

The services wouldn't listen.

I had to do the unthinkable.

I had to kill him.

"So, I think you need to show me how much you appreciate all I do for you," Alex said. His chewing was loud, the fat and gristle slopping between his jaws. "Hey," he said, clicking his fingers in my face. I snatched my head up. I had been slouching. I'm struggling to stay awake. The drugs at the hospital still running through my system. "You aren't eating your food." I looked again at my food. It might as well have been a plate of writhing maggots and rupturing pupas. I don't know why I did what I did next.

I pushed the plate away from me.

Alex stopped eating. His mouth filled with meat that dipped past his filled lips like a bursting cyst. "Eat your food," he said and pushed the plate back towards me. I didn't move. My heart beginning to quicken. Alex let out a long exhale of breath and wiped his mouth on a napkin. "Look," he said with an exhale. "I'm sorry," he said, with the same emotion as if he was discussing the weather. "Your hair." He placed his hand over mine. His touch hot on my icy skin. "I know you didn't want to do that, but I'm happy you did. Plus, you have enough on your plate. Always preening yourself. Always making yourself look pretty with your hair. To be honest, I don't know who you're doing it for." He squeezed my hand tighter. I felt my knuckles crushing together like a serpent straining against a rodent's ribs. I held back the emotion. Staring at the knife on the table. The serrated edge begging for me to grab it. I could. I could grab it. I could end all of this right now. Alex let out a laugh. There was that smile again. The smile he did before he got really mad. "You make a good point," he said, speaking to my absence. "Things have been stressful recently, and I know I can be rough with my rules at times. But this whole thing isn't easy for me either. Work is crazy, and I bust my arse every day to make us money. On the phone to businesses all around the world all hours of the day to make sure we have a good life, and I am being made to be the bad person because I asked you to show a trivial sacrifice for me." He squeezed my hand harder. His knuckles turning white. He wanted me to squeal. But I focused my pain on the knife. "You might not see it now," he said, with more venom, "but *I'm trying to help you.*" He shook his head, then leant in, waiting for a reply. Still, I remained still. "Aren't you going to say anything?" He hissed. A beat of unbroken silence followed.

Alex stood up quickly, kicking the stool backwards, crashes and rattling onto the kitchen tiles. He drove his hand into the salmon and picked it up, is meshing and mincing between his fingers. His face red, his teeth gritted. His hand drove to my mouth, forcing the putrid overcooked fish past my tight lips. "Eat it!" He screamed. He released my hand and grabbed the back of my head, forcing my skull backward. His breath rancid with alcohol. He had been drinking while I had been upstairs.

I stiffened, my eyes bulging. Reflexively, I brought a hand up to my mouth, but he was too strong. The fish forced its way into my mouth. Its texture slimy on my tongue and between my teeth. The taste powerful and repugnant. His hand closed around my nose. He was screaming something. The worst insults imaginable. But I couldn't breathe. Desperately, I clawed at him, trying to force him away. The world moving on fast forward. Heart hammering in my chest. Feeling returned, like a shower of heat through my body, as if I had been ice cold my entire life, then thrown into a fire. But it was not a feeling of pain that coursed through my veins. It was something new. Something I hadn't felt in a long, long time.

Rage.

My hand found the steak knife. I don't know what happened next, only that Alex released me, and I collapsed to the ground, coughing, and spluttering, as the matted meat expelled from my mouth Alex stood in front of me, holding his chest, red bleeding through his fingers like a punctured paint can. I tightly clutched the bloodied steak knife in my fist.

Chapter Nine
Laura

Laura moved back into the ward. The sound of beeping machines, air conditioning chilling her. Harsh lights boring into her eyes. She could even taste the bleach in the air. Every one of her senses being assaulted. Francis was standing talking to Natalie, the nurse, holding a cup of black coffee in a Styrofoam cup. She relayed the details of the silent Clara Weaver that was staring at the ceiling in her bed.

"What do we have?" Laura said, interjecting herself into the conversation like a drunk guest at a wedding. Francis took out a bundle of papers, and checking that Clara wasn't listening, he relayed the information.

"She's fucking nuts, Sergeant," he said. "Self-harm. Suicide attempts. Mental health issues." He eyed Clara like she was a viper in the corner, and to speak too loudly would cause her to leap from the bed and choke the life out of him. Laura took the notes off him and read through them quickly. It had everything – her date of birth. Blood type. A long list of prescribed medication that were collected at the pharmacy a few miles away religiously every month. A long shopping list of meds for depression, anxiety, anorexia nervosa, bulimia nervosa, and suspected psychotic breaks.

"Natalie," Laura said. "When we brought her in, you were happy to see her. Relieved, in fact. Why?" Natalie looked around her, as if to speak too loudly would be committing some kind of treason.

"She was here yesterday," Natalie said. "She came in following a suspected suicide attempt. She was brought here by the ambulance and was undergoing treatment. She had swallowed bleach. A lot of it. Had to have her stomach pumped." Laura felt a chill run down her spine. She eyed the notes again.

Suicide attempts.

"She was being seen to by the nurse in charge. But then the fire alarm went off, and when we went to find her, she was gone. Her husband came to visit her, and we wanted to speak to Clara alone but he wouldn't let us. We had to get security involved and tell him we had called the police." Natalie cleared her throat. "By the time we had gotten to the sickest patients and went to get Clara out, both her and her husband were gone." Laura felt a sickening feeling growing in her stomach, like a balloon filled with bile ready to burst.

"Did you call the police?"

"When we discovered her missing, yes."

"And?"

"We were told someone would be dispatched. No one ever came. We were really busy. After the next lot of patients came in, we thought it was being looked into, so we didn't make a follow-up."

"A patient goes missing, and you don't think to make a follow up?" Laura said, anger rising. Natalie's face turned ashen.

"With all due respect, detective, we have several mental health patients walking out every day. We simply can't keep track." Laura hated the answer, but she was a practical woman, not an idealist. The system was being screwed from each way by politicians that used the NHS as a political football. But only the people on the ground knew what was really going on, and put simply, they cannot cope with the demand. Laura swallowed the barrage of insults and calls of ineptitude down.

"Check that call," Laura said to Francis. Francis nodded and disappeared from the ward. A beat of silence passed between Laura and Natalie. Laura scanned the notes before stabbing her finger at the paper. "Is this her address?" The nurse studied the paper and nodded. "Next of Kin?"

"Husband. Alex Weaver." Laura felt the cold return to her bones.

The blood. She thought. *It's not hers.* Laura took out her radio and called up the control room. Something she didn't want to do. No doubt the new DCI was listening in, waiting to hear Laura's voice, confirming she was at the hospital despite being told not to go there. She was going to be in the shit, but self-preservation was never her strong suit.

"DS Warburton to control."

"Go ahead," the operator said.

"I need officers to attend The Grange, Appleton Road in relation to the woman found on the bridge. Take MOE and get CSI on the way. I'll be there soon to meet patrols."

"What's this about Sergeant?" *Sergeant.* The title cut through her. She had been a DI for years. It was like she was being dead named and couldn't do anything about it.

"Suspected homicide," Laura said. "I'll explain more in a moment. Just get patrols there, now." The radio cut out, a long bleep in her ear. The light at the top of the radio was solid red. "Fucking signal." A woman who doesn't talk, covered in blood with a history of psychosis, who was taken from the hospital following a suicide attempt by her husband. Why would he do that? Why would he not leave her here to be looked after? It didn't make sense to her.

Unless he was scared of what she might say. Laura felt her skin begin to prickle. The blood. The silence. The husband. They were going to find a body when they got to the address. But that didn't explain the bigger picture as to *why.*

The smell of salt found her nostrils. The crashing of waves in the distance. She steadied herself on the ward counter, nearly knocking off the computer monitor. The sound of the rain bombarding the ship. The screams of her ex and the sea that swallowed him.

Him. It was happening again.

She needed a drink.

"Are you okay, detective?" A voice said. "You look pale."

Is she the perpetrator? Is she the victim? What is locked behind those tight lips? He didn't want her to talk. Her head is shaved. Her tiny thin frame is matted with old bruising, black, and yellow smudges on her like smeared baby shit.

"You should sit down…"

I have to know. I have to find out what happened. A body is nothing without a motive. A reason. A god damn reason as to what has happened. I can help her. Save her. I can save someone when I couldn't save myself.

Laura pushed past Natalie and moved to Clara, who was staring at the ceiling. Laura pulled up the chair and leaned over her.

"Clara, I need you to talk to me. My name is Laura. I'm a detective. I'm here to help you." She was speaking so fast. Her heart hammering in her chest. The sound of waves crashing, growing louder. "Talk to me. Tell me what happened. Why were you on the bridge? Whose blood is this? Did he hurt you? Your husband, Alex? Did he do something to you?" Clara's eyes flickered. Laura studied Clara's body. She saw something that didn't fit. She had dirt under her toenails. Pulling her attention away from her feet, she looked at Clara's scalped head. "Did he do this to your hair?" Laura touched Clara's scalp.

Like her hand was made from the burning fires of hell itself, Clara shot up, her eyes burning red. She gripped Laura by the collar, then her hands found her neck and she squeezed. Laura recoiled back, clambering to her feet. Her eyes locked with Clara's. In them, she saw hatred. A deep hatred she couldn't even begin to comprehend. The pain of a woman who had seen the worst of humanity, all locked behind those eyes, screaming to get out. The sound of screaming. Of shouting. An alarm blaring. Laura fell to her back, her hands wrapping around Clara's as she postured over her. The sharp stench of blood finding her nose. The blood. Someone else's blood. Laura couldn't think, her face beginning to swell from the pressure. Clara's fingers digging into her windpipe. Her face was wrapped in madness. Teeth bared.

An endless moment later, the pressure around Laura's throat released. She fumbled onto her knees, heaving heavy breaths, choking, coughing, gasping for air like her lungs were filled with razor blades. Clara was dragged off her, scooped up by a security guard as big as a house, like a rat pulled from a crevice in the drywall by an exterminator. She was thrust back onto the bed. Her hands wild. Her screams. Oh, her screams. Her vocal cords stretching, burning, shrieking to abyssal tomes that Laura didn't know were possible. Wails of pain. Of rage. More security staff raced in, each grabbing a limb while Clara thrashed and kicked, scratched, and bit, like she was on fire trying to be put out by someone pouring petrol on her. Machines blaring. Wires and IV drips tangling around limbs like a bloodied tapeworm ejected from its host, desperate for life.

Laura got to her feet, Francis rushing in and taking hold of her. Natalie rushed to the melee on the bed, a syringe as thick as a throbbing dick plunged into Clara's body. After a moment, her screams turned to a guttural rasp, then a low whimper, and finally died all together.

Security stepped back, wiping blood from their arms, nurses wiping the sweat from their brow. They moved away like a parting tide, each eyeing Laura with venom. Laura stared at Clara, her body still, while staff reattached the wires and drips that had come loose.

"What the fuck happened?" Francis said, his face etched with both concern and anger.

"Get some uniform here to guard her," Laura said, forcing the words out through her aching throat. "We have to go."

Chapter Ten
Laura

Officers arrived on scene and took over the guard. They raced out of the hospital with Francis nipping at her heel and putting Google maps on her phone. The location wasn't far away, and officers had already begun to arrive on scene, passing updates. Laura heard the voice come through the radio. DCI Burnell was attending. Laura bit down on her lip. She was going to get her arse grilled.

The pair of them slipped into the car, Laura in the driver's seat, Francis demoted to the passenger seat. Laura fumbled with the keys and stabbed them into the ignition. She slammed the car into first gear and revved the engine so fiercely the exhaust popped, and the tires screeched like a Banshee's wail.

They were in an unmarked car, so Laura turned on the flashing lights and sirens that flickered to life in the grill and the rear of the vehicle. Other motorists slammed on their brakes fiercely as they took a hard left out of the hospital car park onto the main road. The car bounced off the slight lip of the road onto the main highway, testing the suspension. Laura slammed it straight into third gear, the world blurring past them. Her mind turned faster than the speeding wheels under her. Something was wrong. Terribly wrong. This wasn't just a murder and attempted suicide. There was more to this. She didn't know how, but she could feel it, like tasting something in the air.

"Right," Francis finally said after chewing his nails down to the bone. "I have to ask. What the hell happened back there? One minute Clara was a statue, the next minute, she's on you like a rash." Laura didn't know what to say, or how to describe it.

I was triggered into a memory of some CPTSD that counselling hadn't touched? She killed her husband, but I think she was provoked? I see her as me, and I want to help her because I couldn't help myself? Well, none of those explanations would work now, would they?

"She just flipped," Laura lied. "I don't know why. I went over to her to get her to talk, and then she turned on me." Francis eyed the side of her face.

"With all due respect, Sergeant," he said. "I think you're talking shit." Laura laughed out loud at the audacity of such a remark.

"I think you need to remember who you're talking to, *constable.*" She shifted gears, moving to the opposite end of the road and swerving back to the correct lane with the blare of horns from oncoming traffic. "She's been the victim of abuse," Laura said with a long breath. "I can see it. The blank stares. The history of mental health issues in the past few years. Her emaciation. The abduction from the hospital." She was shaking her head. "Something about this whole thing stinks, and I can smell it from a mile away."

"Where are you getting that from?" Francis said. "People have psychotic breakdowns. There's no history on her or her partner. Both aren't known PNC. No domestic history. No calls were ever made from neighbours. No disclosures were ever made to medical staff. We're assuming she was abducted. She could have easily just walked out of the hospital, and the nurse said the husband was happy to let her speak to hospital staff alone. A controlling partner wouldn't do that!"

"You don't know that," Laura bit. "You don't know

what it's like." Tears were burning in her eyes.

"While you were speaking to the nurse, I did a little digging online about Alex Weaver. He is everywhere on Google. Philanthropist. Supporter of the Wigtown hospital trust. Opened charity organisations. Hell, even injected some money into the rehab clinics that got set up because of what you went through with the *Straw Man* murders."

"What're you implying?" Laura said, her knuckles turning white around the steering wheel. Francis took a deep breath, and Laura waited for the bomb to explode.

"I think you need to go back to the station," Francis said. "You need to sit this one out."

"I can't do that," Laura said quickly, the pain in her throat growing.

"Let's look at what we have," Francis said. "We have a woman who isn't talking, covered in blood. We have a history of mental instability and some insinuation that her husband took her from the hospital. We have no witnesses of that. We also have no records of any form of domestic incident ever with the two of them. In fact, that whole thing has come from you. Not Clara. Not the police. No witnesses or professionals. Just you." He took a breath. "You have a bad past. What happened between you and your ex, Craig, and Alice. Not to mention your drinking." He waited for Laura to rip his throat out, but she fixated her growing rage on the road in front. The engine growing louder. "I think you're projecting your own demons onto Clara's case. I think you're chasing ghosts." Laura let the words sink in. Was she projecting? Was this some kind of saviour complex or survivors' guilt? The therapist had said she should be careful of triggers. That if she felt herself slipping, then she should call them or book in for another session. The demons may have been exorcized, but that didn't mean they were gone forever. She had scoffed at this. Giving up the booze was the hardest thing she had ever done. She remembered laying in the small room she had at the clinic which overlooked a large green meadow and a pond in the centre. Night had fallen, and she was suffering from both insomnia and withdrawal. The only thing she could do was stare at the pond and force herself to focus on it, lest she tries to break through the glass to find the nearest off licence.

The medication they had her on wasn't enough. Years of substance abuse, drinking bottle after bottle to make her sleep, to make her function, to make her feel somewhat alive, had been taken away. There was more to withdrawal than just the physical effects. She still got the shakes. The vomiting. The long nights staring into the darkness. It was the monsters in her mind too. The ones that had been numbed and quieted by the cascading and ready supply of booze to keep them stupefied. In that blackness, alone in that eight by ten room with nothing but a single bed, a writing desk, and a window that overlooked a vast emptiness, did they come to visit her. She saw the deepest, most insidious devils of her mind in that place. She wrote some of it down. Hell, even drew pictures of them sometimes. Sometimes she was smiling. Other times she was screaming, being eaten alive by wolves. She didn't show those to the therapist. She didn't need to share her nightmares with them, too.

After the first week of utter hell of no sleep and vomiting and shitting herself several times a day, she was finally able to sleep for a few hours. Two CBT sessions a day for one hour a time, then it was recreational activities, sports, and time to do what you liked. Laura mainly read in the corner. Old paperbacks. Nothing new. Occasionally disturbed by one of the newcomers to the clinic, who had to be restrained because they attacked another service user. Turned out they were also withdrawing off crack, - and they were only there because it would mean going back to prison should they give a positive sample.

Laura kept herself to herself. No friends, other than the occasional 'hello' here or there. By the end of the third week, she had dropped what weight she had gained from the booze. By the end of the first month, she was sleeping through the night and was reading self-help books and journalling. Speaking to the therapist only once every two days and finding herself booked into further education sessions to pass the time.

She came out of that place after ten months feeling put together, then a further three months at home with check in sessions. And now, her first week she gets involved in a job that hits home, and all her work seems to be unravelling again around her like a bandage that was loosely tied on, revealing an old wound had become infected again. She pushed the image away, Francis still talking. He meant well. She knew he did, but there was no way she was going to let this case pass her by. As if it was some kind of mission for her to complete. Even if she lost herself in the process. But that was what being a police officer meant, right? Giving yourself to the public you serve and forgoing all self-preservation. To not discriminate. To act with righteousness and good deeds, forgoing all prejudice and discrimination.

Laura was the *perfect* person to help discover the truth behind Clara, even if that meant destroying herself in the process.

"I have a duty to protect the people in this town, Francis," she whispered.

"I understand that," he said. "But are you ready for this kind of job, given what you've been through?" He sighed, seeing that she wasn't heading to the station, and they were closing in on the incident location with each passing red light. "Look, it's none of my business what you do," he said, concern in his voice. "But you need to think about this. You already have the DCI on your back, and I know something happened in that hospital that you're not telling me." Laura chewed on those words for a moment.

"You're right," she snapped. "It isn't any of your business. I'm staying on this case. The DCI can suspend me for all I care."

"You don't mean that," Francis barked. "Listen to you!"

"No!" Laura barked. "You listen to me!" She slammed her palm on the dashboard, the loud crack sending Francis' nerves wild. "I decide my fate. Not you, not anyone else. I decide what case to work on. I decide whether I want to get fucked by the new bitch in town. Me. Not you, not anyone else. Me. Now if you're going to be in my ear all the way there, then I'll pull the car over. Stop thinking about me. I'm fine. We are potentially walking into a murder scene. I need to know you're in it with me." Francis went to speak, but the burning in Laura's eyes stole his voice away.

Salt water. Violent waves.

Kiss Kiss.

The distance on the Google maps struggled to keep up with their speed. Units began to arrive at the location. A large, gated estate with several high-end cars in the driveway. They were shouting up on the radio if they knew the code for the gate. Unfortunately, they did not, and the officers were trapped outside of the home on the street knowing there was someone needing their help inside. Laura's blood pressure rose so high her heart was about to pop.

"Warburton to control," she shouted over the radio. "Tell those officers to get through that gate."

"We can't, Sergeant," one of them shouted up. "It's locked up tight. Our rams won't break through it. We don't know what to do." Laura checked the sat nav. Less than a minute away.

"Well figure it out. I want you in that house before I arrive." Francis shot her a look of worry. "Do it now. I want an update on the radio in thirty seconds." Laura killed the transmission. Francis looked at the speedometer. She was doing three times the speed limit with no sign of slowing down. Up ahead he saw something that sent his nerves wild.

"Slow down!" Francis balled. Laura saw her emerging from the side of the road behind a car. She saw the pram first. Then the mother, with her eyes glued to her phone and her headphones in. She couldn't see them. "Look out!" Francis screamed, recoiling back into his seat. He slammed his foot into a brake that wasn't there and pointed at the woman, who was completely oblivious. She was straight in front of them. The woman looked up, and Laura saw sheer terror on her face. She was young, probably a new mother. The pram was black, a little bundle of joy inside. Laura pulled on the wheel. The screeching of the tyres cut through the wail of the sirens. The woman screamed. Francis screamed. The car bounced onto the kerb, narrowly missing the woman and the pram by a couple of inches.

Laura kept on going, her face like stone.

"What the fuck!" Francis screamed.

"She's fine," Laura said, like the whole thing had been a figment of his imagination.

"Pull the car over," he said firmly.

"No."

"Pull the damn car over!" Laura continued driving. Francis shook his head, his heart in his throat. "I'll be reporting you when we get back."

"Join the queue."

"Laura!" He blasted. "What the hell is wrong with you? We can't help anyone if you are like this."

Doing nothing didn't help me before.

Laura slammed on the brakes. The motion jerkin Francis in his seat, the seat belt gripping him. They screeched to a stop. The stench of rubber and a burned-out clutch assaulting them.

"Get out," Laura said. Francis looked at her with horror.

"You need help," he said, unclipping his belt and stepping out into the street. He hadn't even closed his door before Laura sped off again, leaving him looking bewildered in the rear-view mirror.

She drove on. Her knuckles turning white from gripping the steering wheel. What was she doing? Had she lost her mind completely? She had been fine. But now? She was being self-destructive, and she knew it. She was 'losing her shit' as her therapist had so eloquently put it, following Laura flipping a table during a therapy session.

Why do you feel you have to help everyone? They had said.

Because I couldn't help myself.

That's what she was doing now. But she had to. She couldn't explain it or begin to rationalise it. She simply *had* to find out the truth behind what had happened. Maybe she was losing herself in the case? Maybe the triple threat of suicide, abduction, and potential murder was too much for her fragile mind to overcome?

She arrived at the scene. Officers stood outside the large steel front gates like they were a rabble of Jehovah's Witnesses trying to save someone from their sins of gluttony and greed. One officer was trying to pry the gates open. Another was trying to climb over the gates, but kept slipping. Laura furrowed her brow.

If they can't climb the gate, then how did Clara get out? Another piece of the jigsaw she now had to fit together. She viewed the estate with a sense of strange contempt. The graffiti smeared betting and charity shops she was used to seeing had been replaced by stone walled post offices, florists, and small mini-markets. The grey walls and wire fencing, litter, and a crowd outside of Weatherspoon's early in the morning were replaced by families walking their dogs to heel. Green, flourishing trees that arched over the road and mailmen that whistled in their step. All the people were staring at the house where the police stood out front. All wondering why chaos had come to suburbia. Laura left the engine running and stepped out into the street.

"What's going on?" She bit, looking at the faces of the officers. Most of them were new in service. Some with only a few years in. The most senior officer she could spot was a cop that had around five years' service. The state of modern policing was a shambles. Not to say that they should return to the rose-tinted spectacles of older times, but the fact that she had more service than all the officers at the scene combined was more than worrying. To the public, they all looked capable. But this was part of the big lie. The public gets the service they need and thinks it's the best service they can get. But it wasn't, and she knew it. The fact that officers hadn't got into the address was testament to that.

"We've tried knocking on the neighbours to see if they know how to get into the address," one officer said. A young man. Laura recognised him. He had been the first on scene following a domestic murder she had seen on the television. A man, Christian Peters, had relentlessly manipulated and stalked a woman he had become infatuated with, named Lorna Withers. In the end, Lorna had to take matters into her own hands and fight her assailant, eventually driving her friend's car into him. He was now serving life in prison for the murder of her husband, Mark, and the abduction and attempted murder of others. A case that made her sick to the stomach. It was easy to see how controlling and coercive behaviour can result in homicide. She had read many books about it. It was like the victim was being force-fed poison. The dose and timing just varied.

"Any luck?" She said, eyeing the vast house in front of her. The estate gave her chills. She dreaded to think what horrors awaited her inside those walls. They needed to get in, and quick.

Laura's phone rang. She took it out. It was Jeremy. Her face scrunched together like she had bitten into a sour toffee.

"Go on," she said, trying to drown out the calls from officers around her. He sounded out of breath.

"Are you at the house?" He said.

"Of course."

"You were given explicit instructions *not* to go there," he barked. "I've got the DCI breathing down my neck. I can't protect you if you go any further."

"I'm a big girl Jeremy," Laura said. "I can look after

myself." Laura could almost feel the heat coming from him. She waited for steam to push through the handset.

"It's *inspector,*" he seethed. Laura rolled her eyes.

"I'm a big girl, *sir,*" she reiterated. Laura covered the mouthpiece, barking to the officers that were slamming the ram against the front gate, the rattle of the steel mocking them. "Stop that!" She called. The officer, panting, face red, turned to her. "If it hasn't opened so far, it's not going to open now, is it? Try something else. Contingencies, for fuck's sake." She rolled her eyes, returning to Jeremy, who was still talking.

"- not to mention you were on the verge of being dismissed last time –"

"Have you spoken to Francis?" She interjected, cutting him off.

"No," he said, stammering at the question. "Why?"

He hadn't ratted her out. This was good.

"It doesn't matter. Do we have any level one MOE? We can't get through the gate." Jeremy ignored the question, continuing to rattle on about procedures, rank structure, potential dismissal, etc. Laura droned it out, and then terminated the call. She would deal with the burns later, but right now, they had to get through those damn gates. "How long have they lived here?" Laura said, moving to another officer. Young. Not a fleck of hair on his chin. He searched his mind, seeing the Sergeant he had heard so much about asking him a direct question he didn't know the answer too.

"Around four years, I think."

"You *think?*" The officer could feel the heat of her stare. Laura took a piece of paper from her pocket and began to scribble down some questions. "Names. Family. Patterns of movements. Entrances and exits. CCTV. Knock on every house you can see. Do some police work. Investigate. You aren't just here to catch the bad guy and get a statistic." She thrust the paper into the cops dithering hand. "Now!" Like he had had a rocket shoved up his backside, the cop ran like the wind to the houses, which had neighbours staring out at the carnage that had come to their quiet street.

"Sergeant," an officer said. Older looking. Possibly a late joiner. Body armour as black as night. "I have just spoken to the neighbour next door. Said that they only ever saw the husband coming and going. Only saw the wife once." Laura felt like a dull blade was gliding against her nerves.

"So, it's like she's invisible." She said. "What about the one time she saw her?"

"Said she was standing out front and she stole some food from a baby in a pram, and then ran back into the house." Alarm bells rang in Laura's mind.

"No one knows she is here. Isolated. Alone. Controlled." The officer scratched his head.

"I don't know if it's that bad," he said. "She could just be crazy. A recluse." Laura had to stop herself from driving her fist through his face.

"Watch your tongue," she bit. "You don't know how people would take things like that." Laura moved away from the group and looked at the gates. She wrapped her fingers around the cold metal and surveyed the building. She turned. "Anyone have any chains?" The cops looked at her, perplexed.

"What for?" One said.

"To attach to the car. We can pull the gates free from their hinges." A cop let out a laugh, then saw Laura's expression, and her laugh cut away. A beat of silence. "No one?" Only the wind answered. Laura pinched the bridge of her nose and looked up at the monolith before her. Her heart caught in her throat. She saw something moving inside. The movement of a shadow through one of the windows, gliding like a spectre. She turned. None of the other officers had seen it. Each lost in their own conversations. Laura turned back to the house, her hands wrapping around the cold steel bars. Had she imagined it? No. She couldn't have. She had seen that shadow moving through the house with the same certainty that she could feel hot air filling her lungs. *Someone is still in there.* She turned to the officers. "Someone is inside." The cops stopped chattering to each other and eyed her like she had just said the sky was pink.

"I thought this was a murder?" Laura shook her head.

"Have we found a way in yet?" Laura barked. Her patience completely gone. The officer's expressions changed. The Sergeant who was known for losing her head was having another episode right here in real time. They didn't need to say it. She could see it on their faces. They didn't believe her, and if someone was dead inside, then they weren't going to get more dead, so who gave a shit if they took a little longer?

"We have level one MOE on the way Sergeant," an officer said. "We will have to wait."

One thing Laura Warburton was never good at was letting someone else tell her what to do. Especially when it was from someone with a third of her service and rank below. Laura slipped away through the crowd of onlookers and officers. The cops watched her go.

"She's fucked in the head," one of them said. A tall officer with a shaved head. "We need to get in, but we've tried. We can't climb the gates. Have you seen those things? Not in all my kit."

"Those spikes don't look nice," said another officer,

young, blonde. The rounding of her shoulders and firmness of her thighs, would insinuate she was a gym bunny. Three times a week and long runs on the weekends. "Did you hear about that Sergeant? She lost her head at a job. Said she saw a ghost in a closet."

"She got shot, didn't she?" The tall officer said. "Likes the bottle, too. How she hasn't been sacked, I have no idea." The blonde officer went to laugh, but everyone's attention was drawn to the loud blasting of a car horn, and the revving of the vehicle hurtling towards them. DS Warburton behind the wheel.

"Fucking move!" The blonde officer shouted. The group of cops raced out of the way as Laura drove the unmarked car through the locked gate, which exploded in a detonation of brick and warped metal.

Chapter Eleven
Laura

Laura forced the car door open. Glass raining onto the ground, her feet crunching on the tiny shards like diamonds on granite. She steadied herself. The air bag had punched her hard. She touched her head, feeling the hot crimson that was sticky on her fingers. The hissing of the car engine, steam from the radiator pushing into the cool air from the bonnet that looked like it had been gnawed by giant jaws.

Laura stumbled towards the front of the house, calls and shouts coming from behind her that seemed so far away. The radio blaring in her ear, which she threw to the ground. She got to the door and listened but couldn't hear anything. She tried the door handle. Locked. Laura looked through her swaying vision. The upstairs windows were high, overlooking a balcony that went directly over the hard paving of the driveway. Clara hadn't gone out the front door, and to jump from the window would have broken both her legs. Even if she made the jump, she couldn't have scaled that gate. So how did she get out? A hand grabbed her, spinning her on her heel. It was Francis. He was out of breath. His shirt sticking to him. His shoes and pants covered in mud. He had ran here after her. His eyes bulging. Face flushed with red. Laura couldn't hear what he was saying. It all seemed to be one loud crescendo.

"Get that door open," she said, wearily to Francis, and pointed at the front door.

"You need to go to the hospital!" He said, grabbing hold of her coat. Laura shrugged him off. She stumbled backwards, hardly able to keep herself upright. The ringing in her ears prevailing. She looked around. No one was moving. All staring at her with horror on their faces.

"Fine," Laura said. She pushed Francis away and racked her baton. Eight ounces of bone breaking steel. She turned, like a batter about to hit a home run, and swung with everything she could muster at the ground floor window. The tip of the baton collided with the window, and a spiderweb crack appeared on the glass. More calls around her for her to stop. But she didn't listen. She *had* to get into that house. She had to find out what was going on behind those walls. She swung again, screaming as she did, the taste of blood found her tongue. The baton struck, and the glass fell away in a littering rain of shards.

Without missing a beat, Laura slammed the butt of the baton into the broken glass, cleaning it away. Breaking off large chunks like cracking open a frozen river to rescue someone trapped underneath in the dark depths. She removed her coat, throwing it over the gap, and disappeared inside the maw.

Francis watched her go, shouting after her through the shards. He grabbed the glass and recoiled in pain, a shard cutting into his hand. He wafted it in the air, flicking flecks of blood onto the paving under his feet. Laura was moving deeper into the home. He called for her, as if she was vanishing into a cave of monsters. His radio came to life.

"All officers at the scene. This is DCI Amy Burnell. If any officer follows Sergeant Warburton into that crime scene, you will have your dismissal served by me personally." The officers that had been moving to the house suddenly stepped back, like being told they were walking into a minefield. Francis watched Laura move into the blackness.

"Laura," he croaked. She stopped and turned. Her head bleeding. Face ashen. Clothing peppered with fine glass. "Please…" She regarded him. Her mouth tight. Eyes glistening. She turned and continued into the house.

A sickness befell her as she moved through the living room. The plush carpet under her feet littered with glass shards. The house was dark, other than the lazy light that dared venture through the windows. On the walls hung photos of Clara and a man, holding each other in an embrace. Faces a picture of a happy marriage. Very Instagramable. The envy of others that should cast their eyes on their perfect life. But Laura knew that was all for show. She had had the same with Ron. Posting photos online. Posing together with ice creams in some old style village in the Mediterranean. But in those photos, one might see happiness and love. But there be monsters lying in plain sight. And it was the photos with that monster that let other creatures find her. She eyed the photo on its gold frame on the marble fireplace. He was older. Grey haired with a salt and pepper beard. He was handsome, even by Laura's standards. His eyes were a piercing blue that almost drew you in, as if at any moment the smiling man in the picture would change to a malevolent grin, thrust out his hand and drag her into his embrace. Laura put the photo back on the fireplace. She noticed it then. Ornaments. Pictures. They were all perfectly spaced out, like someone had obsessively agonised about every minute detail. There wasn't a single fleck of dust or grime on any surface, and on the sleek white walls around the room. Not a fingerprint on the light switches. Not a speck of dust on the skirting boards. Not even a mark on the wall at the back of the couch. It was as if someone had removed all evidence of human life from the room and turned it sterile. But then she saw one that was out of place. On the floor by her feet. A frame that held a cracked photo of Alex and Clara Weaver at the bottom of the fire place. Laura studied it. They looked happy. But looks can be deceptive. Why was it on the floor when everything else was so perfect? And why was the glass cracked?

Voices of the officers bombarded her, screaming at her to leave the scene. She placed the picture down where she found it. The sound of more sirens filtered through the air. She let them decide their own destinies. She had settled for her own bespoke form of Armageddon.

She stumbled, catching herself on the door that led out of the living room. Her vision began to sway. She closed her eyes and took a deep breath.

Not yet, she thought. *I've got to do this my way before the rest of them come in. If I don't find something now, then all this will have been for nothing.* Slowly, she peeled the door open, before walking into the rest of the house of horrors.

Her heels clicked under her feet as she walked along the polished hallways flooring. The front door to her right, with the silhouettes of officers behind the frosted glass. She envied their love for the job. She had had enough of it all. The pain. The misery. The politics. The fighting for what you knew was right only to have a boss above you throw you to the wolves because it didn't align with their current agenda. Since coming out of rehab, she had fallen out of love with the police force. She loved helping people, but these days it was fewer and farther between where she got to really help a genuine victim of crime. Clara Weaver, she thought, would be her last case to work on. And it would be the case that made or destroyed her faith in the justice system. She knew something was going on. Why wasn't she speaking? What was locked behind those lips? Something she had learned in therapy is that people hold trauma differently. Some self-harm. Some take drugs, have lots of sex, and self-destruct themselves. Some channel it into new relationships, inflicting what they had done to them onto those that they have around them. Some end up in prison. Some end up taking their own lives. Some live perfectly happy and normal lives. But then there were some who shut down. Like a beaten dog that pisses itself every time it hears a noise. They simply crumble and become a shell of their former selves. That was what she saw in Clara Weaver. She saw a woman that had been broken. Destroyed so intensely that she couldn't even fathom speaking a single word to anyone about the horror that she had been subjected to inside these walls.

She couldn't explain it, but the house felt *sick*. Like it was cursed. Like all the terrible things that happened within these walls had somehow left a stain on its existence. She wanted to light a match and burn the place to the ground. But only after she figured out what had happened here.

As a police officer, if wasn't often that she spent time seeing how the other half lived. She had often driven through the suburban, countryside estates that had their huge homes, expensive cars and their whitewash walls and giant plots of land surrounding their homes. It was to evoke envy. It was all for show. Very rarely, if ever, did she get a call to one of these homes. Which on the face of it, one might think it was because their lives were perfect and that they were living the high life. No arguments. A ton of money and three holidays a year to the Maldives. A life of paradise. But you can't spell life of paradise without the word 'lie.' It was all for show. Those that lived in those giant houses with their big fancy homes didn't have the perfect life. They were just better at hiding it from the world. It was the minute details she had to look out for. Things that seemed amiss.

If Clara was in an abusive relationship with Alex Weaver, then there was so much to uncover. The Cycle of Abuse. The intricacies of deny, attack, reverse. All the anagrams. All the training and experience she had amassed in her career. Laura would have to look beyond what she could see already. Look beyond what surface information she was perceiving.

Again, she noticed not a single blemish on the walls, on the oak spindle stair guard, or a single piece of lint of hair on the flooring. It appeared obsessive. But was it an unstable mind? Obsessive-compulsive? Or was it the symptom of control? It was sick. A sick game that she had to find out the secret to beating. It was a puzzle, and Laura needed to find the clues to solve it.

All the doors were open. A small home gym, and a home cinema. A basement. A spare sitting room with couches that looked more expensive than an entire year of her soon to be obsolete salary. Even a walk-in shower and spare bathroom. Everything looked perfect, like something you could see in a magazine while travelling through the airport.

The door at the end of the hallway was closed. No

light graced under the gap of the door, like it had forsaken the walls that were beyond. Laura's mouth went acrid. Her hand hovering over the door handle. She caught herself and put on a pair of rubber gloves. She knew that something was beyond that door, and she would see it for the rest of her life.

Chapter Twelve
Clara
Then

I'm a murderer.

I don't know how long I stayed there. Time seemed to stop. But after an endless moment, I saw the light break through the surrounding tree, slipping through the back patio doors. The light was golden, heavenly, and yet for some reason, its warmth seemed hostile, like a vampire stepping out into the sun would burst into flames. The light fell over your body. Your face was ashen and grey. Your eyes like empty windows. The red snakes that slithered out of your puncture wounds had stopped. As I watched you in that silent space, that should I lay my trembling hands on you cold flesh, would you wrap your cold, cruel fingers around me? Such a ridiculous thought, and yet one I couldn't shake. As much as I reasoned with the thought, the more absurd it became, but then I would have never believed this reality I found myself currently in.

Something moved. In that stillness. In that stillness where I sat, unmoving, barely breathing, only the silence whispering back to me, holding me tightly. I wanted to look around the room but dared not remove my gaze from your body. Fearing if I did, my gaze would return to find you smiling at me.

I fixed my gaze on your grey skin, and nothing moved in that space. The sunlight creeping ever so closely, stopping at the tips of my feet. Even the light wouldn't touch me. I was an outcast. I had committed the worst crime imaginable, and I would be punished for it. The freedom I had longed for so viciously had now been taken away by my own hand.

I blinked. My eyes burning. The cold cut through me like a bolt of ice that shattered and splintered, fragmenting into my blood. Your eyes moved. I was certain. Concrete filled my bones.

The sound again. Closer this time. The sound of something *snapping*.

It was inside the room with me. Were the police here? I had been screaming. Wait, had I? Had I made a sound? Any other sound than the sound of the knife slipping between your ribs? Oh god, how many times had I stabbed you? Could I even hide a body if I wanted to? You would be missed, and your family would hire someone to come looking. Even if they didn't get the police involved, they would hire the best private investigator money could buy. They would find me, no matter how far I ran, and they would tear me limb from limb until there was nothing left but scraps of bones and meat. I was lost. I was forsaken. I was damned.

Snap.

Something moved out the corner of my eye. I had seen it. I was certain.

Snap.

Your head had moved. I wasn't seeing things. I didn't take my eyes off you. Not for a moment. Your head was turned to me. Your smile a long, sharp grin. Your face like that of putty, morphed and shaped into something sinister and cruel, like a Halloween mask.

Snap.

Fingers popped, like a spider that had been dead still, was now waking up and ready to feed. I couldn't believe what I was seeing. I had killed you. I had murdered you. Stabbed you more times than I could remember. Stabbed you in every place I could. But you were alive? Your mouth opened along the floor. your jaw impossibly wide. Cheeks stretching, the skin growing thin as it began to rip and tear. Teeth pushing loose from gums. Your tongue was grey and fat, falling limp onto the floor like a sack of bleached leather.

I watched from the black mouth, a slithering, bald head began to crown. I saw the lump growing from your throat, like a snake regurgitating a kill. It emerged from your gullet. I felt excruciating pain erupt in my abdomen, like someone was taking a blade to my skin. I clutched it with both hands. Blood gushed out of me, drenching my clothes in scarlet. It pooled around me, haemorrhaging a lake of red. I screamed, but nothing came. The sunlight had vanished, and the blackness of midnight returned. The sound of snapping grew louder. Your dead jaws now peeled back. A screaming child flooded and covered in thick mucus writhed on the kitchen floor, bathing in my blood.

It crawled on all fours towards me. Each fat slap of its deformed fingers and feet into the pool of blood. The baby's face, if a word could be used for such an abomination, smiled at me. It's features, eyes, mouth, and nose warped in indescribable horror. I felt the last piece of my sanity explode in glistening shards that cut through every part of my sanity.

The writhing infant moved slowly. I tried to push through the wall, kicking my legs back, my mouth agape, a scream begging to be released but wouldn't come. I looked for the door, but there was none. When I returned my petrified gaze, you were standing over me with the knife I had butchered you with. The infant was screaming, you holding it by its leg. You drove the knife into the abomination's stomach, gutting it like a fish from naval to throat, and letting all its rancid insides and slippery organs rain down onto me.

"You won't get away with this," you hissed in a low, abyssal tone. "They're coming for you."

Hands erupted out from the river of boiling blood that was beneath me. It blistered and cracked my skin as the hands grabbed hold of my flailing limbs. Another hand took hold, but not before I managed to claw at someone's face, their skin carving under my nails, red streaks appearing along their face. Another hand pinned her down, and then a hand smothered my face, pressing down on my skull and burying me into the plush hospital pillow. My mouth meets the mattress. I couldn't breathe. I fought harder, pulling and twisting and thrashing at the demons that wanted to consume me, desperate and fighting for a single breath and single gulp of air, but none came. Hot tears stained my cheeks and burned my bloodshot eyes. Then, the bite of a needle found my leg, and my screams faded into stifled croaks and squeaks until, finally, the darkness returned, and I slipped back into the world of monsters that dragged me through the ground into a spiralling chasm of darkness and screaming.

Chapter Thirteen
Laura

The door to the kitchen had opened halfway before stopping dead, hitting something on the floor. A sinking feeling plummeted in Laura's stomach. She squeezed through the gap to discover Alex Weaver on the ground. His blood soaked into the kitchen tiling, and streams of crimson had snaked through the grooves around him, spreading along the floor like a bloated spider's web. Laura stepped over him. He was dead. No need for CPR. No need to touch him. Forensics would look over him. Establish time of death. Cause of death? It was obvious to anyone with half a brain – the guy had been opened up like a paint can and spilled onto the ground. Fat, muscle, and flesh bursting from the wounds that could be seen on his arms, throat, stomach, and legs, like he had swallowed a vial of vicious tapeworms that ate their way out of him.

He was a large man. Fat, but definitely used to work out. His shoulders were broad. His skin was pasty like clay. A dead body often resembled a washed-out version of a person. Because of gravity, their blood pooled to the ground, making their skin and extremities a pus pasty colour. His lips were grey. His eyes had closed, meaning he had been dead for a little while. Nature had a way of giving its own respects to the dead. Closing their eyes naturally after a few hours. Providing the flies didn't get to them first.

Laura looked around the room. The kitchen light was still on, so it was likely the death occurred on the evening, or possibly in the early morning. But the clothes he wore – A tee shirt with a collar, and jeans that she thought were blue, turned a deep black from the dried blood. He had a gold chain and rings on, which would suggest that he was already fully dressed when he was killed. Laura saw a broken plate on the ground, the pungent stench of fish assaulting her nostrils. He had been murdered over dinner. Clara must have been an excellent cook. The food was to die for.

She continued looking, being extra careful not to disturb anything. The light from the patio doors seeped through into the kitchen. Laura moved to the doors, depressed the handle, and pulled. The door slid open. She stepped out into the garden. It was vast. Summer chairs and tables are laid out, and a log fire pit is in the centre. Next to it, a half empty crate of lager. Some German brand. Laura felt the urge to grab one, snap off the lid, press the bottle to her lips until the bottom faced the heavens. She licked her arid lips. She was so thirsty. Maybe just a sip…

She forced her attention away like a suicide being dragged from the rails of an oncoming train. Her head was still spinning, and now there was a beating of a drum to accompany it. Laura forced herself to look out into the garden. It was freshly cut. She could tell from the smell of grass. No lawnmower was out. A gardener? Maybe? She couldn't see any sign of grass or dirt inside the kitchen. Other than the dead body, the blood, and the smashed plate of food, it looked the same as the living room and the rest of the house. Everything in its place. Obsessively so. There were padlocks on the fridge and cupboards. Food was rationed or scheduled. Given the state of Clara, Laura doubted she had a key.

Food was a weapon. She took a moment, perplexed.

If this place is locked up tight – the gate. The doors. The walls. How did she get out? Remembering the flecks of dirt on Clara's legs, Laura stepped back outside into the back garden. The hedges surrounding her were thick and high. There was no kind of exit that she could see. So short of leaping over the gates like a cat racing from a hungry dog or evaporating through them like a vampire in a movie, she still had no idea how she got out. But in her state, that would have been impossible, which left her to the question of *how?*

The breeze licked her face like a ghost, and Laura closed the patio doors, silencing the outside world and returning to the tomb of silence of the kitchen. She moved around further, checking the sideboards and the cupboards. Nothing jumped out at her. But she knew there was something missing in this perfect picture. Something which was niggling at her, like a song that was scratching at her skull, but she couldn't remember the words.

Then she noticed it. The knife rack by the side of the sink. There was one missing. On the ground, she saw a knife and fork scattered onto the ground amongst the smashed porcelain plate and spoiled food. She inspected the knife on the ground. It was sharp, and yes, there was a fleck of blood on it. Laura eyed up Alex's cadaver, gently peeling away the blood sodden clothing. Pulling back the collar of his shirt. His body was cold. People describe the touch of the dead as ice cold when it's simply room temperature. The coldness of a body is a direct reflection of the cold, bitter, and brutal world we walk through each day, but our beating heart shields us from its clutches. There was something poetic about that.

A small cut. Not much deeper than a scratch on Alex's shoulder. She checked the serration and grooves of the knife again. She was no forensic expert, but she would put money on that this knife was not the one that opened him up. They looked deep. Caused by a much fiercer weapon. She got back up, steadying herself again on the sideboards, less she collapses into the chilling, bloodied embrace of Alex.

The missing knife in the knife rack. It looked like it should have been a steak knife of some kind. Something sharp. Something deadlier. Laura looked around the rest of the room. She couldn't see it anywhere. The murder weapon was missing. Had Clara disposed of it? Or had someone taken it away already? She furrowed her brow. Clara had come straight from the house and been found outside by a member of the public, whose identity they still didn't know. A call had been made to the ambulance from an unregistered number, and they had left before the ambulance arrived. Now pair that with a missing murder weapon. Something wasn't adding up. There was someone else involved in this case. Laura could taste it like the iron in the air from the blood. Laura turned back to the patio doors. Her head really beginning to boom. Squinting her eyes, she studied the surrounding hedges.

"How the hell did you get out?" She was going to whisper more, but the train of vomit came up before she could stop it. She folded in half, expelling a splatter of vomit onto the ground of a murder scene. A fucking murder scene. Long strings of bile falling from her lips and landing onto the sleek white tiles. Laura wiped her mouth on her coat jacket. She needed to get out of here. Fear gripping her. She could have fucked this entire investigation up. She righted herself, her forehead pissing with sweat. Her breath shallow. Head dancing like it was on a fairground ride. She couldn't stop it. Couldn't help it. She collapsed to the ground, head hurtling for the tiles.

Chapter Fourteen
Laura

Laura sat at her desk and stared into the black coffee cup in front of her. A sense of déjà vu that she couldn't shake. How many times had she been here, in this office, staring into a cup filled with tar following something terrible happening?

She had had to change her clothes and hand them over to forensics, peeling off her blood and vomit coated shirt, blazer, pants and even heels. Thankfully, she didn't have to strip off her underwear too. She didn't have a spare set of those in her locker. Being on CID for most of her career had taught her to be prepared for messy days. The term 'messy' was subjective, depending on who you asked. It could be breaking down a door to find an old lady who hadn't been seen in months, to discover her melted into the carpet, maggots long vacating their home in her stomach. Incidents like that weren't just a change of clothes. They were a case of burning everything you were wearing. The stench of death could cling to someone's clothes no matter how much they were bleached and scrubbed. It was a stench that every emergency personal worker knew all too well. A stench that you can't describe but can recall in a moment. A lingering of someone once being alive, like their ghost had leeched onto you and was jealous of the air you still got to breathe.

Then there were the instances like serious car accidents, and she had had to scoop bits of body parts and put them into bin bags that were sodden with diesel fuel or brake dust. Or she had to try and stop the bleeding at a stabbing, and she had nothing other than her finger to jam into the gushing wound to try and buy the ambulance service a couple more precious minutes to get to them. And then there were the instances like today, where every fibre of her would need to be examined, swabbed, and photographed by the forensic unit. The old phrase remains the same and very true. *Blood doesn't lie.*

She took a hefty drink from the coffee. It was turning cold, the steam gathering around the cup's rim. How long had she sat here? The door burst open. It was Jeremy, and he was pissed.

"You have one chance to save your skin. I have the DCI, the Superintendent, the home office, and the fucking media breathing down my neck and calling for you to be paraded out into the street and dragged away by your feet by runaway horses." He slammed his hands on the table. Laura had never seen him this angry before. She was used to him dithering and freaking out when he had too many emails to open. It was different to see him angry and growing a pair of balls. It was refreshing. "What the fuck were you thinking? Why shouldn't I have you arrested? You have been back a week! A fucking week! Did they not teach you anything in rehab? How *not* to fuck everything up wherever you go? I mean, Jesus Christ, Laura." He pinched his fingers to the bridge of his nose. Laura stared at the cup of black in her hand. It had gone cold. She hadn't touched it. All she could think about was Clara, and how Laura had failed her. "Are you even listening to me?" Laura snapped her attention back to him.

"Every word," she said, numbly. The stench of blood. Of vomit. She could still smell it. The hot iron, metallic pungent stench soaked in stomach acid.

"Well?" Laura let out a long breath.

"The second I saw that woman on the bridge, I knew something was wrong." Jeremy let out a bark of stressed laugher.

"That doesn't take a genius now, does it?" He was mocking her. Since he had been promoted, he had become more vicious. No one wanted to work on the MIU with him as the superior. Catherine had jumped ship. Francis was close to retirement. There were a couple of detectives that had been and gone in the months Laura had left and Jeremy had taken control. He was poison, seeping into the blood of whoever worked with him, making them erode from the inside out.

"She is emaciated," Laura continued, pushing the thoughts away of diving over the desk and slamming the coffee cup over his skull. "She has a shaved head. What woman shaves her head?"

"Plenty."

"And leaves long strands?" Laura shook her head. "Clara hasn't said a word. The nurse indicated that the partner had abducted her from the hospital following a suicide attempt. Suicide attempts that have only started recently. Her weight has dropped dramatically over the last few months, according to her medical notes. Coincidence?"

"She's crazy," Jeremy said, dismissing the enquiry. Laura continued, regardless.

"We have a woman who has had a significant decline in her health, attempting to end her life and tried to jump off a bridge. If I hadn't stopped her, we would have two bodies, and not one. You're welcome, by the way." Laura watched the comment land like a bomb in

Jeremy's mind. His face twitched. Only a little, but there. "At the hospital, she freaked out and went after me when I mentioned the dead husband. Something inside her snapped. We get to the house, and no one can get in the place. It's like a fortress. A prison. The house immaculate. Unnervingly so. Everything is pristine. There are locks on the cupboards. It isn't a home. It's a prison. A prison I had to break into."

"You caused a lot of damage."

"If it weren't for me, we would still be outside that place scratching our heads!" Laura heard her voice boom around the room like the reverb of a grenade detonating. Jeremy took it, used to the shockwaves of Laura's outbursts. "I smashed the window to get in. No officer followed me through."

"They value their careers." Laura wanted to punch his fat fuck of a face.

"Correct," she said. "But they didn't get to see what I saw." Jeremy's brow raised.

"Go on."

"It's perfect inside." Jeremy let out a laugh.

"You cause absolute carnage, and you find a nice-looking house? You need to go back on response for some perspective. A nice house isn't that unordinary in everyday life. Just uncommon with the shits we go to." *Shits.* A slander term for those police deal with. Laura never liked the term and never used it herself. It was dehumanising. Same as saying someone's incident, the worst day of their life that they had to call the police for help, was a 'job' or a 'task,' on the live list. These were people's lives. Not just a 'job.'

"No, Jeremy."

"It's sir." Laura clutched the cup in her hand tighter.

"The house was immaculate. Not a single thing out of

place. Not a spec of dirt. Dust. Even the ornaments on the mantelpiece were arranged perfectly. I bet if you measured them with a ruler…"

"Get to the point. I don't have all day. And you have even less." He pulled out the chair and folded his arms.

"There was a knife missing from the knife rack."

"Forensics have recovered the murder weapon."

"It isn't the murder weapon," Laura said. "The knife in the kitchen didn't kill Alex." Jeremy let out a laugh.

"You're a forensic expert now?"

"No, but…"

"Leave the technical stuff to the experts." Laura's breath caught in her throat.

"Locks on the cupboards," she said. "There was a photo frame that was cracked on the floor."

"And your house is perfect?" Jeremy said. Why was he dismissing her?

"Jeremy," Laura bit. "Clara was being controlled so viciously by Alex. She has been a victim of serious coercive and controlling behaviour. She is extremely traumatised to the point she can't speak. Everything about what I have seen points to that."

"The DCI has ruled Clara murdered Alex, and anyone else who stands in the way of that obvious fact will be held accountable." The words were like a ten ton brick landing on Laura's body. She was being told *not* to investigate, and *not* to follow lines of enquiry.

"That makes no sense," Laura said, her voice beginning to shake. "Clara is the victim here." Jeremy scrunched up his face, like he was dealing with a child having a tantrum at bed time.

"I'll humour you," Jeremy said. He let out a long breath. "You're saying she killed him for… what? She snapped? Loss of control? I don't think the CPS will buy that." He said. "Unless she talks, which she is yet to, it's pure conjecture. Alex was stabbed over thirty times and counting. That's not loss of control. That's murder. That's a sustained, frenzied attack. And Clara, regardless of circumstances, is going to prison for it. She could have told the hospital staff. Told a neighbour. Told *anyone* about what was going on at home, but she didn't." Laura couldn't believe what she was hearing. Jeremy was suggesting that because she didn't try to escape someone who was abusing her, then she is to blame, like she welcomed this fate onto herself.

"Is that what you think about me?" Laura bit, her breath hot, her fingers shaking around the coffee mug. "That what Ron put me through was my fault?" His name was like vomit on her tongue. "That *I* welcomed his abuse because I didn't tell anyone about it?" Jeremy held her gaze. His silence speaking volumes.

"I didn't say that," he rebuked after a stretch of quiet. The buzzing of the strip lighting above them like a buzz saw into Laura's skull. "It's just more complicated." Laura swallowed every insult she was going to hurl at him.

"You're right," she whispered, fighting back the tears. "It is." The two sat in silence for a moment. Laura struggling with the runaway narrative in her head. She was fighting a losing battle. There was only so much she could do, and if no one was going to listen to her, then she was truly alone. She had no one to call upon. No one to help her hash out her thoughts, and those who were meant to protect her were saying she was thinking too much into things. That she had got it wrong, and she would be punished for it. No matter how far she ran from manipulation, she found herself right back in its arms. "Speaking of complicated, have they found how Clara got *out* of the address?" Jeremy looked like he had lost interest in the conversation, reluctantly shifting in his chair.

"How so?" He said.

"The door was locked. No back exit. Windows so high that jumping from them would have broken her legs. That gate, those walls. Well, we saw what we had to do to get through that." The corner of Laura's mouth curled into a smile. "So, if you've got it all figured out, *sir*, how did she get out?" His face looked like someone had sat on the remote and pressed the pause button, before it jumping back to life.

"We'll figure it out," Jeremy said.

No, Laura thought. *No, you won't. Because you have your suspect who isn't talking, a dead body and his blood all over her. You don't need to explain the gaps. She'll be found guilty at trail every day of the week. If it even goes that far. She might go to prison, or she might end up in a psych ward and left to rot, doped up on medication for the rest of her life. All because Jeremy Marriot wanted to get a promotion and had forgotten the reason why he became a cop. To help people around him unselfishly and without prejudice. Funny how power corrupts the righteous.*

"Have we found who called the ambulance yet?" Laura said, staring at a single point on the table. Jeremy stood up, stretching himself out like an aged seal.

"We're looking into all leads, *Sergeant.*" He said her title with a hint of joy. He was above her now. Calling the shots. Oh, how she was *so* happy for him. "I'll let you know what the forensics say," he said, moving to the window that looked out onto the grey skyline of Wigtown. It was always so grey here. Like the sun had forsaken this place. Laura thought about mentioning the dirt she saw under Clara's nails. But she kept that information to herself. She didn't trust Jeremy. If she gave any information that pointed away from Clara Weaver being a cold-blooded killer, she wouldn't put it past him to ignore it or completely cover it up. He was out for himself. That was apparent, and he wouldn't let anything stand in the way of his rung up the promotional ladder, no matter how immoral it was. "I can get Catherine to give you a lift home." He said. Laura hadn't said two words to Catherine since her return. She had been put onto the proactive CID unit. She was hardly in the office. Instead, she walked around the most rundown parts of Wigtown doing stop and searches, or 'turning over' as it was known locally, anyone that looked a little dodgy. They had had some great results and there were more drugs off the streets and some seriously nasty bastards behind bars. Problem was, and what she was finding, was as soon as you put one pusher in prison, there's another three ready and waiting to fulfil the gap in the market. Not to mention following the breakdown of the Heywoods. It was a free for all out there now. Like the wild west. Everyone fighting over the same street corner to push whatever smack they had to sell. At least the Heywoods kept a hold on things, or whatever group they worked for. That was the thing about dictatorships and tyrants. Yes, they're evil, but there is law and order. If you cut off the head of snake, there's no one to eat the rats. Jeremy moved to the door of the office, resting his hand on the door frame.

"I was going to tell you tomorrow after you had had some rest," Jeremy said. "But I thought I would tell you now," he sounded firm. Emotionless. "The DCI wants your head on a plate. She said that if you don't hand in your resignation by the end of the week, she will look at charges of gross misconduct, criminal damage, and disgrace in a public office, amongst other things." The words slammed into Laura's chest. The gravity of the situation pressing down on her from every direction, like she was caught in a giants grip and being crushed from all sides. "The only hope you have of keeping your job is that you apologise. Use your mental health as a crux, or whatever you want to do. And you would have to stop your involvement in this case and let others handle it."

Translation – Spread your cheeks and get fucked up the arse till you're bloody.

"I have never begged in my life, *sir*," she hissed. "I'm not going to use my mental state as a get out of jail free card." Jeremy's eyes lingered on her for a moment, the silence so thick they were choking on it.

"That's your choice," he said. "This is your doing. No one else's."

"It's the firing line or the furnace. One kills me quickly. The other…" Jeremy let out a long sigh so hot it could melt ice.

"You have until the end of the week. If I hear you even whisper about this case again, I'll fire you personally." His eyes lingered on her, waiting for a response. When none came, he slipped out of the office.

Laura sat there in her silence, her fingers arced in a steeple, pressed against her lips. Everything that had happened. Everything that she had been through. Every case she had solved. Every life she had saved. Every crook, thief, fraudster, thug, bully, and abuser she had put behind bars. Every celebration. Every tired glass of wine to forget what she had seen. Every single bit of it was going to be undone, because Laura wanted to do the right thing, and now she was going to be hung out to dry for it. She couldn't even begin to attempt to unravel the ball of barbed wire that it was.

I can't do this anymore, she thought. *I just can't.* Laura heard the sound of something tearing. Her eyes found the sound. It was Catherine. She was standing at the foot of the MIU office and was taking off her body armour. Laura hadn't noticed her come in. She was to lost, swimming in her own agony.

"Are you okay?" Catherine said. Laura blinked back the tears that were brewing in her burning eyes. She forced a smile, admiring Catherine. She had lost weight. She looked great. At least that made one of them.

"You have a taser now," Laura said, eyeing the bright yellow banana gun on her belt. "You've come a long way from crosswords and painting your nails."

"It's online chess now," Catherine said, a smile carving along her face. A bright smile. A smile that told Laura that Catherine still had admiration for her old superior. That regardless of the hell she had walked through the past year, she knew it came from a place of good. That no one was perfect. That everyone can get burned. "Come on, *ma'am*," Catherine said. "Let's get you home." Laura reached down to finish her cold coffee. Catherine extended her arm. Laura looked up.

Her face was ashen. Eyes sunken in her head. Her mouth hanging wide open, and fat flies crawling from the pitch-black maw. Blood. So much blood. It was all over her...

Laura recoiled back, knocking the coffee onto the ground. Catherine's hand reaching out to her, the skin blackened. Brown fat and decayed muscle around protruding bone. She stumbled off her chair, knocking it to the ground, Laura falling onto the carpet. She slammed her eyes shut, bringing her hands to her face, a wail of terror blasting through the air.

"Woah!" Catherine barked. "You okay?" A moment of stunned silence. Laura lay on the ground, fingers digging into the carpet under her. She breathed slowly, trying to get a hold of her nerves. Slowly, she peeled her eyes open. Catherine standing over her, her face warped with worry. Laura's body drenched with sweat. Her eyes darting around the room like a pinball.

"Sorry," she said, breathlessly. "I don't know what came over me."

In the car, Catherine tried to make some small talk, but Laura was so far removed from such things. What have you been up to recently? How's things at work? Do you think you'll be placed on a protected wing in prison or mixed with the general population?

Through the rain battered window, Laura watched the world around them go on as normal, its image blurred, like Van Gough's night sky. People milling around with shopping bags. Young couples falling in love sitting opposite each other in the bright windows of restaurants, their whole lives ahead of them. Love, heartbreak, and everything in between. People walking their dogs through deep puddles. Teenagers vaping. Local drunks slumped against the glass of a bus shelter. The young man in his gym gear with biceps that could crush an egg, supporting Beats headphones and staring at the world through his phone on social media.

As men are born, the world continues to turn. As men grow old, the world continues to turn. As men fall and their bodies nourish the land around them, the world continues to turn. The sun awakens and dies each day. The seasons change as empires rise and fall. As hearts are broken and children cry. The world will turn, and the continuum continues on for the eternal eon. But like an old photograph, Laura was locked in time. Locked in a life which she had nothing to return to but her empty shell of a home that held so many bad memories. The thought of sitting alone inside those walls made her skin crawl.

The rain pelted the window like angry fists trying to break it through. Catherine still talking. Rambling about someone she had stopped and searched, and it turns out they were wanted for war crimes.

"She crocheted farm animals, for god's sake!" She said, laughing. "Not a blip on her record. War crimes!" Laura watched the world go by. Catherine slowed the car down approaching a set of traffic lights. "She came quietly, though, and we had a very good talk about TikTok and romance novels. I haven't ever really been into romance books. I prefer horror books or dark fantasy. Do you know of any? Any new writers?"

"Not any good ones," Laura said, bluntly. Catherine paused. She had been spouting hot air into the cab of the car for so long, she almost forgot what it was like to hear someone answer back.

"I'm sure you have a read a few good ones in your time," she laughed, then, after a long pause and licking her lips from her mouth that had become acrid. "So, about what had happened…" Laura's body tensed.

"I'm not supposed to talk about the case."

"You aren't," Catherine said, "I am. You're just listening." Laura peered over at Catherine. A slight smile curled along Catherine's face. Hearing no resistance, Catherine continued. "I did some digging. The new DCI? She has more to do with the case than you think. A few years back. Remember the massacre on the edge of town? The huge house that went up in flames?" Laura *did* know the case she was talking about. She hadn't worked on it personally. She was still in the Met police. But it had made the headlines for weeks.

Hugo Black. He was a prominent figure in the local community, and he had friends in high places. Including the *then* mayor candidate for the Conservative party, Brian Callahan. Hugo's home was set on fire and everyone inside the house burned to death. Eight in total. The culprit, Annabelle Jones, was murdered in prison a few months later. The official story was that she locked all the doors and slaughtered the residents and guests. The online forums, however, claim something much deeper and darker was at play that night.

"I remember," Laura said. "What about it?"

"Well, she was the lead investigator on the case. Detective Sergeant Burnell, at the time. She's since got a promotion. Now she's working on *this* case."

"So, she likes big cases?" Laura wasn't connecting the dots.

"Not just big cases," Catherine said, setting the car into first gear and moving slowly in the Wigtown traffic. The brake lights bleeding through the spattering of rain that seemed almost biblical, like God was sending down a flood to wash away all the sinners of the world, before she stopped abruptly to let a couple of teenagers pass who cut in front of the car, meaning they got caught at the lights again. Catherine let out a frustrated huff, like a Spaniel who wanted to play with their favourite ball but wasn't allowed. "Turns out, Alex Weaver was a silent partner in Hugo Black's companies. And now Burnell has such a vested interest in his murder?" Catherine shook her head. "Doesn't make sense to me?"

"What're you implying?" Laura said, the jigsaw in her mind not fitting together, the pieces jagged like razor blades.

"All I'm saying," Catherine uttered, "is that DCI Burnell is obviously more invested in Alex Weaver being dead than simple professional obligation." Laura's eyes lingered on Catherine for a long moment before returning to the wet world outside. Darkness fell on the town, and a blanket of clouds eclipsed what little of the dying sun fought to get through, rendering the streets a muted twilight. The bodies that shuffled under the downpour of winter rain were as silent as ghosts.

"I want to say thank you for giving me a ride home," Laura said. "Means a lot."

"Don't mention it," Catherine said. "It's nice to see you. How're you doing? Anything you want to talk about?"

"To my therapist, yes." Laura didn't mean the venom that lingered in the response, but she wasn't sorry about it either. She had learned to keep work colleagues as just that. Colleagues. No nights out. No meeting up outside of work. They existed when she clocked in, and vanished when she clocked out. Today was exceptional circumstances. Nothing more.

"I think that's a good idea, "Catherine began. "I always found it good to speak to someone..." She continued with her babbling again. They got through the next set of lights, stopping in the middle of the road. The car's indicator blinked to life to turn onto a dual carriageway. The clicking of the signal like a ticking clock that grated on Laura's bones. Laura turned her attention back to the street.

And then, like a ghost from her past, she saw *her.*

"Let me out," Laura said, suddenly bursting to life.

Her heart picked up. Adrenaline flooded her body, pulling at the car handle like the car engine had begun to smoulder, and they were going to be burned alive at any moment.

"What's wrong?" Catherine said quickly, worry saturating her voice.

"Let me out!" Laura said, knocking on the window loudly, shouting her name. She couldn't control it. It was like an impulse. The sight of her taking over her. Dissolving any reservation she had of maintaining an ounce of self-control. Catherine went to protest further, to talk some sense into her, but Laura pressed the locking button on the dashboard and dove out of the car. Cars narrowly missed her, their horns cutting through the air like a dying scream, headlights devouring her fleeing body. Catherine shouted through the pouring rain after her, and then a cacophony of blaring horns followed.

Laura gave chase. She had seen her, walking with her long coat. Someone she used to know, disappearing into the crowd. Her umbrella bounced with her step. Rain droplets exploded on impact like detonating grenades.

"Celine!"

Chapter Fifteen
Laura

What the hell am I doing? Oh god, why am I doing this? She's so close. Why?

The thoughts raced around Laura's mind quickly as she ran through the busy Wigtown high street. People cast their eyes on her as she moved. Celine's long coat swayed as she moved through the grey streets. Laura called her name, but her voice was lost in the cacophony of rain, screeching cars, revving engines, and passersby who eyed her curiously.

Laura picked up the pace, her legs burning. Her feet slammed into the deep puddles that exploded as her feet plunged into them, dousing her legs in ice cold rainwater. The rain pelted Laura's face; the droplets finding her mouth, which spluttered out with each hot exhalation into the cold air around her.

Celine turned a corner by the side of a Marks and Spencer supermarket at a crossroad. Catherine pulled up at the side of the curb and wound down the window, shouting to Laura.

"What're you doing?" She yelled. "Get in! You're going to catch hypothermia!" Laura ignored the comment and raced past her like a bloodhound hot on a fox's trail. She disappeared down the street, and Catherine pulled back into the busy stream of traffic. A blaring of a horn. An obscene gesture.

Laura saw Celine stop at a crossing set of traffic lights. She could make out her shape clearer now. She was taller than she remembered. Her figure unmistakable. Her braids pinned back in a scrunched bobble. Her

face, even from this distance, was smooth like caramel. Her lips, plump with a delicate dark rouge lipstick. What was she going to say to her when she caught up with her, looking like a frantic drowned rat that had just been pulled from a river?

Hi! Sorry for ditching you in the hospital. I had some stuff I needed to take care of. Can I pick you up again after tossing you in the trash pile?

Sure! How about a drink?

No. I can't do that. Although I could murder one. Speaking of which...

Laura grabbed Celine's shoulder. Her fingers dug into the padding. Celine turned around, and both their eyes met with shock. It wasn't Celine.

"What the hell!" The woman bolstered, recoiling away. She woman clutched her handbag tighter to her chest, her umbrella shaking lingering raindrops onto Laura's confused face. She tried to speak, but instead, she stood staring at the stranger. "Well?" The woman barked. Laura stepped backward. The woman eyed her like a snake that had slithered into her bedroom at night and was coiling up by her bed. The woman eyed her. "Freak." Without another word, she turned on her heel and marched quickly across the road, waving to a car that slowed to let her past. The same car wound down the window. It was Catherine.

"Get in!" Catherine yelled. Laura stood as she watched the woman disappear into the mass of bodies that passed through the town centre like cells in a bloodstream. The sharp blast of a horn pulled her from her gaze. Catherine put her hazard lights on and jumped out of the car. Laura watched her approach, unable to move. Catherine guided her to the car and opened the passenger seat and shut her in, almost afraid that if she didn't, she would go AWOL again.

Catherine slipped back into the driver's side. The sound of the engine ticking over gently beneath them. The windscreen wipers hummed as they cleared away the downpour.

"What was that about?" Catherine shouted. "Could have got yourself killed!" Laura stared through the haze of the rain on the glass. The world around her messy, like someone had put a film over a wet oil painting, blending it all together. The rain dripped from Laura's clothes. But she couldn't feel it. She was far away, in a world that only existed in the silence between breaths. Why had she been so convinced it was Celine? Why was she so desperate to see her? She had, in all honestly, hardly thought about her since coming out of rehab. Convincing herself that she had cut that cancer out of her life for good. But seeing her. The *thought* of seeing her. She completely lost control.

Maybe it was the case? Maybe it was digging up the bones of her past? Maybe it was the stress? The trauma? Or was it because since she moved up to this hellhole, that Celine was the only person who had made her feel anything but numb? Like a crack addict destroys their life for their fix, Laura would run into traffic to touch the woman that made her life hell one more time.

Laura stared out of the rain drenched window. Her neck was stiff from the cold. Opposite them, a Bargain Booze. A plethora of red wine in the window. Flickering lights boasting discount poison. Her old friend. The friend that she forgot she had. Without thinking, she found her hand snaking towards the door handle.

Catherine shifted the car into first gear. Laura's fingers still lingered on the exit. The car pulled forward, and she watched the booze store disappear from view.

"Look," Catherine said. "If you don't want to tell me what the hell was going on, then fine. But I'm locking the doors, and don't do that shit again." A beat of silence. "Sergeant."

"I thought I saw a ghost," Laura said, more thinking it rather than meaning to say it out loud.

"A ghost?" Laura's hairs stood up on her arms. The air from the heater was returning the feeling in her body. "What do you mean?"

"It doesn't matter," Laura whispered. Batting the question away. "Just an echo from a previous life."

Around twenty minutes later, Laura walked through her front door and stripped out of her sodden clothes. She placed them on the bottom step of the staircase and grabbed her long coat from the wall hook. She wrapped it around her, fastening it tightly.

Bagpipe was exactly where she had left him that morning. She doubted he had realised she was gone, other than the empty food bowl. He was curled up on the sofa, his large eyes like marbles on a black canvas. Laura ruffled her fingers through the cat's fur. It was soft to the touch, the fibres gliding through her fingertips. Laura settled back into the back of the couch, and she felt the weight of the day pulling her eyelids closed.

She had removed all traces of Celine from her mind, and in her absence, she convinced herself that she was gone. The thought of her like a passing ship on the dock that disappears into the horizon without much attention. But now, it was like she was beached on the shores of her brain, her carcass rotting, picked apart by fat seagulls.

And what about DCI Burnell? Why was she so

involved in the case? Surely, she should *want* Laura to explore every avenue to prove or disprove something, not ignore the evidence around her and lock Clara up and throw away the key. Celine. Clara. Burnell. Weaver. It was like she was trying to find a piece of hay in a pile of needles. Every way she turned, she was getting shredded and bloodied.

She could just forget about it. Forget the whole thing. Ignore her intuition and let the system do its job. Save her own skin. She could file her report and save herself. Throw Clara to the flames. But that thought made her mind fracture. But just like the cracked photo frame, *something* was wrong with this picture.

She made me do it...

Those words ran around Laura's mind like a toddler with a hammer in an antique store. Who was *she?* What did she mean? The only words she had spoken, and it was a cry for help. Laura felt her blood run cold.

DCI Burnell. She had been there on the bridge, and she was invested in Clara being put behind bars. The closer Laura got to discovering the truth, the more she wanted to stop her. Something was wrong with this case. Very, very wrong indeed. She pulled out her mobile phone. She bit down, thumbing through her contacts. Was there anyone left that she could trust? She dialled Francis.

"I'm not supposed to talk to you," he said as soon as he answered the phone, him whispering fiercely. There were eyes on him. She could tell.

"I need you to do something for me," Laura said. Francis let out a stifled laugh.

"You're joking, right? I'm twelve months off getting my pension."

"If I wasn't desperate, then I wouldn't ask." She let

the comment linger in the dead silence between them. Francis' breathing picked up.

"Make it quick."

"I need you to do some digging on the DCI for me." Laura could feel the handset almost melt with how red Francis' face was going.

"Goodbye," he said quickly.

"No!" Laura blasted. "Please!" Silence met her ear. Gingerly, she checked the call. It was still connected.

"If this gets me in the shit..." He said sourly.

"It won't, I promise. If it does, I'll take the blame." She waited. He gave no objection. The game was on. "Find out what cases she has worked on and if she has had any involvement in the past with either Weaver or Clara."

"What for?" Francis hissed urgently.

"Just trust me." *Trust me. Would she trust herself? Not at all. In fact, she would have hung up the call as soon as she saw it was her calling. But Francis wasn't leaving her in the sun covered in honey next to an ant's nest.* A moment passed. Laura held her breath until finally she heard –

"You're going to get me sacked."

Chapter Sixteen
Laura

Laura awoke from a dreamless sleep to the sound of her phone going. She flicked on the bedside lamp and eyed the phone with one eye open. She checked the time. It had just gone two in the morning. She had been asleep for a little over an hour. She answered the call. It was Jeremy.

"Were you asleep?"

"No," Laura lied, rubbing her eyes and sitting up in the bed. She reached over and took a drink of water from the nightstand. "To what do I owe the pleasure?"

"No," he said with a sigh. "Clara Weaver has assaulted a cop and a nurse in the hospital. She's been sedated, but she's been elevated to always having three officers with her."

"Everyone okay?" Laura said matter-of-factly.

"Yes," Jeremy said. "The cop got a nasty bite to his hand and will need stitches and the nurse had her make up ruined. Other than that, everyone is peachy." Laura nodded.

"I'll do the eight-point checklist in the morning," she said. "Is that all? I was about to head to bed."

"There is one more thing."

Brilliant, Laura thought.

"There's the small matter of your resignation. Have you given it any more thought?" Laura felt her insides churn.

"Plenty of thought," she said.

"And?" *And what?* Laura thought.

"It needs more thought." Jeremy scoffed down the

phone.

"You don't think you can actually redeem yourself from this, do you? Driving the fucking car through the gates of the house. Breaking into a crime scene? Telling the DCI to fuck off. People have been skinned alive for less."

"Is that an offer?" Laura said sourly. She knew what she was doing. But she was already being thrown into the fire. She might as well get a tan out of it. "If *your* officers hadn't been so inept at getting inside the house, I wouldn't have had to fuck the gate." It was true, regardless of if Jeremy wanted to admit it. If Laura hadn't done what she did, they would still be fighting to enter the house, and Alex Weaver would have been feasted on by insects. Because of her, forensic could do their work faster. Because of her, Clara wasn't being fished out of the river. Without her, Jeremy would have been skinned and made into a coat by the Straw Man. Because of her, Clara Weaver would be able to speak about what she had been subjected to, and they can form an idea around her motives.

"You have caused an absolute shit storm, Laura," he said. She could almost feel the heat from his reddening face coming through the phone.

"You're in charge now," she bit. "That's your problem."

"I beg your pardon?" He blasted. "You remember who you're speaking to?" Laura scrunched her eyes tight. God, she was tired. She was so damn tired of all of this. She just wanted to sleep. To fall into a sleep so deep that she didn't ever wake up.

"I know very well that you're my superior, Jeremy," she said, her hand tightening around the glass of water. "I gave up my rank to you, remember?"

"You think I earned this through charity?"

"If the shoe fits." Jeremy let out a long exhale, followed by a strong expletive that would make a sailor blush.

"The only reason you weren't sacked is because of the work you did with Jamie Green and Craig Sinick. Your reputation is the only thing that saved you when it came to light that you were not only drinking on the job but taking advantage of those beneath you. Well, not anymore. You have gone too far this time. Crossed the line. You're chasing ghosts and can't see this for what it is. A murder. A domestic homicide. You're too caught up in your own fantasy of saving your past self from Ron, because you were too *weak* to walk away. You're letting it cloud your mind. You have become unhinged and dangerous."

Unhinged and dangerous. Laura smiled in the dim glow of her bedroom lamp. Weak for not leaving a domestic abusive relationship. Is that what he really thought? Is that what he thought when he dealt with a case of coercive control? That the victim welcomed it by never leaving the abuser? Is that what he thought of her? They were trained in trauma bonding, adverse childhood experiences, domestic homicide stages, obsession, power dynamics, co-dependency, and personality disorders. All of it forgotten because he's got a fucking promotion.

The unit was a shit show before she came. She was the injection of medicine that was needed to purify the septic veins from the body. Since Jeremy had been promoted, the unit was falling to pieces. No one wants to work there. Obsessed with statistics and detections. Getting another step up the ladder. Rubbing shoulders with the big bosses and forsaking what it meant to be a police officer. To protect the most vulnerable members of society. The reason he had such disdain for her was because she reminded him of everything that he wasn't. A leader. Someone who puts themselves in the firing line to protect those below them. Someone who will do whatever it takes, forgoing rank, privilege, or self-preservation, to make the world a better place, piece by piece.

"You know what the worst part of you being my superior is, Jeremy?" Laura seethed, "is that you don't have balls. You throw around your weight like you actually earned your position. When in fact, it was *me* who handed that to you. The unit was on the verge of disbandment and in disrepair until I joined, but now we struggle to retain detectives for more than a few weeks when I'm not around. You're poison. Yes, I fucked up. Yes, I am lucky to still have my warrant card and be able to say that I am a police officer, but you Jeremy? You were the captain of a sinking ship, and the only reason you're back in control is because of the lifeline that I threw to you. And even without a paddle, I was able to keep myself afloat and sort my own shit out. Now do me a favour. When I leave the office and I get a phone call at two in the fucking morning, make sure it's something that can't wait for the next day when I am on shift. It's bad for my rehabilitation." Silence followed. A long moment of silence. Laura could hear the pipes creaking in the bathroom, resetting from her shower before she had gone to bed. The blood running through her veins, hot and bubbling.

God, I need a drink, a voice in her mind whispered, like an old friend who wasn't welcome, but she always had so much fun with.

"First thing in the morning," he said. "I want you in the office, and I want you gone." The call ended. The silence in the room was so loud it was deafening. Laura tossed the phone onto the covers. Then the pain started. Usually, it starts slow, then builds like turning up the heat of a thermostat. But not this time. This was like a bolt of agony that shook her by the head and rattled her brain.

"Fuck!" She cried, and then she felt the pain. Blood poured from her fist, and she opened it slowly, the crushed glass of water in her uncoiling fist sticking into her palm and between her fingers. The bed was drenched in both water and crimson.

She dove out of bed and ran to the bathroom, shards of glass falling around her feet like knives. She thrust her hand in the sink and put the tap on full blast. She screamed. She screamed as the water burned her bloodied hand and she pulled knives from her flesh. She would need to go to the goddamn hospital, but there was no way she could drive. Not with the busted hand, and an ambulance wouldn't come out for this. Not unless she wanted to wait for twelve hours, of which time she would be late for her dry ass fucking in the morning.

Laura picked out the larger shards of glass, the took out her eyebrow tweezers and with the precision of a surgeon with Parkinsons, she pulled out the other little sharp bastards that had managed to bury themselves deep. Her hand was pissing blood, spouting crimson all over the porcelain like she had been trying to gut a sink of fat leeches. Blood, fat and flesh fell into the bowl, and then she rinsed off again for another round of holy hellfire. Sweating, crying, and on the verge of passing out, she thought she had gotten rid of all the glass that had made its new home inside her skin.

She reached over to her wash basket and pulled out a pair of black tights and tied it around her bicep, forcing the artery tight in a makeshift tourniquet, and placed it over her head to let gravity do some of the work. Some blood rained onto her head and face, giving her the appearance of a weeping blood angel. Hell, it looked almost biblical. If she wasn't in such a foul mood, she might have even taken a selfie and posted it on Instagram with some vague caption and hashtags.

Laura moved back into the bedroom, careful not to shred her feet on the glass on the floor and hurried downstairs, nearly tripping over Bagpipe in the process. That's all she needed. Surviving killers and gang members to be taken down by a sleeping cat on the stairs because she crushed a god damn glass in her hand. She found the first aid kit that Celine had insisted she buy when she lived here. Laura thought it a stupid idea, because she wasn't a dumb bitch who had accidents in the home. Well, shoes on the other foot now! She laid out the bandages, alcohol gel, and plasters onto the work top of the kitchen bar. Knowing the pain she was about to inflict on herself, she got a wooden spoon and clenched it between her teeth. Breathing fiercely, she took hold of the alcohol gel and flicked open the cap. Then, taking a deep breath, poured the contents over the wound. Laura kicked and screamed and bit into that wooden spoon so fiercely she wondered which would crack first – the utensil or her teeth.

She tied a bandage the best she could around her hand and spat the spoon out of her mouth. She could feel the splintered wood between her teeth, and fished out the shards the best she could. God, she could murder a glass of wine. She could drink and drink until there wasn't a drop left in this entire town.

Drinking when stressed won't make things better. The sound of her therapist's voice rattled in her mind.

No, she thought. *But it wouldn't make it any worse, either.*

She tied and taped the bandage, placing plasters over the gashes, then let out a breath. Blood had splattered on the basin, the kitchen bar, her clothes, and all around the stairs. Laura looked like she had just walked through an abattoir where the butchers used chainsaws instead of knives. She needed to go the hospital. She had lost easily a pint of blood, if not more, and the plasters and bandages wouldn't hold forever.

Laura walked upstairs, moving quickly, the blood already starting to seep through the bandage. She took her phone from the bed and clicked on Google for local taxi companies. She found one and clicked CALL, but it was engaged. She tried another, and then a third. Frustrated, she let out a huff and took a seat on the bed, behaving like a teenager whose boyfriend was online but not replying to her messages.

She had another thought. As if pulled by an invisible force, a compulsion that she thought she had destroyed in rehab and therapy impelled her to go through her bedroom cabinet. She sifted through old photos, receipts, and envelopes until she found it. She hadn't thrown it away, although she had told everyone that she had. Like shredding the last part of her old self. The final nail in the coffin of her old life, and yet, she hadn't been able to part with it. Since getting sober, she hadn't looked at it, but its existence haunted her like a persistent ghost in the dark. Despite her injured hand, she managed to hold the paper and enter the numbers on her phone. Each digit entered was a step back into chaos. But this time was different. This time, it wasn't just a compulsion to walk into the darkness again. It was desperation. Necessity. She had lost a lot of blood, and needed to get help as soon as she could.

Or so she convinced herself.

Laura dialled the number. Each ring sawing at her nerves, begging her to end the call. To turn her phone off. To get help from someone else. *Anyone else.* And yet, the phone stayed glued to her ear, her body still like stone. Once the door had been reopened, then it would be almost impossible to close it again.

The voicemail came through. Laura felt her stomach plummet. She ended the call, and then with a heavy breath, she began to download the Uber app. The icon opened on her home screen and, like a doomsday clock, the timer ticked down. She fell backwards onto the bed, tears stinging her eyes. Not because of the pain in her hand, or because she was in for a world of shit at work, but because she had caved. She wanted to step back into that old life. She wanted to *feel* something. She attempted to pry the door open to the life she wanted to leave behind, like an addict doing everything they could to avoid their fix but then giving in and rushing to get it, blocking out all the screams in their head telling them to stop. Compulsion. Addiction. Trauma. They were all incredibly powerful driving forces. That's why they worked so well. Sex. Drugs. Gambling. Booze. They were the anaesthetic to an unsatisfied life. It all to appeal to our inner thoughts of that *we are not good enough*, and that was exactly what Laura had fallen foul of again. She had opened the door a crack, but now she must seal it back up again and nail it shut.

She stood and grabbed the paper, tore it into pieces,

and flushed it down the toilet. Then she went to her phone and deleted the call log. Satisfied, she sat back on the bed, watching the Uber app fill up slowly. The bed was comfortable under her body, like a hug she wanted to fall into. She let her eyes begin to close, and her breathing slowed.

The phone screen lit up, a number flashing along the front. Laura pulled it to her face. Her blood ran cold. Her mouth ran dry. She hovered her finger over the call. Decline or accept?

You need to go to the hospital, her mind whispered. She could almost hear its growl.

She clicked the button and placed to the phone to her ear.

"Hello?" She whispered.

"Hey stranger," Celine said. "It's been a while."

Chapter Seventeen
Clara
Now

I snapped my eyes open and lunged upright like the reanimated dead. I could still feel it on me. The blood. The slippery organs. The writhing flesh that constricted around me. I couldn't breathe, and I heaved gulps and gasps of hot air into my lungs, which felt like they wouldn't inflate. I pulled at my hands but couldn't move them, something biting into them. Raw. Cold. Something holding me in place, like I was Jesus Christ nailed to the cross in the scorching sun of the desert.

"There, there," a voice said, filtering through my despair. I bit my lip, teeth digging into the trembling flesh so hard I felt a burst of iron explode into my mouth. I froze, listening to that voice, like it was God himself whispering to me. I felt His warmth, His love taking hold of me, like a crying infant, lost in the middle of a violent storm, is hoisted up into a warm blanket and carried off into safety. "There, it's okay," the voice continued. I slammed my eyes shut, holding onto that voice, until I slowed my breathing and take a full breath. "There we go," the voice continued. "Just slow it down. You've had a lot of medication. Take it easy." Tentatively, I peeled my eyes open. It felt like there was a plastic film over my eyes, and the bright light above me started to fade, then grew bigger and brighter, like a supernova heading straight for me. I blinked furiously. The cold bite of metal stopped me from trying to wipe my eyes. Panic was rising in my chest again, ready to pull me back into the darkness of my mind. I recoiled and flinched when something wet and soft touched my eyes, but that voice kept soothing me, bringing me back from the edge of madness.

I saw the bed. My legs. The *blood*. *Oh god, what have I done? What have they done to me?*

"Take it easy," the voice continued. "You need to relax. You'll hurt yourself." Who said that? My body felt strange, like I was seeing the world from the bottom of a deep well, staring up at the passing shadows above. My body didn't feel my own, like I was numbed to the bone.

I turned my head. Blue curtains surrounded me. I saw a large male in black body armour talking on his radio and then he vanished out of sight. A nurse sat opposite the bed, typing away on her computer that looked older than her. She had a white plaster on her face, which was stuck to her skin with clear tape. What had happened to her? The thing was the size of a palm. Had someone done that to her? Had *I* done that to her?

Why am I in the hospital? I tried to remember, but the harder I tried to search the recesses of my mind, I found only a void so black and empty, it would swallow me whole and never let me go. The nurse didn't respond, only continued to move out from the view of the curtains I was entombed between. I moved my arms but found a biting of metal around my wrists. I was handcuffed. Why was I handcuffed? What was going on? I rattled at the cuffs, the sense of panic pushing through the heaviness in my body. I went to speak, but my mouth couldn't find words again. The nurse eyed me, her face indifferent, but her gaze bubbling over with hatred. Why did she hate me? Why was I in this place? What had I done? I felt the churning of sickness in my stomach begin to rise. I pulled at my arms again.

"You'll hurt yourself if you keep doing that," the familiar voice said. I snapped my head to the sound, a bolt of pain shooting up my neck. "You just need to stay calm. The drugs will wear off soon." I studied her face, taking a moment to realise I was looking at another human being. It was like looking at a photo that looks like two different pictures until you see what you're meant to and can't see anything but. She was young, not a wrinkle on her face. Her makeup was slight but just enough. Her hair was pitch black. Eyes a deep emerald green. My eyes must have spoken for me because the police officer smiled a kind grin. "I'm PC Amanda Shaffer," she said. "And you need to try to relax. It took three of us to pin you down and give you some drugs to make you fall asleep. That's why you're feeling out of sorts." Amanda spoke softly, yet with authority. I imagined she only had to stare at someone just the right way, and they would comply. A skill only developed by those who are used to wrestling with the worst the world has to offer. And now she was with me. Was I the worst? It took three of them? What had I done? Why was I covered in blood? I couldn't remember anything. As hard as I tried to think, to recall, all I found was emptiness lurking there, waiting for me. I retreated before teeth could appear from the blackness and sink into me. "You're in the hospital," PC Shaffer said. She pointed to my handcuffs. "We aren't going to take these off. You got very upset before." Whether she realised it or not, her eyes drifted to where the nurse sat. The plaster on her face. Had I done that? Somehow, I knew. The taste of blood in my mouth. It wasn't from me. Oh god, what had I done? "We're just going getting a doctor, and some others, to come and speak to you and explain fully why you're here," Amanda said. "For now, just relax, okay?" I don't know what to do. Didn't know what I *could* do. I have never been in this situation before. I have never spoken to the police, and now I was chained to a bed, and I had sunk my teeth into a nurse's face.

Between my breaths, I heard beeping. Trolleys rattling. The sounds of groaning. Then, slipping through the ensemble of the hospital, I heard footsteps clicking on the floor. With each approaching step, I felt the swelling of dread in my chest. Was it *you?* Were you coming to claim me again?

She appeared from the side of the curtain, standing in front of me at the end of the bed. She was older. Thick glasses and wore a black pencil skirt and a white shirt. Her hair was the colour of rust dusted with snow. Her wrinkles so deep if you peeled her face off and rolled it thin, it would play Mozart's Lacrimosa. She was thin, and her eyes were as grey and cold as a winter sky. The larger officer returned to the woman's side. Shaffer sat back.

"Clara Weaver," she said, in a tone as welcoming as the inside of a coffin. "My name is detective chief inspector Burnell." She regarded Clara with a cruel gaze, like a kid with a pair of plyers about to play doctor on a trapped rodent. "Firstly, I am glad you're awake. I've been dying to speak to you. Secondly. Your baby is dead. You aren't pregnant anymore. You lost it when you were fighting with my officers and the hospital staff... Lastly..."

Baby...

It all came rushing back to me. The dead infant in my dream Screaming at me, grabbing me by the head and shaking me violently, demanding my attention. The child birthing from the warped head of Alex. The blood. The stench of the blood in my nostril, like a drill bit being hammered into my skull. I felt sick. The wave of heat and nausea rampaging again. My body felt cold, then unbearably hot. Pregnant. I hadn't *been* pregnant. I couldn't *get* pregnant. You kept me on birth control. But what if this was your next plan? Your next move? To put a baby in me when you would consume me with your body. There was no intimacy. No love. It was about power.

"Oh," Burnell said, the word creeping out of her mouth like she had just seen a disappointing magic trick. "I'm guessing you didn't know." She shrugged. "Only a couple of months. You would have had it taken off you in prison, I suppose." My eyes fixed on the bloodstains around my legs, the bed sheets blotched with a child's life that would never be allowed the chance to live. My eyes burned with fiery tears. My body was no longer in the well, but now climbed out, digging my nails, and scraping my body over the stony lip into a violent storm that poured acid rain. I felt *everything*. I felt pain. I felt hatred. I felt contempt for mankind. I wanted to watch the world burn. Watch it fucking burn to the ground and laugh at all the withering souls that melted under my inferno like rats stranded inside a burning building.

"I am arresting you for the murder of Alex Weaver," DCI Burnell continued. "You do not have to…" I snapped one cuff free, and then heaved as hard as I could and pulled the other loose. Like a raging banshee, a scream so fierce, so hellish, escaped my throat like a wind of razor blades that carved and sliced as it moved. I found my feet, and I lunged at the bitch. The hateful wretch. The disgusting piece of vehement shit that stood before me and spouted such filth. We fell to the ground, my hands finding her face. Her eyes. Her lips. She thrashed and screamed and kicked and pushed. I felt hands on me. The blare of an alarm as I was grabbed by the shoulders. I bit and thrashed and clawed and spat all limbs that dared try to fucking pull me off this vindictive evil cunt. She screamed, and I liked it. I loved hearing her scream. To give pain, to give a little bit of something back to the world that had been inflicted on me. To hurt. Cause agony. To make someone finally realise what it was like to be me all these years.

My eyes exploded in a fiery blast of searing agony and slammed shut, shutting the world away in mute darkness. The word sounding far away. My face burning red. Arms grabbed hold of me as the sound of the screaming detective chief bitch Burnell fell away. I thrashed and clawed all who tried to pin me back down. I felt the familiar stab of the needle bite my skin. The volatile storm I found myself in burned away to the bone, only to disappear as the ground opened up. I fell into the black abyss filled with snapping teeth and monsters.

DIARY

I've met someone!

I know, I didn't think it would be possible either. The last few times I have been interested in someone, they have been unavailable, some kind of strange obsessive bastard, or they have been interested in only one thing.

But today, I was in the Wigtown centre grabbing a Costa, when I bumped into him and spilled my drink on his shoes. Not exactly Romeo and Juliet is it, but it would appear that fate or some divine being brought us into each other's lives. I believe in all of that stuff. Divinity in life. Fate. Twin souls. Reincarnated lovers destined to find each other. I thought I had found it once. But you know about that…

He was tall, a little older than me, and he had salt and pepper stubble and short hair, cut like he was out of the army or something. I stood there looking at him like a deer stuck in headlights. The smell of the spilt coffee emanating off his leather shoes. They looked really expensive, and here I was just gawping at him. He was the one to make the first move. A chess set ready to be played. A battle of love to be waged.

"I'll clean that up, shall I?"

Pawn to e4.

At first, I thought he was being condescending and arrogant, but then I noticed the flash of a smile across his face and a twinkle in his eye. He was flirting with me. It was like he could feel it, too. The fact that I have been brought into his life, and he mine, at that exact moment. What are the odds? Like, seriously? What are the odds of this happening? I could feel the pull to him, like there was already a connection between the two of us. In this coffee shop, of all places, the world seemed to stand still.

"I'm so sorry," I finally squeaked, my heart jackhammering in my chest. He cleaned the coffee off his shoes while he stood towering over me.

"Watch where you're going," he said. Again, to an onlooker, you might think that he was being abrasive, rude. But to us, me and him, we knew that he was being playful. He couldn't just ask me right out there and then, but he wanted me to do the dance with him. He wanted me to make the next move. Love was a strategy. A sequence of moves, fakes, and tactics. You wanted to appear strong, but at some point, you had to sacrifice a piece of you in order to move along the board.

He moved to the waste bin and put the napkin in it. A walked to him. I felt like I was floating.

"I'm sorry," I said, unable to pry my eyes away from his. They were mesmerising, like losing myself in a vast oasis when I had been walking through the desert for so long. I was dying, and he was here to save me.

"Do you know how much these shoes cost?" He said. I seem to have got some on his lapel, too. I pointed to the stray droplets of coffee.

"I have got some on your jacket too," I said, reaching out my hand to wipe them away. He pushed my hand away.

Bishop to G7.

"I've got it, thanks." He wiped it away. He looked up, and we locked eyes. I wanted to tell him there and then. Wanted to tell him everything I was thinking, but I needed to play it cool. He was still figuring me out, that we were on the same wavelength. I couldn't be too rushed. I had to play it cool.

"Can I buy you your coffee?" I asked, trying to remain as collected as possible. He thought about it for a second. He let out a laugh and then nodded.

Queen to A5.

"I guess you better had," he said. My heart did backflips.

"Grab a table," I said. "I'll be right back." After grabbing his coffee, we sat and watched the world move past outside the rain splattered window. He was local. His name was Alex. He said that he was back in town after completing some business stuff, but he didn't go into much detail. I lapped up every word, nodding, probing, and asking questions. People love to talk about themselves. Love to tell others about them, and Alex was an expert at that. He hardly asked me a single thing. But I didn't mind. To be in his company was amazing. It was like I was on a gondola in Venice with my true love, gliding through the streets with the sound of Italian symphonies floating through the air. It was bliss, and time stopped.

"What do you do for a living?" He said, his fingers wrapped around the coffee cup. I didn't know what to say. He was taking an interest in me.

"Investigations," I said, leaving the comment to linger. I didn't need to give much away straight off the bat. He had been very forthcoming, but I wanted to pique his interest a little. Keep him thinking about me. Both about who I was, and what I would look like walking to him on a bed with no clothes on. I could see him undressing me with his eyes. He might not have known he was doing it, but he was postulating. His body was giving his intention away. The mouth may spout falseness, but the eyes never lie, and he had been flitting those pearly blues to my chest from the moment we had set down. He wanted to fuck me. There was no denying that.

"I see," he said, a smirk appearing on his face.

Check.

He was going to ask me out for another coffee. I could feel it. I knew what the next words out of his mouth would be.

"Well," he said, "thank you for the coffee. I better be going." He stood. My heart began to break. I had the urge to leap up and grab his hand and tell him that the moves he was making were all wrong, but I relaxed the spiders in my stomach. He was doing his own dance to his own tune. Playing his own game. Now, he wanted me to think about him, and he was doing a perfect job. "I'll see you around," he said, before nodding to me, and then leaving the coffee shop.

I watched him go, and I watched him flag down a taxi that stopped outside the shop. I noted the registration plate, the ID number and the taxi firm of the car. He wanted me to find him. To play this game. This was good. I enjoyed playing games.

Chapter Eighteen
Laura

She had spent the last fifteen minutes pacing around the house. She should have told her no, that she would get a taxi to A&E, but something compelled her to resist the urge. Was it lust? Longing for human connection? Or was it stepping back into familiar territory? What was it that kept her from picking the phone back up and telling Celine that she had made a mistake, that she shouldn't have called her? But when she saw those headlights pull up outside her home, she would be lying if she didn't feel an ounce of excitement rush through her.

Laura threw on her coat, her bandaged hand tucked underneath. As she approached the door, she looked in the mirror. She wasn't wearing any makeup, which she didn't mind. The fucked hand would be the main focus anyway, and she would be given a pass for not making an effort given that she had lost at least a pint of blood. Priorities and all that. But again, why did she care? And why was she puffing out her hair to make it look fuller? This was purely a meeting of circumstance. Purely asking for help. Nothing more, and she would make that clear.

Laura slipped into the car. She had upgraded. The last she had seen Celine driving was a beaten-up Nissan Micra. This, however, was a sleek new BMW. The sight of her took Laura's breath away. It was like seeing a ghost. She looked exactly as she remembered. There was so much unsaid between them, so Laura went with the obvious opener.

"Nice car," she said as she closed the door and ran her healthy hand around the interior. She could smell the freshness of the leather.

"Thanks," Celine said, her tone flat. She said nothing else, and the silence that followed was deafening. Laura had explained to her on the phone that she needed a ride to the hospital. Celine had queried why she didn't get an ambulance or a taxi. Laura had lied. There were no Taxi's available, and an ambulance would take hours. One of those were true. "So," she said, putting the car into drive. Automatic. *Nice.* "How have you been? I heard you went away for a little while after we last spoke." *After we last spoke,* Laura thought. Jesus Christ, she could cut through the subtext with a knife, fry it up and chew on it. Bloody and raw.

"Yeah," she said. "I got sober. Worked some stuff out."

"What kind of stuff?"

Like me, you mean.

"Relationships. Pressures of the job. Bagpipes last lot of injections." Laura said bluntly. "The usual *stuff.*" Was Laura flirting with her? Playing it cool, casual. Cracking jokes?

"And how are you now?" Her lips were still. Not a crack of emotion on her face.

I'm sitting here with you. That's how well it's going.

"Just taking it one day at a time. Work is mayhem. Speaking of which," she ran her hand over the interior again. "You didn't get this car on a forensic investigator's wage."

"Such a detective," Celine said. Laura could almost hear the rolling of her eyes. She had cut her hair shorter. Her clothing was so new it should still have a tag on it. "No," she said, turning onto the dual carriageway to the town centre. "I decided to take a new career path. Went travelling for a few weeks. Nothing major. Just a little bit of Asia, America. Did some soul searching. Worked some stuff out."

"That sounds amazing." Laura said. She wasn't lying, either. She was genuinely impressed.

"It was okay," Celine said, downplaying it. "It helped me move past a lot of things." Laura could feel the daggers sticking into her. "After that, I used what money I had left to set up a business consulting on investigations. Looking through records. Freelancing my forensic services to private companies. A month or two later, I landed a couple of big clients, and the rest is history." She said the last sentence like she was teasing it out of her mouth. Why? Did she want to make Laura jealous? Was she so audacious in that she had moved on with her life? If she was, she wasn't doing a good job of it. Laura was sitting in her car at three in the morning and she was taking her to the hospital. But then again, Laura could exactly say the same thing. That is why people don't like seeing their failures laid out in front of them. It's a mar to their ego, like a crack in a mirror.

"Sorry about what happened," Laura said. She figured she would rather attack the elephant in the room than try to move around it. Call it bolshy. Call it insensitive. But put your cards on the table and you can get on with your life. Laura was expecting Celine to respond with some witty comment. Respond with some underhanded, smart ass, passive aggressiveness. But she didn't. Instead, she sat there watching the black tarmac move past like a dark river.

"I forgive you," she said. Laura felt a flare of anger. She wasn't asking for forgiveness. This was meant to be a mutual thing. *I fucked up, you fucked up, let's move on with our lives*, sort of thing. No. *Laura* was the bad one. How the hell did that happen? "I wasn't in the best place myself." She let out a sigh. "I hadn't been taking my medication. Things were moving too fast, and I should have put on the brakes, I needed someone to fix me, and I know you needed someone to help you too. We were both as bad as each other, and we took different paths to mutual destruction." She let out a sigh. "So yeah. I'm so sorry too. You didn't deserve what I put you through, and I know you didn't mean what you did to me, either." Laura was taken aback. She felt that old scar being ripped open. She wanted to cry. To hug her. To fuck her right there on the driver's seat while the car cruised at eighty. But she sat quietly and was suffocated by the silence that followed.

"That means a lot," she said, pushing through the closing of her throat. It was like someone had released the tap off the pressure cooker. Therapy can do all the work in the world. But nothing will beat the feeling of the person you wanted, to acknowledge the pain they caused you and absolve you of your own failings.

"So," Celine said after a moment. "How did you mess your hand up?" Laura had forgotten about the throbbing pain in her hand, but now her attention was brought back to it. The person helping her to get treated was the person who kept reminding her of her pain. Irony, if there ever was any.

"Tried using a glass as a stress ball."

"Doesn't sound like you," Celine said, a small smirk appearing on her face. They pulled off onto the busy streets that ran through the centre. Signs for the hospital coming into view. The streets were lively. People out drinking in the twenty-four-hour bars.

Shops that never closed. Bright lights and brighter smiles. The cops would have a fun one tonight. There was something in the air. "What made you do that?"

"Police may have been called to a home with a suspected domestic murder, with the male bleeding out inside. They may not have been able to get access. I may or may not have driven the car through the gates, and I may or may not be in the shit for it." Celine nodded silently, soaking it up.

"Sounds like you had no other choice." Laura ran her fingers through her hair.

"I couldn't see one."

"So, you did a good thing." Laura let that sink in and watched the passing streets blur past. Streetlights changed. Drinks and smiles flowed.

"Yeah. I guess I did."

"Why did she kill him?" Celine said. Laura felt her skin prickle.

"That's the big question." Celine's mouth curled into a smile.

"The things people do for love." Now Celine was flirting back in her strange, unique way. The look in her eye twinkled at Laura. Laura felt her heart pick up. Her legs flooding with warmth.

"We were never that bad," Laura said. Celine shrugged.

"Love. Lust. Chaos. Passion. All the same, just different names of the same diode. Plus," Celine trained her gaze on Laura. "Always the ones you least suspect."

"Exactly. Anyway," Laura said, quickly moving to less jagged topics of conversation. "Because of that, I am in hot water, and despite what I managed to do, I got an ear full of Jeremy, and I crushed the glass in my hand. Hence, my phone call to you."

"Is that the only reason why you called me?" Celine said, pulling into the car park of the hospital. Laura didn't even realise they were so close, lost in the ball of barbed wire of toxic exes reuniting. But she thought of the question.

"I told you," Laura said. "There were no taxis available." Celine pulled into a car park space, the engine silent. She pulled the handbrake and the sounds of ambulances in the distance.

"If you say so." Celine reached over to her, the movement taking Laura by surprise. She was an inch from her face. Celine's hot breath mixed with Laura's. Laura felt the swelling in her legs grow into a steady throbbing. She swallowed hard, and Celine drew her face closer. Her fingers on the edge of her seat, depressing the fabric, the tips of her fingers gracing her outer thigh. A delicate dance of who shouted 'stop' first. But Celine wasn't going to anchor the brakes, and Laura didn't utter a word. Laura's heartbeat picked up. What was she doing, and why wasn't she stopping her? She had wanted this for so long. Like a forbidden fruit. Despite what she had told herself, told her therapist and written in her journal before bed, she *hadn't* moved on. It was the scar she wanted to tear open. Celine was the only woman that had made her feel anything again since Ron. It was like she had forgotten how to breathe since she left, and she had been suffocating ever since.

"Laura?" Celine said. She was staring at her. Laura noticed she was pressed against the inside passenger seat. Her breathing heavy. The seatbelt wrapped around her shoulder where Celine had pushed the depressor.

"What?" Laura said, coming back to the moment. The fantasy dying away. The cold reality hit her like a truck. Celine let out a stifled laugh, gesturing to the hospital across the way.

"You going in, or what?" Laura felt embarrassed. Then, a swelling of shame ran through her bloodstream, dousing the heat in her vein, and rendering them cold and brittle.

"Thanks for the lift," Laura said and slipped out into the night.

"Wait!" Celine said, grabbing her good arm. Her touch nailed Laura to the spot. She turned. Celine's face, the first time she had seen it properly in months, lit up by the interior cab light of the BMW. The sight of her took Laura's breath away. She felt a tide of emotion drown her. "I know this is a little much and tell me to fuck off it you like. Since what happened, I have kind of been keeping myself to myself, but I would like to get out of the house. I'm going crazy – between work and, well… work. I haven't been out much at all."

"Are you asking me for a drink?"

"A soft drink, yes. Just two old friends catching up. No funny business, I promise." Laura thought about this for a second. But before she could process the emotions that were creating a cocktail of excitement, guilt, remorse, and lust inside her, she spoke.

"Okay." Celine smiled. Her teeth were impeccably white. She reached into her pocket and took out her business card and passed it to her.

"Just in case you lose my number," she said, a lilt of teasing carried on a bright smile. "Pick you up at seven?" Laura put the card in her pocket and ran her fingers through her auburn hair.

"Should be fine." Laura didn't think it *would* be fine, but after she had her arse handed to her at work, she could do with something to delay the reality of being single, unemployed, and in recovery with a cat. "See you later," she said. "Thanks for the ride." Celine said nothing else. She just eyed Laura with the same look that she had every time Laura had come into the bedroom in a set of lingerie, with a bottle of wine and two glasses in her hand. A look they both knew all too well. This encounter wasn't going to be a '*no funny business*' sort of affair. As she made her way to the hospital entrance, she thought of nothing else but what that affair would entail.

Chapter Nineteen
Laura

Laura walked into the entrance of the Accident and Emergency department and tried her best not to throw up. It was odd being on this side of the reception desk. Usually, she would be in the backroom with a prisoner who had developed a case of 'incarseritis,' the sudden onset of symptoms when arrested. She remembered one man claiming to have schizophrenia, saying that the voices in his head were telling him to hurt his family. Laura had carefully and politely asked where the voices were coming from.

"In my head," the man said, with such certainty of his insanity, continued holding his tattooed hands to his mouth, muttering through his sausage fingers.

"I thought those with schizophrenia heard voices *outside* their heads?" The brute slowly pulled his hands from his face, the sobs stopping abruptly, like someone had pulled the power cord on a stereo. His pale blue eyes, piercing.

"What're you saying?" As if Laura needed to clarify. But as the phrase went, 'you can't fix stupid, but you can lock it up.'

"I'm saying you aren't schizophrenic." Her colleague at the time, a newbie detective with less hair on his chin than on his balls, shot a look at her. She was sure he stopped breathing, too.

"You saying I'm making it up?" The thug reiterated, suddenly having dry cheeks and not a single tear in his eyes.

"That's not how I would put it."

"And how would you put it?" He hissed. Laura noted where her cuffs and gas were on her body armour.

"I'm saying you are categorically, one hundred percent, spouting absolute bullshit." Laura rolled around with him on the floor for four minutes before the hospital security came. She was taken back to the station for one of her many detentions in the office *Room of Doom*, where her supervisor tore her a new arsehole. As far as she was aware, that criminal never faked being mentally ill again. He just tore his veins out in the custody cell with his teeth so they could see he needed to go to the hospital. Laura thought that to be some sort of progress.

Sitting in the waiting room, however, she looked around her. Nobody ever sat here when they were having a good day.

"Oh, how are you?" A nurse would say.

"Perfectly peachy," the patient would respond. "Just thought I would come in and check out the décor. Is that blood? Does the vending machine work? Didn't think so. Can you turn this rerun of Coronation Street up, please? I can't quite hear it over the screaming." That little scenario made her smile and took the icing off the cake made of shit she found herself chewing on of late. She checked herself in at the reception desk, giving her name and details.

"Next of Kin?" The receptionist asked. A handsome man with a rainbow pride lanyard. Laura pondered the question. It was still Celine. She reiterated there had been no change. She would sort that out later. She didn't think she would ever see her again, and now she was going for a drink with her this evening. "Take a seat," the receptionist said, pointing to a blue plastic chair that was bolted to the floor against the wall. Laura nodded, moving to the waiting area.

Was she seriously thinking about heading for a drink with Celine? After everything that had happened? But then a part of her whispered in her mind. She had changed. They both had. Two broken people don't make a whole relationship. But two fixed people? Could that save them both from the scrap pile? She dared to fantasise about the idea, while someone erupted into a coughing fit across the room, and the machines in the back buzzed and bleeped. She began thinking of what drink she was going to order. Non-alcoholic, obviously. She felt strong enough to resist the urge. She hadn't been into a pub or restaurant since she got out of rehab, but she couldn't hide away forever. She wasn't necessarily a pint girl, although she could sink one in a couple of seconds, something she discovered in her partying years at university. However, cocktails were more her thing, those sugary, fruity little bombshells. But it would be *Mocktails* for her. Same thing, less regret. Maybe even finish off with a diet coke before bedtime. Oh, how she knew how to party. And what about food? It wasn't a *date*, or so she kept telling herself. But she didn't want to go for something sloppy. The last thing you want if you run into an ex is them thinking you to be a pig. No. Some part of her wanted Celine to *miss* what she had been so cruel towards. Sitting opposite her, looking a solid ten out of ten. Hair done. Makeup perfect. Smelling of roses and freshly shaven legs and pussy. Maybe pizza? She had heard of a new pizza place that had opened in the centre of Wigtown. 'Ego's,' she thinks it was called. Stone baked meat feast pizza made with signature dough, and homemade BBQ sauce to dip, with some halloumi sticks with sweet chilli dip on the side. The thought of the food was making her mouth water. But that wasn't all that was tantalising her senses. As much as she tried to deny it in her mind, her body told a different story. She couldn't wait to sit down with Celine again. Seeing her tonight, unlocking *that* door, and allowing for all those feelings she had kept locked away to come flooding back through.

If things progressed from this one dinner date, and that was a big *if*, then things would be different. Celine knew the pressures of her job, and by the sounds of it, Celine had a pretty high stakes job too. So, they would have plenty to talk about, and they couldn't afford to lose their heads again because they had more to lose than last time. Laura's career was hanging by a thread, and Celine looked like she had cleaned her act up and was on her way up in the world. They would rejoin each other's lives as equals, each with their own wants, wishes and boundaries, instead of two broken souls trying to fix each other and fit into each other's lives. She felt good. Excited at the possibility. She just hoped that it wasn't all an illusion and she, or Celine, were just playing a very good fake. She had been fooled before. More times than she would like to admit.

I wonder where Clara is? She thought, returning to the job. She was in this hospital, and Laura was off duty, about to be sent to a ward. Maybe a little walk about. Maybe she could speak to her? The thought made her stomach churn. It was too risky. In the hospital, she would be guarded around the clock by cops. They would have been informed about Laura, no doubt. Jeremy wasn't stupid. He would be expecting her to go rogue. But then again, was he? Maybe he was so up his own arse about his promotion, that he couldn't tear himself away from the vision of him wanking naked in the mirror with his new pips on his shoulder long enough to look around him and take note of what the rest of the world was doing.

A nurse emerged from the side triage room holding a clipboard. The whole room looked up like meerkats hearing the rustling of a crisp packet.

"Miss Warburton." Laura smiled and stood up and walked to the nurse, those that had been waiting longer stabbing her in the back with their gaze. She slipped through the door and closed the waiting room away. The nurse pulled the blue curtain across, sealing them away from prying eyes. The nurse unravelled the bandages around Laura's hand and openly grimaced.

"Ugly, right?" Laura said. The nurse responded by lifting her eyebrows and then a sharp intake of breath through tight teeth. She began to prod and poke at the wound, stopping when Laura would let out a noise indicative to receiving a quick headbutt to the nose if the nurse continued.

"How did this happen?" The nurse said. She eyed her curiously.

"I was busy in the kitchen, and the cat jumped out at me. I was startled and crushed the glass in my hand." An unlikely story, but it was the only one she could think of.

"Must have been some startle," she said. She didn't believe Laura. That was apparent. Nevertheless, she didn't pry any further. "What's your cat's name?"

"Bagpipe. He's a black moggie."

"That's a strange name for a cat."

"It's strange we name animals anyway," she said. "And besides, you can call a cat whatever you like, it won't come to you. So, I called him *Bagpipe*." The nurse nodded.

"You'll need stitches."

"I thought as much." The nurse continued looking over the injury.

"I think it's safe that you haven't any glass in the wound. I can't feel anything. But you may have damaged a nerve or tendon, so you'll need an x-ray, and then we can get a fresh dressing on and antibiotics."

"Understood." The nurse turned and typed away on the computer.

"I need you to take yourself to Majors, and then someone will be with you." Laura stood and moved to the door. She depressed the handle and turned back to the nurse's computer. She had Laura's notes open, typing them away in the box. Laura squinted at the other names quickly, and then she saw her. Clara Weaver. Ward A2. Sensing she wasn't alone, the nurse turned in her chair.

"Can I help you with something else?" She said politely. Laura smiled and shook her head.

"No," she said. "You've helped plenty."

A few hours of staring at a wall later, Laura was X-rayed. Nothing of note. Just some swelling that would go down in a few days, and she was patched up and discharged. She moved to the exit and then grabbed the attention of a passing doctor.

"Excuse me," she said, fumbling through her coat pocket. She pulled out her warrant card. The doctor straightened. "I need to find where the officers are with the patient Clara Weaver." The doctor – A woman with blonde hair, tall, athletic. Her name tag 'DR. E. Hughes' She eyed her bandaged arm.

"Are you on duty?"

"Yes," Laura lied. The doctor eyed her suspiciously and then pointed to the lift.

"Third floor. Turn right. Ward A2. Intensive care

unit." Laura thanked her and moved to the lift. She could feel the doctor's eyes on her back. Why had she lied? Why was she making more trouble for herself? She wasn't on duty. She had no right to ask anything about anyone in the hospital. Using her warrant card to gain access to patients was one thing. Doing it off duty and lying? That was more than simple misconduct. It was criminal.

Moving through the hospital, she kept her head down as she slipped past the doctors and nurses on their rounds. The harsh corridor lighting obscuring the pitch black world outside. She found Ward A2. Just where the doctor had told her. She should leave her a review on the hospital website. She had been so helpful. Laura moved past an out of use vending machine and the large yellow waste bins that were being pulled by the porters who looked like they needed a good night's sleep.

She walked through the narrow ward walkway, flanked each side by different rooms filled with beds, sleeping bodies, and beeping machines. The receptionist eyed her, but Laura walked purposefully, holding her head up high, so she wasn't challenged. Laura knew that most communication is body language. If you look the part, people won't see you're faking it. At the bottom of the walkway, past the bright orange toilet doors and a stack of abandoned trolleys teeming with medication, stood a closed door. A placard stuck to the back that read 'SECURE PATIENT.'

She got to the door and looked through the small window. Clara was lying on the bed, mouth open like a fish out of water. An IV drip feeding into her arm. Handcuffs wrapped around her wrists and attaching her to the bed railing. Two officers. Each talking amongst themselves. She hadn't been seen yet, which was good. One would need to use the bathroom at some point, and then she could cause a distraction, so the other would need to leave for a minute or two. That would be her chance. All she had to do right now was wait. She would sit in one of the wards, right at the back, so nobody would notice her, keeping her eye on the room to see if someone comes out.

She turned quickly, not looking where she was going, and barged right into a woman that was holding a coffee. The coffee ruptured from the paper cup and splattered onto the floor, dousing the pair of them in hot liquid.

"Shit," Laura said, getting her coat and wiping down the other woman. "I am so, so sorry." Laura noted the warrant card dangling from her neck. Her heart stopped. DCI Burnell. The one person she didn't want to see, and Laura had just thrown coffee all over her. Laura met her eye. She was in so much shit she could swim in it.

"Laura." It was funny that someone could say your name and call them a cunt at the same time. "You're off duty. Why are you here?" She pointed to Laura's hand. "You've been in a spot of bother."

"I was in the neighbourhood," Laura said, throwing the comment away. Burnell eyed her with the same fury as finding a maggot in your turkey on Christmas.

"I should have you arrested," Burnell said. "Interfering with a crime scene." Burnell's face soured.

"Last I checked, ma'am, this corridor wasn't a crime scene." She pushed her hair from her face. It was sticking together with the sweat that was pouring out of her. "I hurt my hand, and I was only down the hall in majors. Thought I would come and see if the cops on guard duty wanted a coffee." Laura eyed the half-empty cup of Joe in Burnell's hand. "By the looks of it, you didn't think to ask them." The two women eyed each other. The great white and the barracuda. She needed to get out of there, and quickly. There was no way she could speak to Clara now. Not now that her cover had been blown. "I'll leave you to it." She moved to step past DCI Burnell, but she sidestepped and blocked her path. Laura felt her blood begin to boil.

"You know," Burnell started. "I can understand you driving through the gate and writing off a twelve-thousand-pound vehicle. I can understand you smashing a window and crawling over broken glass and contaminating a crime scene. I can even understand your alcoholism. But what I can't understand," she raised her hand, pointing to the door. "Is why *her?*"

Why her? The question. The perfect question. Why her? Why anyone? Why would an officer care about someone they don't know? Why should any of us care about right and wrong? Empathy? Duty? Consequence? Because of human decency. If you took all of that away. If you stripped away the laws and norms of society, and let savages rule, good men would still help each other.

"Why Clara?" Laura said, running her tongue along the inside of her dry mouth. "Because everyone here is trying to throw her in prison. I am trying to discover the truth." Burnell took a sip of her coffee, her eyes never leaving Laura's for a second. Laura weighed her up. She could tell with the way she stood. The fierceness in Burnell's eyes, that she had a history of running at the wall until it broke down. She had fought tooth and nail for every promotion she got. She was good. Brilliant, in fact, as much as Laura was pained to admit it. To Burnell, Laura was simply in the way of her doing her job, and Laura saw Burnell in the way of her doing hers. But Jeremy? He was weak. A red faced, bulbous man who would throw someone under the bus at a chance of more power. Just like he was doing with Laura, but he hadn't only just thrown her under the bus. He was reversing over her until she was matted into the tarmac.

Power and greed were all consuming, like a hungry shark that didn't know when to stop gorging itself. They knew no boundaries, and Jeremy was itching for another rung up that greasy ladder. It meant ignoring some facts that didn't show Clara Weaver as a cold-blooded killer, then he would silence any voice that shouted the contrary. But the question was why was Burnell so hell bent on this case and showing Clara as guilty? What was it about Alex Weaver that made her so passionate? Almost vengeful...

"I dealt with Annabelle Jones," she said. "For the murders at the home of Hugo Black, a few years back. I know a murdering woman when I see one. This case is open and shut. She's guilty. You're chasing ghosts." Chasing ghosts. She could have only gotten that from Jeremy. Is that what they thought? That Laura was so caught up with her past that she was trying to save herself, through Clara, by proxy? Not a detective doing a good job. Not a detective exploring all connections, lines of inquiry for not only a fair trial but a clear conscience, but because she was traumatised? Laura felt the spit along her tongue, and she was a second from hocking it in Burnell's eye. "Speaking of which," she checked her watch. "You should be on duty in a few hours. I'll be in the office in a few hours, and I expect to see your resignation on my desk. Be sure to double space it. My eyes aren't what they used to be." She let out a satisfied sigh. A long smile crept along her face like a worm splitting open and being pulled apart by hungry birds. "Oh, how I have enjoyed our little encounter tonight." She stepped past Laura and slipped into the room. "I'll see you later," she said, that smile unmoving, before closing the ward door behind her. Laura noticed it then. The smell coming off her. Something fragrant. Something floral.

Chapter Twenty
Laura

Laura arrived home as the sun began to rise. She had caught an Uber. She stopped at the local garage and bought herself a pack of cigarettes. She was going to fight one demon at a time. The nicotine gum tasted like shit and was too hard to find, meaning she had to stockpile it. Cigarettes, however, were sold everywhere, and she could dip in and out of them. That first inhale was heavenly.

As long as she didn't drink, she could stay on track. That was the biggie. No booze. If she touched booze, then there was only one way it would go, and Laura didn't want to go down that path again. Not for all the tea in China. Not for all the money in the world. Not for the sweetest piece of pussy she could get her hands on. No booze. Ever. Again.

"I'll walk the rest of the way, thank you," she said to the Uber driver, who had been waiting patiently for her to come out of the store.

"No problem," he said. "Have a nice day!" The driver indicated, despite the roads being dead, and disappeared into the rising sun. Laura watched him go. The cool air waking up her body, numbing her hand and dulling the throbbing. She walked down the quiet road, smoking away. Hell, she even began humming a song. She actually felt happy. The feeling of the nicotine rushing around her body. A tingling. A sensation she had forgotten.

Laura's phone buzzed. She checked it. It was Celine.

Morning. How was the hospital? How you feeling?

How am I feeling? She laughed. She could feel the tears burning on her eyelids. The short spell of joy evaporated into the wind.

Hey. Thanks for the lift. Means a lot. Hand is patched up. Have some work stuff to deal with. Just heading home and then heading to the station. Speak later.

Immediately, she got a reply.

You need another lift? Laura left Celine on *Read*.

Back at the house, she changed her bedding and had a shower, making sure to keep her hand dry. She walked out of the bedroom and Bagpipe was playing in the discarded bloodstained duvet covers. Laura smiled and crouched down.

"Hey, little guy," she said. Bagpipe purred and moved to her, gliding his fur under her fingertips, and wrapped around her freshly shaven legs. He nestled his head into her palm and began licking at the loose drips of water on her skin. His rough tongue making her itch. "Shall we get you some food?" Bagpipe lifted his head, his fangs poking from under his black lips. His eyes are impossibly yellow.

Downstairs, Laura fed Bagpipe a generous helping of meat and even took out a frozen piece of fish she had been saving but never got around to eating. He devoured it quickly, meowing as she prepped it, circling around her feet like a hungry shark. Laura checked the time. It was nearly time for her judgement. She moved to the kitchen bar and sat down. Although the morning was bright, the room seemed bleaker. The walls that much greyer. The bar that much darker. What was she going to do? She had put her life back together, and she had fired a cannonball into the middle of it. And for what? For doing the right thing? She could feel the hangmen's noose tightening around her neck. If she resigned, an innocent woman could go to prison. A victim. If she didn't resign, then Laura would be sitting in the cell with her. What was she going to do?

Like a death row inmate that was about to face the firing squad, she stood up and let out a deep breath. She didn't like what she was going to have to face, but she wasn't about to run away. She had to try one last time. She took out her phone and hit dial.

"Where are you?" Jeremy barked.

"I'm going to be late this morning."

"Are you taking the fucking piss –"

"I had an accident last night." Jeremy's voice stopped dead.

"What kind of accident?"

The 'I was so angry at you that I crushed a glass in my hand,' kind of accident.

"I was making some food, and the cat startled me. I sliced my palm open. I have been at the hospital all night."

"I know you have." Laura felt her blood run cold.

"Burnell tell you?"

"Why the fuck did you go near the defendant!" He sounded like he was going to the put his hand through the phone and throttle her. "You are completely out of line!"

"I was in the neighbourhood," she spat.

"Cut the attitude, Sergeant," he hissed. "I want you

here in the next ten minutes for your resignation." It didn't matter what time she arrived if it was her last day. Hell, she could turn up in her underwear and throw eggs at him. That would be a real hoot.

"There's more to it than you think, Jeremy."

"Inspector."

"Jeremy," Laura maintained defiantly. "I know it. This isn't as clear cut as we think. Why does she have short hair now? Why have the neighbours never spoken to her? Why was she taken from the hospital?"

"You sound like a broken record! It's all circumstantial," Jeremy said, the frustration straining through his teeth. "I'm not going over this again. The woman is unstable. We have the medical records to prove that."

"But Jeremy…" Laura pleaded.

"Goodbye, Laura," Jeremy said before ending the call. Laura stayed in suspended amazement. The anger bubbled up inside her. She felt the shakes in her legs first, then her heart thumping in her head. It felt like angry fists threatening to smash the glass that protected her brain from full catatonia. The fists continued to pound, and Laura felt something shatter.

She threw her phone across the room, it collided fiercely with the wall and falling to the floor like a shattered brick. She swiped the kitchen bar, glasses, and candles and papers cascading onto the ground. She let out a loud scream, it ringing around the silent house, her throat burning. Her knuckles were white as she pressed them into her eyes until all she could think about was the pain. The sweet, purifying pain. She could hear herself screaming behind those gritted teeth. Her throat was like a hot engine revving loudly with no oil. She could do it. Just walk out of this house right now and buy some booze and drink herself to death. That sweet crimson nectar.

A rush of heat filled her, and she released herself, throwing the stool to the floor, just narrowly missing Bagpipe, who darted like a black shadow out of the way. She slammed her fists against the kitchen bar, hammering them into the surface again and again, before slowing, her breathing deep. Her breath was ragged. Swallowing hard, running her hand over her sweating face, and staring into nothing. Then the tears came. Her bottom lip quivering. Her face scrunching up like a crisp packet thrown into a flame. She slumped onto the ground, laying in the wake of her destruction.

"I can't do this anymore," she sobbed. "I just can't do this…" Laura snaked her hand up to the kitchen counter and hauled herself to her feet. She pulled open the cupboard and found her box of anti-depressants. She was supposed to take them. Had been taking them. But she still felt sad. She would take them all. Force the whole blister pack down and lie on the couch until she felt nothing at all. She pulled out the box and poured herself a drink of water. The pills popped out of the packet easily. Twenty of them in total. Annihilation never looked so appetising.

She should call her sponsor. But she didn't. She stayed in that agony for a second longer. She took a pill and swallowed it with a gulp of water. Then a second. A third. Fighting back the tears. A fourth slipped in, and she felt her stomach wretch. A fifth. Sixth.

"I can't do this…" She whispered between her sobs. "I just want it to end…" Laura felt Bagpipe run his fur around her legs. She pushed her fingers to the back of her throat. Her stomach began to bounce, her gagging making her eyes water, and she vomited into the sink.

She went in for another round, expelling bile and water that splashed around the basin. She forced down another glass of water and stood there, hunched over the sink, gasping for air. She sifted through the vomit and counted five pills. Five out of six. She took the rest of the pills and threw them into the sink, dissolving them in a downpour of water until the plug stopped gurgling. Laura wiped her mouth, stringy phlegm sticking to her fingers.

Laura reached down and scooped Bagpipe up and nestled him into her face. Holding onto him as she sobbed. Staggered, sharp breaths pulsing from her quivering lips.

The doorbell went. Laura snapped her attention to the front door. She opened it, and the cold slapped her sweating body. It was Celine, who eyed her with worry in the morning twilight.

"Are you okay?" The colour drained from her face. No. That wasn't it. She wasn't wearing make-up. Had she been home?

"What are you doing here?" Laura said. Celine queried her.

"I came to make sure you were okay. You didn't respond to my text. I thought you might have collapsed on your walk home or something. You lost a lot of blood."

"I'm fine," Laura said, touching the handle of the door. Why was she here?

"Okay," Celine said. "Glad you're alright. See you later." Celine turned on her heel and made her way back to her car. Laura watched her go. Every part of her told her not to. She shouldn't be alone. Not right now. Every fibre in her being begged her not to call out to her. That this was what she wanted. She wanted

Laura to need her. But she found her lips moving, and her voice carrying along the empty space between them.

"I could do with a ride to work."

Chapter Twenty – One
Laura

"We still good for later?" Celine said as she pulled up to the station. Laura felt like she was being pulled in each direction, like the Hellraiser Pin Head was sticking his hooks into her and pulling her skin from her bones.

"Yeah," Laura said. She feigned a smile. It wasn't that she didn't want to spend some time with Celine or, right now, anyone but her own thoughts. It was the fact that she could feel herself slipping. Re-adjusting her entire world to a new way of life. Simple things, like instead of drinking a bottle of wine to herself after work, she had a glass of water instead. Instead of having a glass of wine before work, she had a cup of juice. Instead of destroying her life at every turn, she opted for yoga. So far, she hated sobriety. Even the calls with her therapist were becoming a chore. She had to fill out a mental health diary every week. So far, after just over three months, she had drawn a picture of Bagpipe and had used it as a doorstopper. Why was she failing so badly? Sobriety was tough. It meant living in the real world. Dancing around in her underwear, a bottle deep to her favourite playlist on YouTube was an escape. It blotted out the reason why she drank, and that reason was pain. She could hide from it. Without the bottle. Without the numb. She had nowhere to hide. And that was agony. But maybe it *wasn't* the booze she was addicted to. Maybe it was the fact that at any moment, everything she had could fall apart. Maybe that was the reason that when she looked into Celine's eyes, she found herself not only wanting to jump back into that abyss, but almost begging it to happen.

"I'm looking forward to it." Celine eyed her, a small smile creeping along her lips.

"I can't wait." Laura stepped out of the car and Celine watched her go into the station. As soon as Celine was out of view, Laura let out a panicked breath. The muted thoughts under Celine's spell now screaming again in her absence.

Why the fuck was she at my house? Because she was worried and I didn't text her back? Bullshit. It was damn near stalking. Laura had unlocked the door to allow Celine back into her life, and Celine had barged through with suitcases and fresh bedding. She knew she needed to call it off. Food? Drinks? Some kind of strange date – but not a date – where they would do anything but talk about the fact how much they loathed each other and tore each other limb from limb? She took out her phone, Celine's number open, her finger hovering over it. She clicked it, typed out a message –

Sorry. I can't do this again. Thanks for the lift. Have a good life.

She stared at the message, then quickly deleted it, feeling the anxiety crush her heart within its grasp. Why had she deleted it? She searched the feeling, opened the box that was wrapped in chains and barbed wire. It was fear. She was scared. Not of Celine, but what Celine meant to her. She was safety. She was familiar. Since getting out of rehab, she had been stripped of everything she clung to. It was like taking the red pill. The pill that made her see the world for what it really was, away from her world of abject comfort. Like when someone gets clean and gets a job when they get out of prison, and they go straight into the local newsagents with a knife and commit an armed robbery. It's because they can't handle the world without the security of their walls. Of the familiarity and predictability of circumstances. That's what Celine was to Laura. She was her prison. Her security. Her solace and protection from a world that was complete chaos. She was her anchor, and as much as she hated to admit it, she needed her, or she would float into the ocean and drown.

She was pulled from her thoughts by a voice calling her name. She looked at the entrance to the station. Jeremy standing there. He looked like he hadn't been home in days.

"Are you going to stand out there all morning? Or are you going to come in?" Laura moved into the station, slipping past Jeremy without a word.

"Jesus," Jeremy said, leaning forward in his chair, looking at Laura's hand. "How many stitches?"

"Seven," she said. Jeremy almost wanted to touch it, like when a friend says they have a bruise that hurts, and you jab your finger into it and wonder why they then punch you.

"What happened?" Jeremy said, eyeing the bandaged wound.

"Bagpipe.," Laura said. "I was making some food, and he jumped up, startled me, and the next thing I know is I am going to the hospital."

"Fuck," he said. His face was draining of colour. Despite the amount of blood he had seen, he hadn't ever got used to the sight of it. "Right then," Jeremy said. He leaned back in his chair, his grey hair wafting in the small desk fan he kept on at all times. The chair crying under his weight. "I don't know how to say this, Laura," he started. His words were slow. Careful. Over the phone, he had so much to say. So vicious. But face to face, he was crumbling like a mean online troll confronted by the receiver holding a baseball bat. "You know what I have asked you to do," he said. "And by no means, Laura, do I make this decision lightly. I think it's in everyone's best interests, given recent events –"

"Do I get a federation rep present?" Laura interjected. Jeremy's voice cut short, like someone had strangled the rest of the words out of him.

"If you feel you need one."

"I don't, but it's nice to have the offer." Laura said, folding her arms. Her red hair hanging over her shoulders.

"Right," Jeremy said, clearing his throat. "Like I was saying –"

"Is DCI Cunt not joining us? Or does she have children to scare before she gets in?" Again, Jeremy's eyes looked like pin balls that had been smashed by an angry child.

"DCI Burnell was on nights last night. You know this. Miss Weaver was taken back to custody this morning. We're going for an extension on her custody clock so that she can be interviewed. Superintendent Bennettt is writing it up now. After that, she'll be charged for the murder of Alex Weaver and sent to prison until her trial date." Laura let those words sink in. She saw an opportunity for leverage. "Now, if I may continue. Your resignation will mean that –"

"I'm not going to resign, Jeremy." The words shot Jeremy like a cannonball to the gut. His eyes went wide.

"You're not?" He said, his voice sounding meek.

"No," Laura said. "At least not right now." She studied Jeremy's perplexed expression, like he was watching a dog do Gangnam Style. Laura leaned forward. She could smell Jeremy. A mixture of sweat and aftershave. "I can't resign whilst Clara Weaver still needs to be interviewed." Jeremy's face went all kinds of crazy before erupting in a loud roar of laughter. His belly bustling up and down, the buttons on his shirt clinging on for dear life.

"You can't be serious!" He said. "The DCI would have my balls if I let you go anywhere near her."

"Sounds to me like you don't have a choice?" Laura rebuked.

"How do you figure?" Laura stabbed her finger onto the coffee-stained table.

"Well, you're looking for an extension. You need to be progressing the case to get one. You aren't going to interview Clara. You don't know the case, and you haven't interviewed anyone in years. You're rusty. You'd have to get a team together. The DCI isn't at work. She was on nights last night. Francis isn't going to interview her. He's good, but this is a complex case. Which, sadly for you, means I'm your only option." Laura leant back, watching the colour drain from Jeremy's eyes for the second time that morning. Probably a third. The first would have been when he saw his disgusting body naked in the mirror. "I have the skills, the knowledge of the case, and frankly, *without* me, you have no reason to keep Clara in custody, as the case isn't being progressed. The detention extension is denied. This gets to the media, and you are the man who let a potential mentally unstable murderer walk the streets again. That wouldn't look good for your next promotion board, now would it?" Jeremy's jaw was hanging so low Laura was surprised it hadn't hit the table. She had got him by the balls, and he knew she had. His ineptitude as a leader had led him to be exploited by his own failings. The silence was deafening, as Jeremy stared at Laura, the cogs turning in his head on the 'I'm Fucked' meter. Laura raised her hands, shrugging. "Or," she said, reaching to Jeremy and pulling the sheet of paper for her resignation towards her. "I can do as you like, end my career right now, and let you pick up the pieces." Jeremy's hand snapped around Laura's. His teeth bared. Laura tried not to laugh.

"You have some nerve." That she did, but she was modest enough not to brag.

"Your choice." Laura looked at the ticking clock on the wall. Silently reminding herself to smash the thing to pieces when she usurped Jeremy back into her rightful place as head of the MIU. "Time's ticking." Jeremy tightened his hand around her wrist.

"And what happens after you speak to her?" Laura smiled. She was inching closer.

"If I speak to her and get nothing, I will resign without question." She raised her hand to her head. "*Sir.*" Jeremy chewed on his response like he was trying to find a missing tooth with his tongue.

"One interview," he said. "But you better not fuck it up."

Chapter Twenty – Two
Clara

The cell walls were a sickly yellow and the mat I was given for a bed reminded me of when I used to do PE in school. It was uncomfortable, and the room was so cold I could see my breath like a plume of ghostly smoke. They told me I wasn't able to have a blanket due to my history. I was under constant supervision by a police officer who sat at the door, silently staring at me. The clothing they gave me was itchy and thin. A grey jumper and a grey pair of joggers with some pumps to go on my feet. I wasn't allowed my clothes that I had been brought in with. They had taken them to be tested.

The custody sergeants were friendly enough. I nodded and shook my head when they asked me questions. They got frustrated with me because I didn't speak. I could see it in their eyes. They thought I was a killer. A killer hiding behind my own silence. But the truly terrifying part? I didn't know if I was responsible for Alex's death or not. There *had* been someone else there. I remember their shape when I awoke on the kitchen floor. But why was I covered in blood? Had I imagined it? I felt like the loneliest person in the world. I wanted to scream and shout, or even ask someone about what was happening. Tell someone what had happened. But I couldn't. To speak it was to make it real, and the reality of this situation was that I was guilty of murdering a man who had made my life a living hell for many years.

"Clara," a voice called, pulling me out of the locked

cell in my head, bringing me back to the literal cell I found myself sitting in. I met her gaze. She was the only female detention officer on duty, and although I could tell that every interaction with me felt like an effort, I liked her. She had kind eyes. Her name is Tanya, and she used to live on a goat farm in the USA. She treated me like I was human, which is more than I had been treated by anyone in so long. I lifted my head and met her gaze. She waited for a response, but I didn't know what to say. Tanya let out a breath and lifted a towel. "Shower time."

I got up and followed Tanya silently out of the cell. I could feel the eyes of the entire suite on me, like I was some kind of rare animal in a zoo to be observed. To be studied. The shower wasn't much to look at. The door was waist height and swung open like something out of a cowboy movie. Tanya stood by the door and I tucked myself into the wall away from the eyes of the rest of the suite. I took off the pumps, the linoleum flooring sticking to my feet like old, cold gum. I stepped through the small door, Tanya not taking her eyes off me for a second. I shivered as I stripped away my jumper and my joggers. Tanya's eyes widening as she saw my prominent collar bones. My ribs. I barely had breasts, and my bra hung off me. I had nothing about me to resemble a woman. I was a shell of a person. Alex had taken everything from me. I undressed completely, and Tanya tuned away from me, giving me some dignity. The shower head was a silver nipple with a black mouth that jutted out from the wall. The tap was one button, coated in filth and grime. I pressed it, and the water spluttered out, dousing me in cold water. I took in a sharp intake of breath as my frame, withered and tiny, shivered under the dousing icy downpour. After a minute, the water began to heat up, and what was once cold and harsh, turned soothing and loving on my skin. There was something poetic about that.

The shower shut off suddenly. It must be on a timer. I pressed the button, hoping to have more heat. More of that warmth that I had been starved of, but none came. I had had my fill, and I was left hungry for more. My legs began to shiver, my feet pattering in the small puddle of residue water still yet to be swallowed up by the tarnished drain. Its ridges cut into the soles of my feet. Tanya passed me the towel, and I dried off, then gave me a small plastic bag containing a finger wrap, which had a nipple end like a shower mat and on it, a dry dot of toothpaste. I put it in my mouth and began to scrub away, spitting bloody foam onto the floor. Feeling somehow filthier than when I started, I got dressed again.

Back in my cell, I resumed my position of sitting and silently observing the wall in front of me. Someone had cut their name into the paint. On the cell door, which was a deep lime green, more had done the same. Names after names after names, chipped into the paint by so many other lost souls. I lay down on the mat, desperately wanting to shut away the bright light that burned into my eyes.

"I need to see your face and hands at all times," the officer said. His voice sounding alien. It was the first time I had heard him speak. With a frustrated, silent scream, I pulled the covers from over my face and threw them onto the floor like a discarded tapeworm. I sat back up, resuming my seated position. The officer resumed his silence, like someone standing behind a two-way mirror watching a patient go slowly insane.

I had no idea of time. There were no windows. No clocks. I wouldn't ask. I dared not to. How had I ended up here? I was in the hospital. The cracked picture frame. The buzz cutter. Then blood. Nothing but blood surrounded me. *I was* pregnant. Tears brimmed on my eyelids. I was pregnant and didn't even know it. I had escaped. Somehow. I can hardly remember. Then I was on the bridge. The wind so cold. So fierce. I dove into oblivion, but something stopped me. Then the hospital again, and now here. Nothing seemed to stay still in my mind, like trying to solve a jigsaw of moving pieces. The confusion was agonising, and all I could do was sit and stare at the wall.

"Miss Weaver," my neck nearly snapped at how fast I turned my head at the sound. A woman was standing there. A red head. I recognised her from somewhere. The sight of her filled me with dread, like she was about to lead me to the gallows. But I will take familiar right now, be it the face of God or the Devil himself. "My name is Detective Sergeant Laura Warburton," the woman said. Although she wasn't a large woman, her energy filled the space. Something about the way she stood. Presented herself. It told me that this woman was either going to save me or bury me. "Do you remember me?" Laura Warburton said. I shook my head. Laura stayed in that intermittent silence between breathing and speaking. She pursed her lips. "Okay," she finally said. "Come on."

Chapter Twenty – Three
Laura

Laura walked through the custody suite and down to the interview room, Clara trailing behind her like a lost lamb. Body shivering. The jumper curled over her hands and her arms tucked tightly into her chest. She could see Jeremy in the side office, with a stack of notes ready for when Laura was done. He wanted her to fail. He hadn't ever come out and said it, but the sharpness of the knives digging in her back told the full story. He was nervous, trying to stop his hands from shaking as he looked through his notes and questions. He had had to break the news to the DCI, waking her up from her post- night shift snooze. A bad idea. When he had told her Laura was leading with the first interview, Laura thought she could hear the ground opening up ready to swallow Jeremy whole. She arrived an hour later, and eyed Laura like she was a maggot in her expensive salad.

Laura passed Burnell, who was sitting in another room. Monitors and CCTV feeds hooked up to the room she was headed to. Jeremy beside her. Laura felt the stabbing of knives in her back. As Laura moved past the consultation rooms, the processing room, and the other interview rooms, she knew that she had one shot to get Clara talking, or they were both going to jail.

People often ask police officers what the thing they are most scared of is? The answer wasn't fighting someone with a knife or going to a violent domestic on their own. They were all hazards of the job. No. The thing officers scared more than being killed or injured in the line of duty was going to prison. Being locked away with all the people they had put away over the years. The thought made Laura shudder. Everything she had done. All the cases she had solved. Her future. Her safety. Her *life* rested on the will of a suspected murderer. She would have to employ every tactic she knew in the interview. Staggered disclosures of evidence. Open ended questions. Special warnings. Tactical silences. All the tricks she had, and even then, it wouldn't be enough. On a case like this, there would usually be someone in the interview with her for support, and two senior detectives watching via a CCTV link. But this time she was on her own, and the two detectives watching her wanted to hang her out to dry. There was playing against the odds, and there was a game that was rigged against you from the start. Still, she had no choice. If she failed to get Clara to talk, she was done for. Her only hope was that Clara, the woman who hadn't said a single word, would sing like a canary.

She pushed open the interview room. It was small. One chair for Laura. One chair for Clara that was bolted to the floor, and a plain wooden desk in the centre which was also bolted to the floor. At the end of the table was a recorder. Above them an unblinking eye of a CCTV camera. The walls were a blinding white. The carpet was a worn blue, and on the back wall, a god damn ticking clock. She could feel Jeremy's gaze bearing down on her as he watched from the back room. No doubt Burnell was also watching. Probably with popcorn to share, as Laura threw her life into the fire.

The sweating on her palms and tightness in her chest told her she was nervous. Still, she walked into that room with her head held high and tried not to look at the camera. She had one task. Make her talk. Anything. Even to say her own name. Get those lips moving, even an inch, and go from there. She knew she could do it. She was confident she could. She had been building a picture of Clara since the moment she met her. A woman who, on the face of it, was mentally unstable with a history of self-harm and suicide attempts. But when you looked closer, they all happened around the time she was reported to have met Alex. Not straight away, of course. An abusive relationship is like drinking water that is poisoned just ever so slightly. At first you don't notice it, but over time, you get sicker and sicker, and suddenly, you forget what it felt like to be healthy. Clara had a shaved head. A newly shaved head. Evidence of which was found in her bedroom. The home was immaculate. Too immaculate. A fridge filled with food, yet Clara looked emaciated. Locks on the cupboards. Not free to come and go as she pleased. A pregnancy she didn't know about. Taken from the hospital. A suicide attempt on the bridge.

She did it.

Who was *she* in this equation? Was it a split in her psyche? *She being Clara? Or was there another in the picture?* A chilling thought ran through Laura as she moved through that silent space.

Is that why Burnell is so invested in putting Clara away? Was there a history between her and Alex Laura didn't know about?

Was her boss a murderer?

She snapped herself out of her train of thought. It was clouding her judgement. Conjecture. Pure lunacy at this time.

But Craig. Mary Dutton. The murders. How well do you know someone?

Ron.

She felt her chest go tighter. Her vision burning under that artificial light. She swallowed hard.

"Sit down, please Mrs. Weaver," Laura said, pointing to the bolted down chair as she let the door close with a quiet thud. Clara did. Laura took a seat and eyed her. Clara stared back at her with vacant eyes. They say the eyes are the window to the soul. Laura saw nothing in them, like two empty windows that had been frosted over in a long, desolate winter. Laura gestured to her paperwork and began filling in her name, station, and the interview reference number. "Have you been interviewed before, Mrs. Weaver?" She called her *Mrs* on purpose, hoping to get some kind of reaction from her. Clara said nothing. *Did* nothing like speaking to a doll. Laura tightened the grip on her pen. "Okay," she said, speaking to the void. "I will start the interview up, and I will introduce me and the tape, and then ask you to introduce yourself. Can you do that for me?" Clara did nothing. The room seemed to shrink. Laura's eyes flitted to the black CCTV camera above her, the unblinking black orb above them. "I will then caution you, and I will ask you questions. Before we begin, you don't want a solicitor here?" Laura was begging for an answer.

Yes, because I need to speak to someone about what happened.

Clara said nothing. Laura let out a sigh. Her hand beginning to tremble around the pen. She pushed the REC button on the interview recorder. The display went off, and then a timer began.

"This interview is being digitally recorded…" Laura began. She rattled off the location, date, reference, and who she was. "Being interviewed today is…" She gestured to Clara. Clara sat motionless, like a piece of furniture. She said nothing. Laura licked her lips. "Clara

Weaver," she said, filling in the empty space. Laura cleared her throat. After cautioning Clara, Laura asked for her to confirm why she was here. Clara sat silently, staring at the table. "I am going to ask you questions about what happened," Laura said. "I want you to tell me in as much detail as you can about the murder of your husband."

I can feel the hair on my arms beginning to stand on end, like there are bugs prickling my skin. She is talking. She won't stop talking. She talks and then she stops. She wants me to speak, but I can't. . No one will believe me, so I don't speak. I can't say a word because if I talk, then it becomes real. If I talk, then I have to relive what happened What I did. What I saw. The woman. I can vaguely see her face. Smooth. Her features blurred in my mind. As hard as I try to focus on it, to bring it to the forefront of my mind, I can't quite catch it, like I am trying to remember a dream. A dream that I never had.

Why is she asking me these questions? Who I am? You think I know the answer to the question? I know who I *was*, but what are identities other than sounds we make with our mouths? I am not a mother. I have no family. I have no partner. I have no job. Work. Home. What am I other than a vessel? An empty shell that has been stripped apart from everything I am, was, or could ever be? So, I can't answer the question of who I am, because I simply don't know. I am nothing. So, I stay in my silence.

Lavender. The memory of the smell. I remember it so vividly as she leant into me. Leant into me and whispered in my ear, that should I speak, should I say a word about what happened, that no one would believe me. I am guilty. I must keep my mouth shut.

Or was I imagining things? Was there another person there? Or was I having another *episode,* as Alex would put it? *You're always forgetting things. It didn't happen like that. I never said that. That never happened.* I have learned to not trust my own mind anymore. It had betrayed me so many times. So how could I be sure about anything anymore?

She is asking me about Alex. How I met him. I blink my eyes. She pauses, as if trying to decode the reflex. She continues. She seems kind. But they all seem kind at the start. Alex was kind. He was loving. He was gentle. But as kind as she is, she wants to put me in prison for the rest of my life. I have no friends here. I am alone. I am nothing. I am silent.

Laura asked Clara list of questions about how her and Alex met, their relationship. Any issues in the relationship, or any history of domestic abuse or issues? Clara maintained her silence. She went through the rest of her questions, going into more sensitive topics. Hoping to get *something* out of Clara. To find that raw nerve. Laura went through the rest of her questions – Her childhood. Her family life. History of self-harm. Clara continued to stare at her, her eyes unmoving. Then she asked how she met Alex, and Clara blinked. Laura paused. Did she mean to do that? Was it just a reflex or some kind of signal? She continued. "You said to me on the bridge before you jumped. It was me that pulled you away. Me that saved your life." Laura let the silence fill the space between them, like a flowing tide. "You said to me '*She did it.*' What did you mean by '*She did it*'?" To Laura's growing frustration and rising pulse, Clara continued to stay silence. Laura glanced at the recorder. They had been talking for an hour, or rather, Laura talking to herself for an hour. Her interview notes were bare. The ticking of the clock filling the silence between them. Laura clenched her teeth together, looking over her interview questions, tapping her pen on the table in an erratic rhythm. She was running out of things to ask. She had nothing extra to go off.

Laura reached under the desk and took out an envelope filled with photos of the crime scene. She started with the layout of the house, the bedroom, asking questions about them. Then she cut straight to the kitchen. The body of Alex Weaver. The blood stains. The splatters on the wall.

"The CSI said it looked like a sustained, frenzied attack," she said, pointing to the photos, but keeping her eyes on Clara. Those eyes remained dead. Unmoving. Laura pointed at the blood splatter patterns on the walls, the cupboards, and the ceilings. "The length and position of the droplets show us that the attack happened quickly, suggesting it was not planned but rather a sudden, sustained and frenzied attack." Laura pointed at the pictures again, stabbing them with her finger. "Alex Weaver, your husband, was stabbed over thirty times to the chest, groin, face, and legs. His DNA, bone and fat were found on the knife that you left on the floor of the kitchen. Your fingerprints on it, coated in Alex's blood." Clara said nothing. "The knife is a —" Laura pulled out the photo of the knife. A nine-inch butchers' knife with a black handle, taken from the knife rack. She queried the weapon. She looked back at the photos and found one of the kitchen cupboards. The knife rack next to the sink. There was indeed a knife missing, but the knives on the block had black handles with red nodules on them. Only slightly, but definitely there. Forensics hadn't drawn the connection. She felt a rush of horror run through her. She was the only one who knew that the knife recovered wasn't the murder weapon, but then why was Clara's bloody fingerprints on the handle, and why was Alex's DNA, blood, and bone on the blade? Had Laura gotten it wrong? Was everyone else right? She was in too deep. She had signed her own death warrant.

"How did Alex make his money?" Laura said, changing the questioning. She still had time to look into the peculiarity later. Right now, she had to focus on getting Clara to fucking talk. "A huge home. Nice cars. Beautiful interior. How did he make his money? Our records show he was an investor. Tell me about that." Clara did nothing. "Such a huge home with so many rooms. Did he have housekeepers? Or was it just you that cleaned it?" Laura tapped her pen again on the table in its atonal rhythm. Clara stared at the wall. Laura leaned forward. "Did you have to clean that whole house yourself? What happened if you didn't clean it well enough?" Laura noticed something happen. It was only slight. Innocuous. Unimportant in any other scenario, or with any other person. But Clara did something that told Laura she was on the right lines. Clara sucked in a sharp breath between tight lips. Laura felt a flurry of exactment run through her. "What was Alex like when he got angry, Mrs. Weaver?" Clara did nothing. "Would he ever lock you in the house? I saw there were padlocks on the cupboards and the fridge filled with food, and yet you look so thin. Could you eat what and when you liked?" Nothing. Laura felt the heat in the room turn up. She had an idea. It might just work, but it was risky. Very risky, and illegal. But she had no choice. She was up against the clock, and she was out of options.

"You're so beautiful, Clara," Laura said. Clara's eyes lifted from the table and met hers. "So, so beautiful. I am so happy I met you. You are the most perfect, most wonderful person I have ever met." Laura walked her fingers along the table. Clara's shoulders dropped. Her breath grew heavy. It was working. "I know you don't want to be here," Laura continued, hand inches from Clara's arm. "All those bruises on you. All those sores. All that pain. I'm sorry. I'm so, so sorry for what I did to you. Such a wonderful, loving, caring woman that I have in my life." Clara's lip began to tremble. Tears formed in her eyes. Laura's face turned hard. She snapped her hand to Clara's arm, gripping her biceps tightly. Laura's knuckles turning white, teeth bared like a growling hound. "So do as I fucking say, or else!" At once, Clara's eyes lit up. She recoiled back, standing like she had been doused in petrol and a match thrown onto her. Clara began thrashing and screaming, hitting herself to the face and head. Head butting the wall, biting hard on her own arms and shoulders, drawing blood that oozed out of the puncture holes and dripped onto the carpet. She turned to Laura, who slammed her hand on the red panic button behind her, the alarm blaring.

Clara crumpled to the floor, pawing at the wall Detention officers burst into the room and grabbed hold of Clara. She was fighting, thrashing, screaming incoherently. Words that were stretched and hoarse, like a string quartet using bricks to play bows made from rusted piano wire.

"Lavender!" Clara screamed, "Lavender!"

Laura stood in the room as the onslaught left. She

turned to the recorder. It was still playing. She turned it off. Her pictures, exhibits, and interview notes were strewn along the table and had been trampled into the ground. Large boot prints on some of them.

The door pushed open. It was Jeremy.

"What the fuck was that, Laura!" He bolstered. "Are you trying to fuck up this entire investigation?!" He stood over Laura as she leaned down and picked up her paperwork. "I knew I should have fired you the moment you drove through that gate, Jesus fucking Christ, what are you playing at? Are you trying to take everyone else down with – Are you even listening to me?" Laura picked up the last of her paperwork and slowly straightened herself to face Jeremy. She moved past him, pushing the notes and paperwork into his chest.

"I've got some things I need to look at," Jeremy watched her leave the room and move down the corridor towards the sound of Clara screaming, being dragged away by officers.

"Where are you going?" Jeremy shouted after her. Laura stopped and turned, her fox tail hair sticking to her face. She brushed it away.

"Upstairs," Laura said, a smile along her lips. "She's just given her defence."

Laura moved through the upstairs offices above the custody suite and found a computer. She pulled out the pictures of the murder scene, and she was right. There was absolutely a different knife missing. She knew she wasn't losing it. The DCI must have told the forensics to not look closer. They had the wrong murder weapon, which poses an even bigger question — where did the new knife come from, and why did it have Clara and

Alex's DNA all over it? She wasn't a forensic specialist. But Celine was. This shit was her bread and butter. She could find out for her. Which meant that Laura would somehow have to get the knife out of the evidence locker at the station. She could take it to Celine, and then, what, she test it and put it back into evidence with no one noticing the fucking murder weapon was missing? She clenched her eyes shut. This was impossible.

Laura tried every interrogation technique she knew, and Clara gave nothing away. Not even a smile. A grin. A scratch of the head. Just stayed sitting there as if she was speaking to a doll. But then when she mentioned Alex specifically went in on their relationship, Clara blinked, and then sucked in air. Further questioning got nowhere. She did the only thing she could think of. She had to replicate the trauma. The abuse of Clara Weaver at the hands of her dead husband. She had to embody *him*, meaning she had to embody *Ron*. She had to become that which she despised in order to save someone. I vile twist of fate, and she could feel the universe mocking her at every turn.

Her elbows dug into the desk. The notes and pictures splayed out in front of her in a gruesome collage of death. "Lavender," she whispered. "Lavender. She did it. She did it. Lavender." How did the two mix together? She leaned back in her chair. "What did that mean?" She pondered this, and then she felt her phone ring. She looked. It was Francis.

"Go on, Francis."

"You're not going to believe this," he said. He sounded out of breath, like he was rushing to be somewhere. Laura tightened her jaw.

"I'm listening."

"The house fire a few years back. With Hugo Black and Annabelle Jones? The DCI was working on that case. Head investigator."

"I know this already, Francis," Laura said.

"I know," he said. "He heard a car door slamming. But there's more." Papers rustling. Fabric gracing the receiver. "She's been promoted since then, of course. I looked into the case file. My advanced clearance, and all. Turns out, Hugo Black had a lot of business interests, from betting companies, finance, electrical. Even medical. One in particular was a company set up by a man named Francis Ward. He was investigated by the police for selling cough medicine contaminated with strychnine. It killed a lot of children."

"I remember hearing about that case," Laura said. "What does this have to do with the DCI?" Francis spoke quickly, as if just saying what he was going to come out with next would lead to him eating a bullet.

"Our victim, Alex Weaver, was a silent partner in Hugo Black business. That's how he got so wealthy. Alex Weaver is directly connected to the enterprise of Hugo Black's that profited off a pharmacy company that killed children. DS Burnell, at the time, worked on that case. Now she's working on this case, trying to put Clara away for his murder. The only link between them is Hugo Black. Why is she so hellbent on this case? It doesn't make sense?"

"It's like she has some kind of vendetta against anyone connected to Black," Laura said, mouth running dry. She looked around. The room still empty. "Where are you now?"

"I'm on my way to the custody suite," he said. "I managed to pull some bank records that I think would be useful to ask Clara about." *Ask Clara about*, Laura thought. *You're a little too late for doing that.* "No problem," Laura said. "I appreciate it. Honestly. Thank you." She hung up the call.

Laura let her mind wander. Clara Weaver, never in trouble with the police before, murders her husband in a frenzied attack. The murder weapon appears to be missing, and another weapon put in its place. Clara Weaver has a history of mental instability, but only since she met Alex Weaver. Alex Weaver is a silent partner in a business that profited off a pharmacy company that killed children with poisoned products. DS Burnell worked on the Hugo Black case. Now, she's working on the Alex Weaver case.

She asked for this case specifically. Isn't that what Francis had told her?? She had asked to work on this case, spe-ci-fi-ca-lly. Laura spelled the word out in her head.

She did it. Lavender. What did that mean? What was the connection? Laura pressed her palms into her temples and ran her hands down the back of her head. She needed a smoke and a glass of wine so badly.

Then like someone had plunged her body into ice, Laura delt the pieces slot together, and she felt that icy chill run through her.

Lavender. Burnell had smelt floral in the hospital. Burnell's connection to the case. Clara. To put her away. Access to the scene of the crime. She could have done it. Killed Alex then removed the knife and framed Clara. It all made sense.

"Oh…. Fuck…." Laura whispered. Her voice trembling. She heard a door swing shut, and the soft cushioning of footsteps on the ground. Like summoning the Devil himself, Burnell entered the office. Her face twisted into a savage sneer. Laura felt the heat in her chest begin to swell. Burnell pulled out a chair, the wheels underneath it squeaking, and the chair yearning with her weight.

"I just wanted to say thank you," she said, fighting back a cackle. "I wanted to say thank you for securing your own place in prison for misconduct." She ran her fingers through her dark hair. Laura could see herself in the reflection of Burnell's thick glasses. She looked like shit. Sleep deprived. Hungry. In need of another six months in rehab. "I gave you the chance to leave with dignity, but you and your pride," she shook her head, looking at the floor. She righted herself. "I'll be interviewing her next, and I will get the truth out of her." She could lock her up right now for Alex's murder. Put an end to all this. But without evidence, she was pissing into the wind. She had to play it cool. Pretend like nothing was wrong.

"She won't talk." Laura spat. "I tried everything."

"And yet she's still screaming?" Burnell said, cocking her head to the side. "How did you manage that?"

By traumatising her again.

"Because I know what I'm doing." Burnell let out a loud bellow of laughter.

"I'm trying to show that there is more to this case than meets the eye," Laura snapped. "You're ignoring things. It isn't right." Burnell pursed her lips.

"Ahh yes. The ex-alcoholic, domestic violence victim is telling *me*, a senior investigator who has worked on some of the deadliest, most horrendous crimes of the modern age, that *I'm* ignoring things." Laura felt her skin beginning to burn. The two stared at each other. The tension was so thick you could cut it with a saw. "Why are you so invested in this case?" Burnell said. "You seem obsessed." Was she obsessed? Was she really looking at things that weren't there? She bit down, swallowing hard.

"She's the victim," Laura said, trying to hold on to her nerve, her frustration bubbling over. It felt like he was smashing her head against a brick wall and getting nowhere.

"You need to escape the world of darkness and light," Burnell said. "This world of dreams and hidden meanings. Retribution. Valiant quests. There's nothing more to this case than a woman who murdered her husband, and she won't tell us why." Burnell stood up. "This is clear cut, and there's nothing that will show you otherwise." With that, Burnell stood up and moved to the office door. She turned and scoured at Laura. "You are suspended immediately. You will be called into the office of Professional Standards in a few days, where you will be interviewed under caution for your misconduct and your crimes. The force will be seeking a prosecution. I would get a solicitor, a good one, if I were you." With that, she disappeared from sight, leaving Laura to chew on her own misery.

Laura sat back, pressing her hands to her face. Her body felt like it was going to convulse. She needed some fresh evidence. Something that would prove Clara was innocent and Burnell was the killer. She needed to go back to the start of the investigation. She needed to go back to basics. She couldn't get the knife from the evidence locker. Her pass to the building will be suspended within the hour. She would probably be escorted out of the suite soon. There must be something that she hadn't seen. Something that she could do. She had only a few hours before Clara was charged and remanded into custody. She needed to find something new. Something was missed. She needed to break into the crime scene.

More footsteps, several of them, came down the hall. At the door emerged Jeremy, followed by two detention officers. Laura eyed them with venom, her eyes puffy. Face stinging with hot tears. Jeremy's face pained. Something had happened, and Laura waited for the knife in her back to be twisted a little sharper.

"It's time to go," Jeremy said, filling the doorway. Laura choked back the tears.

"Jeremy," she croaked.

"It's, Sir." he blasted, his booming voice ricocheting around the room. "Now get up before we drag you out of the building." Laura peeled herself off her chair, the leather sticking to her, like fingers clawing at her to stay. To work on the case. To protect the vulnerable without prejudice.

"I need to wait to see what the CPS say," Laura lied. She had no intention of being around when Clara was charged. She had a house to break into. She was simply being defiant.

"We sent the case to them before you even interviewed her." Laura felt the room close in around her. She had been set up, given false hope, like a starving dog chasing a mechanical hare around the track for the enjoyment of others. Laura stared at the desk. The interview notes, evidence on the computer. It had been pointless. The whole thing. Her notes. Her investigation. It was all for nothing. She had been appeased by Jeremy, so she would stay out of their way while they condemned Clara.

"You fucker…" It was all she could manage.

"I'm sorry," he said. And then, because she hadn't been beaten and broken enough, he rubbed that little more salt in the wound with a final, "Thanks for your efforts." He stepped to the side, opening the doorway.

"Now, please." After everything she had done. After everything she had been through. After every God damn case she had worked on, her fuck ups, her rehab, her putting herself back together like a jigsaw of razor blades. After Sheree. Craig. Jamie and Oliver Green. After all the messes she had put back together, she had been betrayed. She had asked for a chance. A chance to show that Clara Weaver was not the killer she was portrayed as. And for that, she had been nailed to the crucifix while birds pecked out her eyes.

Laura couldn't feel her legs as she stood up and moved to Jeremy like she was on autopilot. Her eyes met his, and she cocked back her fist and buried it in his nose as hard as she could. The sound of cartilage crunching, blood spraying onto the cream coloured walls. Jeremy fell back, stumbling on the ground, blood pouring onto his white shirt. Laura descended on him, driving her fists wherever she could land them. Face. Chest. Ribs. Like a starving, beaten dog that had finally been released and its captor had been covered in bacon grease, until arms wrapped around her and pulled her away.

Chapter Twenty – Four
Laura

"She needs to be arrested!" Burnell shouted from opposite the superintendent's desk back at the station. Jeremy sat next to her, a bloody rag under his nose. Superintendent Bennett eyed her with fire.

"One more word out of you," Bennett roared, "and I'll ship you back to whatever unit you came from, rip those pips off your shoulder and give you stripes instead." His gaze was fierce. His tone was calm, yet powerful, like a silenced pistol. The two gazed at each other before Burnell finally looked away and sank back into her chair. Bennett let his gaze linger before returning it to Laura, who sat quietly, hands folded together, glaring at Burnell. Bennett sat back, running his hand over the back of his neck. His bird nest hair looked like a snowy horseshoe. For a man of slight stature, his presence filled the room. It was more than just the crown on his shoulder. It was the man to whom those crowns belonged. He turned the firing line to Laura. "What the fuck were you thinking?" Laura ran her tongue on the inside of her mouth. Did she expose Burnell right now? No. She had to wait. She needed to get back to the house.

"I lost my temper, sir." Bennett digested those words before standing from his chair and moved to the window. He could get a good look at Wigtown from here, like a king overlooking his people. People *he* had sworn to protect. And here he was, trying to make sure that those in which he intrusted with that very same duty to protect and serve the public didn't destroy each other. He felt like a headmaster scolding school children.

"Where is the investigation up to?" Bennett said. Laura stabbed a look at Jeremy and Burnell. Whereas Bennett didn't need to fill the space around him to seem in control, Jeremy had not yet found such qualities in his new found role. He sat hunched over, eyes already becoming blackened. Laura had clipped him good. He could leave the room. Vanish into thin air, and you wouldn't notice.

"We are seeking a charging decision from the CPS as we speak," Burnell said. "We will need an extension on her custody clock." Bennett's brow raised as he turned back from the window.

"And when were you going to approach me about this?" Burnell froze. Her pulse picking up.

"I was..." she stammered, clearing her throat, pulling her blazer tighter. "We were going to ask you earlier, but..." She glared at Laura.

"You don't have a clue what you're doing, do you?" Bennett said, his words like blades in Burnell's psyche. She squirmed in her chair, trying to think of something she could say or do before the lions ate her alive. The room was silent. Thankfully, Bennett shared Laura's hate for ticking clocks, and he had a small digital clock on the side of his desk. It was late evening, and Laura hadn't slept in over two days, and the thirst for red wine, her old friend to soothe her to sleep, was becoming harder to resist. She was meant to be meeting Celine. That wasn't going to happen.

"We have had some setbacks." She said, trying to resurface over the raging sea she was drowning in. "Sergeant Warburton has derailed this straightforward investigation at every turn. She has disregarded mine and Inspector Marriott's direct orders. She is unhinged. Criminal damage. Assaulting her colleague. Interfering with the suspect." She let out a tight breath. "She needs more than suspending. She needs to be dismissed immediately and prosecuted."

"Are you looking to press charges, Jeremy?" Bennett said. Eyes fell onto Jeremy. His eyes were closed tight. The two pain killers he had crunched barely touching the throbbing in his nose. Laura had broken it, according to the nurse in custody. Nothing long lasting, but he wouldn't be able to smell anything for a few weeks. Laura waited with bated breath. If Jeremy really wanted to throw her under the bus, this was his opportunity. If he wanted to press charges, Laura was out, and he would continue his ascent up that greasy ladder. If he refused, then Burnell would see it as an act of defiance. How the world of morality and corporate interests rarely, *if ever*, line up.

"I haven't decided yet," he croaked from behind the rag. Burnell's lips went tight. "DCI Burnell is the lead on the case," Jeremy quickly rebuked. "There is enough happening already. I don't want to complicate things further at this moment in time." Bennett burst into laughter.

"Aren't you the head of the unit?" He said, moving to Jeremy. "Aren't those pips on your shoulder? Haven't you assumed the lead position of the MIU while Miss Warburton was away getting treatment?"

"Sir, I feel you're missing the point here..." Burnell began before Bennett silenced her words like snapping a singer's neck in the middle of a concert.

"One more word," he said. "One more word." Burnell again quickly learned how to shut the fuck up. He returned his fury to Jeremy. "How can I expect you to serve the people of this town when I don't have faith that you can keep those responsible for their safety under control?" As the last syllable died in the still air, Jeremy's mind began to crack like glass exposed to extreme heat. "So, I return to my initial question, Inspector Marriot. Do you have a single *fucking* clue what you're doing?" Jeremy wanted the world to open up and swallow him whole. Flame geysers to explode from the earth, spouting hellish entities with claws and teeth to drag him down into the City of Dis. Anything would be less painful than this. But his silence was louder than anything he could possibly say in return, and that silence was more powerful than any excuse, reasoning, or defence Jeremy could muster. And that was all the answer Bennett needed. Bennett turned his attention to Laura, who hadn't moved an inch, lost in her own internal battle behind her eyes. Her gaze burning into Burnell.

"Miss Warburton." Bennett said, his tone flat again. "What do you have to say about your actions this evening?" She peeled her gaze from the killer sat apposite her, and met Bennett's eye. Jeremy was on the verge of tears. Burnell sitting back with her arms crossed like a petulant teenager.

"I accept responsibility for what I have done," she said. "I acted inappropriately. I let my emotions and personal pressures get the better of me. I accept whatever punishment you deem appropriate, Mr. Bennett." Bennett's mouth curled into a smile. His yellowed teeth pushing through his lips.

"See," he said. "No excuses. No passing the blame. That sort of honesty is something that is seriously *lacking* in your counterparts." He eyed Laura's bandaged hand. "What happened there?"

This was it. She could throw Jeremy into the inferno and watch the skin bubble and blister as the flames devoured him. His failings as a supervisor were coming for him. He was reaping the sordid shit show he had sewn, and Laura was going to be the one to bury him. But he wasn't the enemy here. He wasn't the one that needed to be thrown into the fire. It was Burnell.

"I was making some food," she said. "And my cat startled me. I cut my hand. Nothing major. Just a scratch." Bennett seemed almost deflated by the lacklustre story.

"Very well," he said. He moved back to his chair and sat down. A world behind his eyes ticking away. Everyone hung on that silence, awaiting his next words. "You are suspended with immediate effect without pay. An internal investigation will be launched, and you will be made to answer for what you have done." Laura tried not to let her emotions show. The lump in her throat growing, like hands closing around her windpipe. She needed to tell him about Burnell and her links to the case. To save herself. But something inside her told her not to. Jeremy hadn't pressed charges. Maybe he believed her. Maybe it was guilt, maybe? Remorse? Fearful of Laura will tear his balls off next? Either way, he had saved her from the firing squad. He was Burnell's puppet right now. *She* was the problem, and at the heart of all of this was a woman in a cell that needed justice, and that trumped Laura's own ideas of revenge.

"I understand, sir," Laura said meekly. Trying to sound like her heart wasn't breaking in two. Burnell was struggling to hold it together, fidgeting in her chair, her breathing fast and shallow. Bennett gestured to the door.

"Laura, thank you for your time," he said. "DCI Burnell? DI Marriot?" The sound of their names like they were being sent to the gallows. They met his eye. "Get out of my office."

Laura smoked a cigarette in the cool night air. The taste now vile, but she did it anyway. She watched as a plane flew overhead, its light blinking and cutting through the carpet of black. Some stars twinkled through the light pollution, yet the dark seemed thicker, like someone had reached into the sky and given it an extra lick of paint. She had been defeated. By corruption and favouritism. Her career was over because her face didn't fit in this world anymore. Because she joined the police to help people and to do the right thing. But that didn't toe the line of internal politics.

She had to clear her name.

The door behind her opened into the car park. She turned and felt like throwing up on the spot. Jeremy stood there. He had opted to simply stuffing tissue up his nose rather than using every rag in the constabulary.

"I'm sorry," he said meekly. He waited for a response. Laura offered him none, simply staring at him, waiting for the knife to be slipped deeper into her back. Maybe he would twist it this time? Mix things up a little. He looked at her cigarette. "Can I have one of those?" Laura furrowed her brow.

"You don't smoke."

"I thought you didn't either." Laura took out a cigarette and flicked it at him. Jeremy fumbled, catching it before it fell to the ground. "Lighter?"

"You want a fucking lung as well?" Jeremy didn't answer. Laura passed him the lighter. He sparked up and took a deep drag and expelled it into the night air.

"Haven't touched one of these in over twenty years," he said.

"You used to smoke?"

"Like a chimney," he said, taking another famine hungry drag. "Since I met Mary. She hated smokers. Whenever I would see her, I would take a smoke to calm my nerves to build up the courage to ask her out. But then when I did, she told me no because I smoked. Irony, eh? So, I quit, asked her out, and we have been together since. Married twenty years this year."

"Congratulations," Laura said, looking back up at the sky. They shared a silent moment between themselves.

"I'm sorry Laura," he said. "I have been a fool. So absorbed in my own career. Things were going to shit with me in charge. I tried to fix it but went the wrong way about it. And that isn't easy for me to admit. Bennett was right. I don't know what I am doing." Laura took a deep drag of her smoke.

"You stabbed me in the fucking back, Jeremy. After everything we have been through together." She turned to face him. "Why aren't you pressing charges?"

"I haven't decided yet," he said, eyeing the floor. Laura stepped towards him, stabbing him in the chest with her finger.

"No," she bit. "You *have* decided, and you're not pressing them. You're just too much of a coward to tell that to the DCI. Tell me why." Jeremy looked like he was chewing on a wasp. He scratched his head, his fingers digging into his thinning grey hair. His scalp flaking into the wind. He looked like shit. He doubted he had been home since Clara was arrested. He was one step away from a heart attack. The pressures of his role crushing him like a vice. Jeremy stayed silent. His breath was warm on her face that was being numbed by the cool air. Laura wanted to press him on it, but in the end, it didn't matter. Not right now, anyway. She knew the reason. He was weak. He was a weak leader. He was a weak friend. He was weak in the face of conflict. He wouldn't press charges on her because he knew that Laura busting his face was the wake up call he needed.

"Your hand," Jeremy said quickly, changing the subject. "You didn't get that from your cat." She let out a frustrated breath, moving away from him.

"Oh, and how the fuck would you know that?"

"I'm not completely useless," he said. "I can still figure out when someone is lying. What happened?" Laura eyed her garment with disdain like it had betrayed her.

"That night when you called me," Laura said, feeling the chest of misery in her mind creak open, and black tar began trickling out. "When you called me unhinged and dangerous, and weak for not leaving Ron."

"I never said…"

"I was drinking a glass of water in bed." Laura eyed her hand. "I crushed the glass in my hand. That was how much you hurt me." Jeremy's mouth hung open like a black pit. His eyes were wide.

"Laura…"

"I went to the hospital," she shouted, almost laughing. Misery pouring out of her mouth. "While I was there, I thought, oh I don't know, try to solve the case? Work, work, work, all the time. That's all I do, isn't it? Work, and save lives, and then this is what I get in return. I get suspended. My friends turn against me. My colleagues ostracise me. It's no wonder I used to drink." She felt her stomach beginning to tighten, like someone had pushed their fist into her gut, grabbed a handful of soft parts, and then began twisting. "God, how much simpler things were when I used to drink!" She declared this to the sky, spreading her arms like she was a bird about to take flight. "How life was so much easier when all I wanted to do was destroy myself!" She stepped to Jeremy, her eyes glistening with pain. "So, you know what I did? I took pills. A lot of pills. I cracked open that blister pack and I swallowed one after the other like I was popping mother fucking sweats. I had enough of it. This job. This case. You. The world. This existence. I wanted to end it all, and I was going to." Her voice was trembling. A cocktail of rage and pain. "But something stopped me, and I forced my fingers down my throat, and I came to work and pretended everything was okay. Then Jeremy, DI Fucking Marriot, you throw me a bone and tell me to go interview Clara. Then I find out you've already made your mind up that she's guilty!" Laura's mouth fell open, her hands grabbing her hair. "You set me up! You knew all along what you were doing! So, no! I don't accept your apology! If I could rip your throat out right here and now!" Laura's voice trembled. Her voice growing louder in the empty car park. "Because why should I bother living if all I have is pain? Why should I bother living if all I have is misery?" Tears were falling down her cheeks like heavy rain. She went quiet then. A silent sob taking over, ravaging her body. She shook her head, trying to find words that wouldn't come, until she croaked – "I just can't do this anymore…"

Jeremy snatched out his hands and held Laura tight in his embrace. She tried pushing him away, fighting him, but he held her tightly, stopping her from tipping over the edge. Slowly, Laura gave into him, the thrashing turning into light thumping, as the pain drowned her.

"It's okay," Jeremy whispered. "I'm sorry. I'm so

sorry Laura. It's okay." He held her while she sobbed and pawed at his shirt and blazer. Through that silent cry, shards of sharp pain pushed through, until Laura was wailing into Jeremy's chest. After a long moment, she peeled herself away, and silently walked back to her car, leaving Jeremy watching her in the cold, dark car park. The clouds glided along the black canvas like smoke, as if the moon was entering a stage in a magic show.

Laura moved to her car, that had been lonely and abandoned in the car park. A whisper of frost beginning to form, which cracked as she pulled the door open. She slipped inside, hands shaking for a cigarette. Jeremy lingered a second longer, like a shadow, before slipping back into the station. The light from inside devouring him, and then he was gone. Laura sat alone with her thoughts. She checked the time. It had gone past nine in the evening, and she felt a swelling of pain in her chest. She had stood Celine up, and then she saw the text messages.

Hey, what time are you getting here? I have ordered us some starters.

Then a few minutes later –

Let me know if you're coming, please. They're asking for the table back if I'm not going to order anything more than breadsticks, lol.

And finally –

I have left now. Don't call me.

Laura rested her head on the seat and let out a long, frustrated breath, closing her eyes tight and pinching the bridge of her nose. She had blown it. Blown something she never would admit she wanted to give another shot. Maybe it was for the best? It was definitely for the best. But that led to the creeping fear in her stomach to swell. It meant that her lifeline to her old world had been severed, meaning that she had to live in the world she found herself in now. Now and forever. And that scared the shit out of her.

Laura put her phone back in her pocket and lit up a smoke. She put the keys in the ignition and turned the engine on. The blowers blasting fierce cold air onto her, which chilled her to the core. She turned them down, and listened to the engine idle and tick away. She cracked a window, the cab filling with cigarette smoke. Taking a long drag, she eyed herself in her wing mirror, her reflection glowing like a blacksmith blowing on hot steel. She continued to smoke, watching the time tick away. Laura checked the pet camera on her phone. Something she had bought after her home had been broken into.

Bagpipe was laying spread out on the couch as if he had been flattened by a speeding car. She turned the camera off, a smile creeping along her face. She saw something moving in the darkness along the car park. Laura followed it with her gaze. And there, standing between two parked cars, was a fox. Its auburn fur ruffling in the light breeze. Hot air expelled from its snout. A long pink tongue hanging from its jaws. Just like her, a red head lost in a terrifying world, trying to find a place to be safe and call home. She watched the creature move, gliding silently between the parked cars, sniffing at the ground. Before long, Laura found it moving towards her, and its eyes that glistened in the moonlight, staring up at her. Curiously observing her, like she had been observing it.

Laura felt a swelling of love in her heart. She had always loved foxes. They represented a world that was ever present, but rarely seen. A world in the dark which no one else saw. Like the two were locked away from each other, and a path between rarely found, but must be seized when it presented itself. Laura flashed her teeth in a wide smile.

"Hey little buddy," she said softly. The fox didn't move, nor did it answer back, which Laura was thankful for. She scanned her car. Finding a half-eaten sandwich in the footwell she hadn't thrown out yet, she peeled the slice of ham from the sticky bread and dangled it out of the window. The fox stepped backwards at first, analysing the giant red-haired woman above her, dangling something from its metallic cage. Gingerly, the rust-coloured fox pawed over slowly, sniffing at the ham. The thing must have been starving, because when it was an inch away, it snatched the ham from Laura, its glistening eyes cutting through the shadows, and scurried back into the dark under a car. It's gaze never moving from Laura. She watched it, the smile on her face wide. Then her thoughts slipped into those decrepit places.

'A world that was ever present, but rarely seen. A world in the dark which no one else saw. Like the two were locked away from each other, and a path between rarely found, but must be seized when it presented itself.'

The cracked photo on the floor. There was something wrong with that picture. With this entire picture. She needed to see the case through. Clara. She may be dead wrong. Maybe throwing herself into the fire with what she had to do next. But she couldn't live with herself if she didn't at least try. She pulled up Google maps and punched in the address of the murder house. Something was missing. Something had been overlooked, and Laura was going to find it.

DIARY

I watched you leave this morning, and I know a thing or two about breaking into houses. I have seen enough of it in my time to know how it's done without leaving any trace.

Your house is amazing. It's like out of a magazine! Have you ever been hungry? This décor. These rooms. Gosh, there are so many rooms! I bet you have cleaners, don't you? There is no way one person can keep a house this fancy, this clean all the time, and yet, I haven't seen a single speck of dust on anything. You should give your housekeeper a raise. That I can say.

I rearranged some of your ornaments, just to see if you noticed. Plus, it might drive you a little crazy. Because, my love, a little madness is a good thing. It keeps us guessing. Keeps us alert. That way, when you see me again, you'll remember me straight away, and you won't be able to stop thinking about me. Just how I can't stop thinking about you.

I moved through the home, and then I saw a photo of you in the arms of another woman. Was this one of your whores? Someone you had been fucking? The white frame it was in must be worth a small fortune. A perfect frame for a perfect picture. Look at the way you smile. Both smile. Look at you. I picked up the fame and slammed it on the corner of the mantle, a nice big crack along the glass. I went back to the kitchen and put it right where you would see it. To fuck with you. Nothing more. You know what you have done to me.

I went up to your bedroom. I put some of your

clothes to my face and took a long inhale of you. It's like you're inside me now. Your scent. Your DNA. Dancing and merging with my own. If we were just connected on a spiritual level, then we are connected in mind, body, and soul.

I lay on your bed, lying on the soft pillows, wondering what it would be like to be close to you. Wondering what it would be like to touch you again, to stroke your brutish body as I run my fingers along your skin as the morning sunbathed us in golden light. I found my hand snaking down to my underwear, and I felt myself between my fingers. I was so wet for you. So wet you wouldn't believe. So wet that you would have no idea how much I wanted you inside me. I came quickly and dried myself on your pillow. The next time you go to bed, you'll be able to smell me. You'll be thinking of me and know that I am thinking of you.

I was going to stay, but I heard the gate opening, and then the sound of your car pulling into the driveway to your home. *Our* home.

But then when I saw you get out of the car, my face soured.

I saw her. The woman from the photograph. She looked ill. Emaciated. You are holding her in your arms, as you scooped her out of the passenger seat and carried her to the door. My heart tore into pieces, Alex. Right then, you shattered everything I wanted for us. I was just some whore. Some cheap whore that you fucked one time after coffee. How could you do this to me? Do this to *us*? Do you know how much you have hurt me? Know how much harm you have done?

I could tell her. I could run right out of the house now and I could confront you with her. See who you really love. See who you really fucking care for! But I decided this isn't the best time. So, I slipped out of the back door and watched you from afar as you carried in your cunt wife. You are filled with dirty little secrets. To think I nearly let myself get carried away with you. You almost had me, too.

But this isn't over. Not by a long shot.

Chapter Twenty – Five
Clara

I hope I killed him. I hope I tore him open and showed the world that his insides were nothing but black and rotten. Part of me hopes I did. Another part of me even thinks I would have enjoyed it.

Chapter Twenty - Six
Laura

Laura pulled onto the street of the murder house. Through the gloom of streetlights, she could see a liveried police car sitting outside the mangled front gates that had been chained together. It was easy overtime. Sit there, eat some food, read a book, or watch something on Netflix, and make sure no one tries to get into the crime scene.

Which is exactly what Laura was there to do. They had missed it. The cracked photo. The fact that inside that home was sterile. Preserved, like a dollhouse, like a show home one might see inside a fancy retail magazine. It was screaming how affluent and wonderful your life would be if you lived here. That you were good enough. Instagramable and Facebook postable. TikTok showable and internet lovable. The kind of house people will envy, and that was exactly the point. The things we see around us online are not real life, and Laura was about to break that shell right open and let the putrid yolk pour out for the world to see.

Laura stared at the dark street. Houses that would take the average person a lifetime to afford sat silent around her, overshadowed by huge trees. Bentleys, Porches, and Rolls-Royce cars sitting proudly behind the gates. Some houses were so set back that you couldn't see them through the thick walls of hedges that cocooned them. The mystery of affluence. It was more subtle, like the unwrapping of a present on Christmas day. A grand unveiling to those that were privy or fortunate enough to see the world which the rest of the public only got to imagine. Just like her job. A world filled with monsters that existed right in front of you, but you were too blind to notice.

She donned a pair of black leather gloves and tied the balaclava tighter around her face, tightening the hood of her black jacket. In her pocket was an evidence bag, some tweezers, and a couple of bent paperclips for some homemade lock picks and tension rods. She had practiced on her own locks in her home before coming out. Bagpipe had sat there confused, wondering what the red haired lady was doing and why she wasn't petting or feeding him. After she had got the hang of it, she made some more and put them into her pocket. You didn't spend fifteen years as a detective without learning how your enemy operates. Plus, YouTube was a great resource for learning criminality.

She moved stealthily under the blanket of darkness, drawing closer to the target. She ducked behind a parked car, observing the glow of the mobile phones of the officers in sat in their vehicle. She could see two occupants on board, and she needed to walk right past them and get over that fence without them noticing her. A fence that had been impossible to get over in daylight, with all the support available to her. She gritted her teeth. How the hell was she going to do that? She had an idea, but if it backfired, she wouldn't just be up shit creek without a paddle, she would be drowning in it.

Just turn back, the voice in her head whispered through that dead silence. *You have so much to lose and nothing to gain. You need to let this go. You're becoming obsessed.*

Laura edged closer to the police car. She was so close she could see the Netflix show on the officer's phone.

If she wasn't there to break into the place, she would knock on the window and tell them to stay vigilant. The monstrous gates flanked the car. The chain dangling like a dormant alarm bell. If she tried to climb it, they would hear the chain rattling, but there was no other way through. She needed to cause a distraction. Something loud. Something they couldn't ignore.

Laura looked around her, and she felt her heart rate spike. Outside of the house was a skip filled with bricks, old plywood, and broken timber. It was perfect, and she thanked God, Buddha, or whoever for her brief flicker of luck. Moving quickly like a fox searching for food, she grabbed a brick and then returned behind the car. With the brick in her hand, she felt the weight of what she was about to do. There was no turning back. There was no other option. This was the only way, and it had to go perfectly. It had to go off like a fucking firework.

She picked her target. A nice shiny Mercedes that had been relegated to the front of a large house which didn't have enough room on its designer driveway for both the Mercedes and the Ferrari. How people trivialise and rank possessions. When you have all the money in the world, even the most expensive of toys become obsolete.

Laura took a deep breath, lined up the shot, and hurled the brick through the air. Those seconds that the brick was airborne were the longest in her life. Her breath was tight in her chest as she watched the missile fall back to earth and smash into the windscreen of the Mercedes. At once, her world got a lot louder as the car alarm blared. The sharp stabbing of the car alarm rang out in ear shattering intervals. Its lights flashing, expelling the surrounding dark in flashes of panic. She saw lights come on in the house. Laura's balaclava creasing into a smirk.

The officers dove out of the car as if it had been set on fire, and raced, confused, to the screaming vehicle. The owners of the car appeared at the front door and moved onto the street. She could hear the voices of furious, affluent homeowners screaming at the officers that their toy had had a fight with a brick and come off worse.

Seizing the opportunity, Laura darted to the murder house gates faster than a high school kid out his girlfriend's window when he hears her father stomping up the stairs. She eyed the mangle of metal in front of her and saw that she had done a brilliant job of rearranging those steel teeth. Looking over her shoulder, she held the chain in place, and managed to slip through a hole just wide enough for her to fit through.

She was on the other side. Now, the real work began. She saw the unblinking eye of the CCTV cameras perched like crows on the lip of the roof. She moved quickly around its flank, racing to the rear of the home. She stopped, catching her breath, her breathing ragged and heavy. *What the hell am I doing?* She forced the thoughts away, throwing first dirt on them, then pouring concrete. She couldn't waver now. She was in too deep.

She moved, sticking close to the brickwork. She turned the corner, standing at the expansive back garden that had fountains, decking, and summer chairs with a small gazebo over the top. A barbecue that looked more expensive than her car. She glided like a shadow and faced the back patio doors. Her figure reflecting back at her through the like a ghost against the darkened glass. Laura knelt on the decking and placed a paperclip fashioned into a pin into the patio lock and then got the improvised tension rod and began to work.

Laura stopped, her breath catching in her throat. She could hear a car coming, the squeaking of brakes and the sharp pulling of a handbrake. Doors opening and closing. Radios filtering through the air, and the deadly silence returning from the absence of a blaring car alarm. They had called for backup. They would be checking the property soon. She was running out of time. Laura could feel the sweat of her palms on the inside of the gloves. She let out a long breath, pushing the pins in the lock, trying to stop her hands from shaking. She needed to remain calm, but her heart jumped out of her chest when she heard the front gate scrape along the driveway, the chain rattling, and the watchful glare of a torch moving towards her.

Chapter Twenty – Seven
Laura

The sound of the footsteps grew closer. The chatter of the radio. The torch cut through the darkness. The gate opened, scraping along the ground, getting stuck on a loose rock that must have been moved when Laura had slipped through, buying her vital seconds. She nearly had it. Just a little more…

The gate dislodged, and the officer's footsteps continued. He was a metre away. Not even that. Laura pushed and applied pressure. Sweat stinging her eyes.

The pin is going to snap. I'm going to get caught. I have to run away. Now. Run! Run right now!

A foot emerged from the corner of the wall. The light fell onto the ground by her feet. The officer turned, and the torchlight devoured the darkness where Laura had been a moment ago. Breathing deeply, she hid behind the inside wall by the French doors. The officer's torch slowly passing through the darkened garden, and then inside the back doors, dousing the sitting room in radiant light. Laura placed her hand over her mouth. She was on the verge of losing it. One slight push, and she would unravel. The officer drew his torch around the still room, illuminating the mist of dust particles that danced in the air.

The officer pressed his face against the glass. His hand snaking to the door handle. She hadn't locked it. Didn't have time. He was less than a foot away. If he stepped over that threshold…

He's going to come inside. He knows someone is in here. He must have heard the door close. He's coming in. Ready or not, here I come!

Laura heard the handle begin to depress. The click of the lock. The lick of the wind on her face. She could hear his breathing, like a hungry dog hunting a terrified mouse. She squeezed her eyes shut, willing herself to evaporate into the air. The door opened more, and the officer took a step inside the room.

Chapter Twenty - Eight
Laura

Laura held her breath as the officer stepped into the darkened room. His torch light scanning the walls, designer couches, ornaments, and carpet. All he had to do was turn his head, and he would see her. One small movement, and it was all over. Laura held her breath tight in her chest, but she couldn't hold it back much longer. She had to release it soon. She couldn't run. This was it. It was all over. She would let out that pressure from her lungs and gasp for air, and then she would be doused in torch light.

The officer's radio buzzed and cut through the air. He pressed his finger to it.

"Go ahead," he said calmly, still scanning the darkness.

"Where are you?" A small mechanical voice said. "Get back out here! I'm not sitting here by myself." The cop curled his mouth into a smile. He gave one more glance to the dark, as if saying goodbye.

She swallowed, biting down on that breath that begged for release.

"Just checking the house," the officer said. "Thought I heard something."

She couldn't hold it. She couldn't hold it any longer.

"Well get back here. You better not be *in* the house! It's a crime scene!"

Laura squeezed her eyes closed as tight as she could. She felt herself drifting away. The feeling in her legs disappeared.

"Jesus," the officer said. "You're worse than my

girlfriend." With that, the cop turned, slipped outside, and closed the door. Laura held onto that screaming breath for an agonising second longer until the torchlight died away. Laura crumbled to the floor, gasping for air, coughing into her shoulder. Her heart was pounding in her chest. Her body drenched with sweat. She unfolded herself from the ground and peered out into the back garden. Nothing moved. No torch lights. No radio. It was as still as a grave. She took out her phone and used the home screen light to illuminate her way. It was dim enough not to be seen, and there were no windows through to the street from here.

Moving through the sitting room connected to the back garden, she was still stunned by how pristine everything seemed. To anyone else, it resembled the perfect home. To Laura, it looked like a prison cell. They say that a person's surroundings are a direct reflection of their mental health. One may assume that someone whose mind is in complete disarray would live in complete disrepair. But it didn't always manifest like that. What Laura was seeing was a fearful, terrified mind. Everything had to be perfect. Obsessively so. Because if it wasn't, then there would be consequences.

And that wouldn't do now, would it?

She stopped dead. In her head. It was Ron's voice. Laura felt spiders crawling along her skin.

Leave me alone, she mouthed to herself. *I don't want you here.*

Baby, Ron's voice hissed in her mind. *The whole reason you're doing this is because of me. I told you, you can't save her, just like you couldn't save yourself from me. I am a part of you now, whether you like it or not. And like I told you; I will have you forever. Kiss, kiss.*

Laura felt the tears burning in her eyes. She steadied herself on the wall. Her breath caught in her throat, her chest suddenly tight like someone had reached in and filled her lungs, were stuffed with cotton wool. The room began to spin. She needed to do something to quiet his voice in her head, less she bolted for the door and run from ghosts.

Laura bit down on her lip, clamping it between her teeth until she felt the pang of iron on her tongue. She pressed her knuckles into her eyes until the sound of Ron's voice picking at her brain like a hungry insect disappeared. She opened her eyes, her vision marred by white and black clouds as she righted herself. Her tears burned her cheeks. After a moment, she continued through the house and made it into the living room. This was where she needed to be. Where the forensic investigators would have missed a vital clue.

The door was open, just the way it had been when she had last been here. Large windows that looked out into the street welcomed her. She pulled her phone light tight to her, being careful to not draw too close to the glass. A fireplace sat like a darkened mouth. Its slate housing reaching up to the high ceiling. The cream-coloured couch stretched the length of the back wall. It was flanked by two single sitting chairs with plush pillows, and a side table perfectly displayed a crystal decanter set filled with whisky. The amber liquid called to her. She would love nothing more than to sink a mouthful. Just one. Just one delicious mouthful.

She pulled away from the temptation, and moved to the fireplace, an iron basket filled with thick cut logs by her feet. Laura glided her eyes along the mantle. Photos upon photos of the couple stood there, their faces twisted in the blackness like devils with cruel sneers.

The photo with the smashed glass tucked at the base of the fireplace. She crouched down, picked it up, and studied it. Running her fingers over the cracked glass. Why was this picture on the ground? Why was the glass cracked? It stood out like a sore thumb. A stain on a pristine white shirt. Why was it here? She turned it over and found what she had been looking for. In the bottom corner, almost invisible to everyone that wasn't looking for it, she found the tip of a smudge. Laura unclipped the back of the picture from the frame and peeled it away. A fingerprint on the back of the photo, and traces of dirt. *Dirt.* In a house that was so clean and tidy, why was there dirt on this photo? The house was obsessively clean. Alex worked with business. He wore designer suits and pressed pants. Clara wouldn't have dared risked bringing dirt into the house, and Laura hadn't seen a single mark of it from the back door to here. So why was it here? The crack on the photo must be fresh. Had they been arguing? What had happened?

She had the pieces of the jigsaw, but couldn't figure out how they fitted together. Then it hit her. She had been right all along. Clara Weaver was innocent, and she knew exactly how to prove it.

Outside, the night air had cooled, and it cut through her sweat sodden clothes. She had to figure out a way to get through the gate and out of the estate undetected. Peering through the side gate into the street, Laura could see the two officers were in the car. She could sneak past them, but that would mean another distraction, and Laura was fresh out of ideas for that. A figure moved along the driveway, and Laura darted behind the wall. They had doubled down on their patrols. She was trapped.

"Fuck!" She hissed. Vital evidence in her hand, and

unable to hand it to the people that needed it. She couldn't wait for them to change shifts. She needed to get out of the fast.

She scanned the uninviting darkness. *There has to be another way out of here*, she thought. *Clara got out of a locked house somehow.*

She was moving to the back of the garden before she even noticed. Moving past the shed and into the thick ferns and bushes, she searched aimlessly for a way, like a rat trapped in a maze inside an oven that was slowly heating up. Something caught her eyes. In the thicket of bushes, caught on a bramble, a small packet of children's biscuits. Laura put them in her pocket, then pulled the thick ferns and shrubbery apart, and she felt the cold ring of a door handle.

"You have got to be fucking kidding me," she said, unable to believe her luck. She placed her hand on a wooden door that had been built into the greenery. Laura turned the ring pull, and the door unlatched, dirt falling onto her. Clara's feet in the hospital. The dirt under her toenails.

Dirt. Dirt on her feet. Dirt on the photo frame. This was how *they* had got in, and how Clara had got out.

Clever girl. She heard the voice float through the dark. Ice filled her body. Gingerly, she looked over her shoulder.

She studied the silhouette. The figure was still, shrouded in darkness like a mannequin in a shop window. It wasn't the police. It was someone else. Laura's mouth worked, but no sound came out. Then the figure spoke.

Kiss kiss.

Laura bolted through the hidden door without looking back.

Chapter Twenty - Nine
Laura

Laura ran through the dark streets, her shoes clicking on the ground. She stopped and crumpled onto the tarmac behind a parked car.

"I'm losing my fucking mind," she said, pressing her hands to her face. She pulled off the balaclava and let herself breathe the cool night air. She welcomed its cold bite on her hot skin. Adrenaline in overdrive. Her body redlining.

The sound of a car in the distance. Laura spotted the headlights bleeding through the blackness as it creeped up the road. She moved quickly, rolling onto the pavement. The cop car gliding past her, its spotlights shining along the street like she was a convict making a break from Alcatraz. When the car had vanished, she took out her phone and called Celine. It rang out twice. She bit down and rang a third time.

"You want to mess with my head all night?" Celine said sharply.

"Shut up a second," Laura said quickly, eyeing the stillness around her like a rodent searching for predators. "I broke into the crime scene, and I—"

"Whoa, whoa," Celine said quickly. "Laura, you did what?"

"Look," she said, squeezing her eyes closed for a second. "I don't have time to explain. Can you test some fingerprints for me at your new lab?"

"What the … Laura, whatever you're getting yourself involved in, I'm not putting my career and business on the line. You need to sort your own shit out, whatever you're trying to do? You need to do it without me…"

"Wait!" Laura called, desperate to keep her on the line. "Just hold on a second." Silence met her ear. Laura frantically checked the call. It was still connected. The seconds on the call timer continued. "I need your help. Seriously. Someone is going to go to prison for something they didn't do if we don't get this tested. It's vital." Laura could hear Celine's jaw tighten.

"What crime scene?"

"The Grange. Appleton Road. Domestic murder. Clara Weaver and Alex Weaver." Seconds went by. "I'll explain everything I promise," Laura said quickly. "I am putting everything on the line here. I won't mention your name, I promise." A beat of silence. "Celine?" She said, tears welling in her eyes, her throat beginning to close up. Her body was trembling. "I'm sorry I missed our dinner. I am so caught up with this. I'll explain everything. Please. Baby? Help me." Laura felt like her chest was on fire. She had run out of lifelines. Celine was telling her no, and she was pushing against it. Once again, she was involving others in her mess. She was the problem, the poison infecting those around her. With all her bridges burned, she was the one to sink into the abyss when the tides of her life consumed her. She was the problem. She was the poison that was infecting those around her, and with all her bridges burned, she was the one that was sink into the abyss when the tides of her life consumed her.

"Be at mine as soon as you can," Celine said. "I have a small home set up." Laura let out a long breath.

"Thank you," she said. "Thank you so, so much." Celine waited a moment before responding. And then —

"Laura…"

"What is it?" She said, running her hand down her

face.

"Don't ever call me baby again."

Laura checked her rear-view mirror, paranoia consuming her. She gripped the steering wheel tightly, her knuckles turning white. Time was ticking, and she only had a few hours left to get to the bottom of what mysteries she had uncovered. Who did the fingerprints belong to?

Burnell. It had to be. She was the one desperate to throw Clara in jail. He had worked on the case of Hugo Black. Alex Weaver had connections to him. She was the common denominator. Was she responsible? Was she the reason Alex was dead? It was the only explanation. Celine would give her the answers she so desperately needed, and then she could call Jeremy and Burnell would be locked up. One of her own. A police officer. A police officer responsible for murder. How could she have been so blind? *Sinick*. *Dutton*. Now *Burnell*. It all made sense. She just needed a motive, and then Clara would be cleared of everything. *She did it*. It was obvious now. That's why Burnell had shunned the idea. Burnell was the *She*. *She* had been there on the bridge when Clara tried to jump. *She* had been the one to ignore Laura's calls for a deeper investigation. *She* had links to every part of the case. *She* was a killer, and Laura was going to rip that smug smile from her face when she wrapped handcuffs around her wrists.

Her phone buzzed next to her on the passenger seat. She took her eyes off the road and checked it. It was Burnell. Of all fucking people.

'**We need to talk.**'

Laura scoffed. "You got that right," she said. She put the phone down and continued on. She didn't notice the headlights behind her until the darkness of the road flooded with reds and blues, and then the squawk of a siren that cut through the air. Her heart hammered in her chest. She was getting pulled over.

"Shit," Laura hissed, slamming her palm on the steering wheel. She pulled over to the kerb. She looked on the passenger seat. The picture frame in the evidence bag. The balaclava still wrapped around her neck, and the leather gloves poking out of her jacket. This officer is going to think it's Christmas when he sees her. She had two choices – Give her real name, and she be brought in for interfering with a crime scene, or lie, and be brought in on suspicion of burglary.

The cop car stopped behind her, and Laura watched the door crack open. Quickly, she stuffed the evidence bag and gloves into the glove box. When she did, she cursed herself. She should have put it under the driver's seat. Cops *always* check the glove box. They *sometimes* check under the driver's seat. It was a game of odds, and Laura was all in against the House.

She could feel the sweat pushing from her brow. *Keep your shit together.* The officer appeared at her driver's side window and gestured for her to wind it down. Laura did, and the cop's face was etched in flickering blue and reds.

"Evening," he said. He was older. His face marred with deep wrinkles. His frame was broad, and his hair salt and pepper. He was clean shaven. No doubt been in the job for several years. "Do you know why I have pulled you over?"

You're not meant to ask me that without cautioning me first, Laura thought. *Don't tell him you're a cop.*

"You tell me, officer," she said with a flat tone. The officer pursed his lips.

"You seemed to have something in your hand as you drove past me," he said. "What was it?" Laura eyed him intently. He stared back. His eyes had a slight ring of red. He was tired. Probably his third or fourth night shift in a row. Maybe has a new baby. Not sleeping well, if at all. She could spot the faint littering of crumbs on his body armour. He hadn't long since eaten. Probably a McDonalds.

Just play it cool.

Laura exhaled.

"Okay," she said, raising her hands and taking her phone out of her pocket. "You caught me. I was on my phone. Just checked a quick text. Shouldn't have done it." The officer nodded.

"You know how dangerous that is?" He said. She did, and the officer berated her about it. He gestured to her glove box. Laura's nerves spiked. "Keep your phone in there when driving. No distractions that way." His eyes scanned the inside of the car.

"Noted," she said. She gestured to the road. "Can I go now?" The officer paused, pondering the question.

"I need your name and address," he said, taking out his notebook from the zip in his body armour. It was fluorescent. Not a mark on it. Maybe he wasn't as experienced as she thought. The lack of blood and grime on his uniform. The fact that he hadn't recognised her when she was on practically every god damn poster in the police station.

"Why do you need that?" She said, playing dumb. She knew exactly why, but wanted to make sure he knew. The officer flicked on his body camera. A brief pause, and then three sharp, fast beeps. Laura's face was caught in the fisheye lens, and she saw her reflection on the small box monitor mounted on the officer's chest.

The officer straightened.

"Just give me your name and address and this will go much, much smoother for you." Laura needed to appease him and to get out of this without giving herself up. Not providing your details to an officer at the roadside was an arrestable offense. Fucking U.K. law. The officer hesitated with his pen, and his eyes flitted to her. "Now," he barked.

"Celine Burrows," Laura said before she could stop herself. She passed her date of birth. The officer scribbled it down.

"Give me a second," he said, moving to the back of the car and jotting down the registration plate. She could hear him talking into the radio. She put her head back on the seat and let out a stifled breath. She had just lied to the police. Lied to the damn police. She couldn't believe what she was doing. How far was she willing to go to get to the truth? And how does one get to the truth by paving the way in a web of lies? A terrible realisation cut through her mind.

He's running the car through. It will come back to me, not Celine. He'll know I'm lying. Shit!

The officer returned, his face like he was chewing on a wasp.

"Your car doesn't come back to you," he said. Laura thought quickly.

"It's my friend Laura's," she said. "I'm heading to her house now." The officer placed a hand on the roof of the car.

"To be perfectly honest with you, Miss Burrows, I think you're lying to me." He took a step back. "Out of the car, please." Laura's mind raced for a way to get out of this, but she couldn't think of one. She was three steps short from fucked.

"Is that necessary?" Laura protested. "You have my details. I have given you an explanation of where I am going. Do you suspect me of a crime?" The officer's face turned sour.

"You have a garment around your neck. You haven't given me a straight answer, you're sweating, and you haven't taken your eyes off that glove box since we began speaking." His hand reached to his utility belt, his fingers caressing the top of his taser. "Now step out of the car. I'm searching you and the vehicle." Laura felt her temperature rising, like she had been thrown into a frying pan. His gaze was cooking her alive. She couldn't flee. She couldn't lie her way out of it. She couldn't fight, charm, or bully her way out of it. She had tied the noose around her neck, and the cop was kicking the chair from under her. "Miss," he said, his tone that of a low growl. "Get out of the car, now." Laura's lip trembled. She had to come clean. She had no choice.

"I need to tell you something," she said quickly. "I have been lying to you." The sudden confession took him by surprise, as his face flashed from anger to shock in a blink.

"Go on." She searched her mind, thinking of how she could say what she needed to say in just the right way.

"I'm not going to my girlfriend's house, Laura," she said. "I have been having an affair. I am going to see them now. My partner is at home in bed, and I am going to a hotel room to meet someone I have met off Tinder." The lies just kept on mounting up. She couldn't help her lips from spinning them. Can a spider get caught in its own web?

"I see," he said.

"The glove box is filled with condoms and sex toys," she reached for it quickly to pull it open. "Here let me –

"

"No," the officer said, raising his hand, trying to hide his embarrassment. "No, that's fine." He placed his notebook back into his pocket. "Just get yourself off the road," he said. "I don't want to see this car again tonight." With that, he turned and moved back to his car. Laura watched him go, and then put the car in gear and peeled away from the curb. She watched as the officer turned off his light bar and flicked on his interior light and pulled out his computer, speaking into his radio. She had done it. She had got away free, but at what cost?

Chapter Thirty
Laura

Laura's phone buzzed as she drove. She looked at the bright screen that cut through the dark. It was Francis. She hung up. She couldn't speak to him. Couldn't tell him where she was going or what she was doing. She had put too much on the line already. She didn't want to drag him down with her. He was a good man, and Laura had ruined too many lives to add another one to her growing list.

She pulled up to Celine's home. The lights were off other than the kitchen, which she could see through the break in the living room blinds. Laura let out a long breath. What the hell was she doing here, really? Why was Celine still helping her? Laura had left her to fend for herself in the hospital, vanished for a few months, then hit her up with a *'hey! I know it's been a while, but I need your help. Drinks? Food? Sure thing! I won't go, and when I don't, I'll call you again asking for your help. No, I'm not the abuser. You are. Remember?'* She felt rotten to the core, and now, she was going to ask her again for her help on a case she had no business being on. She had convinced herself that this whole thing was just work. Nothing more. Platonic, and that her waking moment weren't thinking about getting her head between her thighs. She said to her that this was purely friendship, that they should get to know each other again. To grow together as separate people and not find themselves thrown into the same toxic merry-go-round they had both tried so hard to escape. And when Celine finds out that Laura had given her name to the police to try to get out of being thrown to the wolves, another betrayal. Another lie. Another stab in the back. Celine would be gone. Laura would be jobless. Francis, Jeremy, and hell, even Burnell. They wouldn't ever speak to her again. Either she would end up in a physical prison, or a mental one, all sick of Laura's self-destruction under the guise of 'doing the right thing.'

She felt like a poisonous flower that was beautiful and alluring, only to find that when you touched it, it shredded your skin and scarred you for life. She was toxic. She hadn't done any kind of healing. She had just buried her issues deeper down and found new ways of coping with them. The problem wasn't her past. Ron. Her addiction. It was her. *She was the problem. She was sick.* This was the last case she was going to work on. This was the last time she was going to ask Celine for anything. This was the last time she was going to put her neck on the line. It had to be. But like so many addicts and junkies swear that it's the last time when they beg, borrow, and steal. How much could she believe it? The hundredth last time? The thousandth? It always seemed like the last time, but it never, ever was.

Laura cracked the handle and stepped out into the night air, taking the evidence bag out of the glove box with her. Walking up to the front of the house, she had a growing sense of dread in her stomach, like she was going to puke. She hadn't been alone with Celine, not for any length of time in so long. Not really. There was the drive to the hospital, but just the two of them, in a house alone? With emotions running high? Laura didn't know what would happen. She would either shag her or stab her. She didn't know which she preferred right now. Before, she had been excited to see her, like stepping into a forbidden forest to taste the fine fruit that hung from exotic trees. But this time, she felt like she was stepping into an abandoned building, with nothing but ghosts and devils waiting for her.

She knocked on the door. Silence looming. The moon was shining brightly above her, staring down at her. Its face twisted and contorted into a devilish scream. She squinted her eyes, and scrunched them shut. She shook her head. She was sleep deprived, and she hadn't eaten anything in a while. Fuck, she wanted a drink. A drink of wine so goddamn badly. It was the only thing that calmed her nerves. The medication. The journalling. The meditation. The exercise. The monthly meetings with her sponsor. The crisis line. Samaritans. AA. The pamphlets and emails she got telling her to stay strong. Occupational health. All of it paled in comparison to what she *really* wanted. To what she craved. Laura's phone buzzed again. She checked it without thinking. It was Burnell.

'I know you're reading these messages. Call me back immediately.'

"We can talk on interview you murdering fuck. Once I have the evidence, I'll charge you personally." Another message came through.

'Where are you?'

She stuffed her phone into her pocket, and knocked on the door again, anger pounding into the silence. The door handle depressed. Laura put her phone away quickly. Celine stood there in a tight white tee shirt that rounded and clung to her breasts. Her hair was braided, and they fell over her shoulders like tightly coiled rope. Her jeans were a dark blue, waist high, tight around her legs and hips. Laura wanted to peel them off with her teeth. She stuffed the thought away.

"Can you knock harder? I have neighbours, you

know," she said. She eyed Laura, either with contempt or indifference. Laura couldn't tell. "Are you standing there, or are you coming in?" Celine said, stepping out of Laura's way, inviting her into her home like a vampire. The door closed behind them, sealing them both inside. Laura looked at the décor. Dark mahogany walls with splashes of gold. Pictures hung up on of Celine at her graduation. Other photos of people with her, presumably family. No one she had ever met. The boxes next to the stairs suggested she still hadn't unpacked, and yet, she had made this place look more homely than Laura had with her own house.

Because you got it from his bereavement money. You're living in the home given to you by the man who took everything from you. You are living in a tomb.

"Can I get you a drink?" Celine said. Laura turned on her heel.

"A drink?" Laura said, her mouth salivating.

"Non-alcoholic," she said. "I know you're in recovery." Laura stared at her, her mouth trying to find a word that said both 'Fuck you' and 'Thank you' at the same time.

"That would be nice," she settled on. "Water, please." Celine held her smile, her teeth perfect, straight, and gleaming through the dim light that filtered through from the kitchen.

They stepped through the house. She could smell the scent of something. Her brow fused together. In the kitchen, she saw the oven was on, and some pizza was crisping nicely. Thin base. Bright and colourful. It was also two in the morning.

"A little late for food, isn't it?"

"You were supposed to be meeting me for food earlier," she said, her smile wavering. "You want my help; you will sit down with me and have something to eat." Her tone was final. This wasn't a negotiation. Laura would have to sit around and play happy families, forcing pizza down her neck and make small talk. She noticed the littering of leaves and flour on the kitchen counter.

"You made them fresh?" Celine was taking out glasses from the cupboard. She fished out a couple of candles and lit them, their wicks sizzling and flaring to life. The flame dancing on them as she placed them down on the table. Laura heard it then, the faint sound of music filtering through the air. This was a fucking date.

"Music and candles?"

"Do you want my help?" Celine said, her eyes flaring. Laura's voice caught in her throat, her fingers wrapping around the evidence bag. Her silence told all. "We eat with music and candles, or you can leave." She straightened her back, moved to the counter, and pulled out some cutlery, and set it on the table. "I made them from scratch using a recipe I found online," she said, gesturing to the oven, then gathered the candles and set them on the table, reaching over to the centre. Laura noticed her shirt stretch up, revealing her smooth dark skin, and the burgundy underwear that was lacy and studded. She wanted her to see it. Just a flash of what Laura would have if she played her cards right. The thought made her flush with heat. But she couldn't discern if it was that of passion, or of repulsion.

"I really need you to check this photo frame," Laura said, holding out the evidence bag. "It's important. It has a fingerprint on it." Celine paused and eyed Laura.

"A fingerprint on a photo frame?" She let out a laugh. "What's so special about that?"

"That's the point," Laura said, holding it out with

desperation. "To anyone else, nothing. But I think something terrible has happened, and someone responsible is trying to cover it up." She stabbed the photo frame with her finger. "The house is pristine, Celine. Nothing is out of place, except this photo frame. It's cracked, and there's a smudge on it. A fingerprint. When I was there today –"

"The crime scene you broke into?" Laura felt the bullet cut straight through her.

"Yes," she barked. "The crime scene. I left via a back door that was hidden in the brambles. No one would have known it was there, and when I went through it, soil rained on me. If we can attribute the soil on this fingerprint to someone external, that would prove that there is someone else involved in this case. Plus, the body has stab wounds. Tonnes of them, from neck, torso, and groin. A frenzied attack. Not planned." Celine let out a long breath and rested her hand on the table.

"A fingerprint doesn't seem much to go off."

"It isn't, which is why I need your help."

"You could just take it to the force CSI." Laura furrowed her brow. The one person who knew her best in the whole world wasn't believing her. She felt like she was smashing her head through a brick wall.

"CSI will only do what the commander tells them to do. Now if the commander is responsible for the murder…" Celine held her hand up.

"Slow down," Celine said, a blast of laughter erupting as she pulled plates out of the cupboard. "Are you telling me that the leading investigating officer is guilty of the crime?" Laura nodded, pulling out a chair, placing the frame on the table and turned to meet Celine's gaze.

"That's what I'm thinking, yes. She has tried to stop me every second of the investigation. She has been involved in multiple other incidents that either directly or indirectly involve the victim." Laura held her hands up. "I just need you to check this over and see who the fingerprint comes back to." Celine pondered this, running the idea around her mind.

"Say she is responsible for the murder," Celine said. "What motive do you have?" Laura pursed her lips, resting her elbows on the table and put her fingers to her mouth.

"That's the one part of the puzzle I'm missing. But if we can get the DNA, we can ask that on interview."

"I suppose," Celine said, taking the oven gloves from the oven door and opening it up like a roaring mouth, placing the plates on the counter. "Has the suspect said anything on interview?" Laura's fingers rattled the table.

"She hasn't said anything."

"Nothing? No comment?" Laura shook her head.

"Nothing. To anyone."

"Why doesn't she just talk?" Laura searched her mind.

"Maybe because she knows if she opens her mouth, then something bad will happen? I don't think she's *hiding* anything. I think she's absolutely terrified. Think about it – the man who provided your home was controlling and abusive. Every bit of your daily life was monitored and controlled. She has been hospitalised three times to try to escape the relationship, and every time she ended up back in that house. And now, if she has witnessed something, she has been threatened to keep her mouth shut. Why would someone believe her? She is the perfect suspect, and her mental state is clearly questionable." Celine shrugged.

"I don't know," she said, taking a knife out of the

knife rack and digging it into the pizzas. "Maybe you're looking too much into it. Maybe you're looking into things that aren't there." The comment flared Laura's temper.

You sound just like the rest of them, she thought. She checked the time. She didn't have long before the CPS charged Clara with murder. Her phone buzzed again. Burnell blowing it up. Laura killed the call and put it back into her pocket.

Celine brought the food over and cut it into slices. Stunned at the decoration of different vegetables and meats. She couldn't hide the look on her face. She was impressed.

"Where did you learn to cook?" Laura said, mouth watering.

"You'd be amazed what I have been up to since we last met." Laura was passed two large slices of the vegetable pizza, and a slice of meat. She was hungry. Ravenous.

"This looks…" she said, marvelling at the food. "It looks amazing. Thank you for doing this."

"My pleasure," she said. She sat down opposite Laura and placed the glass of water by her plate. The sound of the music pushing through even more. A song by Talor Swift. One she hadn't heard before. Laura heard Celine singing along to it. The humming of the oven, and the clinking of Celine's cutlery as she dug into the meat pizza. "Dig in." Laura went straight for the meat. It was succulent, cooked to perfection. The dough was chewy, a little tough, but just the way she liked it. It was the best damn meal she had eaten in years. She took a sip of her water.

"So," Laura said, gingerly. "When can you do these tests?" Laura waited for the explosion. Celine sat back.

"Is that all you care about?" She said, her eyes wide. "You came back into my life, remember? You asked for my help, and I have made you this meal, and you can't even take a minute and enjoy spending some time with me. You haven't asked me how my day has been." Laura felt herself gripping the fork tighter. Celine stared at her, then nodded her head. "Well?"

"Are you going to help me or not?" Celine clenched her jaw.

"After we've eaten. I want you to finish every bite." Laura's brow furrowed.

"I'm not a kid."

"No," Celine said, "but you are here for my help. Eat the meal you promised me. You aren't using me again." Laura bit down on the fork, the sensation grabbing her by the crown and rattling her head. She let go of the knife in her other hand and dropped it onto the floor. They both eyed the insulting utensil.

"Oh dear," Celine said, her eyes hard. "Go get another one out of the drawer." Celine pointed to the cupboards. Laura pushed the chair out quickly, eyeing Celine with venom. The pizza, once delicious in her mouth, now tasted rancid, like rotting vegetables. Their bitter taste lingering on her tongue. She stood, moving to the cupboard, and opened it up. She plunged her hand into grab a knife, and she saw it. Right there in front of her. Laura heard Celine humming the song that was playing on the Alexa. Her fingers tracing the instrument. She touched it. It had been cleaned. Its blade sharp. Small red dots on the black handle.

"I feel the Lavender haze creepin' up on me. Surreal, I'm damned if I do give a damn what people say." Laura felt her stomach plunge into icy waters. She swallowed hard and turned around.

"Actually," she said, putting her hand to her head. "I think I need to get going." Celine looked up at her from her chair, still singing.

"I love this song," she said. "I heard it a few days ago. Can't get it out of my head." She stood and moved to Laura; her face fixed in a sneer. Laura had the urge to grab a knife and slice her throat open. She pressed against the counter, looking at Celine with terror. She couldn't speak. Her body rattled with shock. How could she? All this time, Laura had been looking at the wrong person. But why? It didn't make any sense. Celine moved to the cupboard next to Laura. "What's wrong?" Celine said. "You don't look too good."

"I just," Laura said, feeling flushes of heat. "I just think I need to go home. I should go to the CSI. You're right. I'm being silly." Laura moved to leave when Celine blocked her way.

"You haven't finished your food," she gestured to the evidence bag. "I want you to tell me *everything* about the case. About this suspect you have." She leaned in. "Stay a while." Her mouth stretched. Her teeth looking like daggers of bone. "I've locked the door anyway," she said, an insane titter slipping from her lips. "Can't be too careful. Lots of crazies out there." The two shared a long look. Laura couldn't fight her way out of this one. She had to ride it out. Play happy families, and somehow duck away and call for help. But the smile on Celine's face told her she knew she was onto her. Something she said earlier, in passing. It had burrowed in Laura's brain like a maggot in rotten meat.

"Okay," Laura said. "I suppose I better had finish up." She moved to the table and took another seat. Her body was rigid whilst Celine continued to sing to Alexa. The same song, *Lavender Haze* by *Taylor Swift,* repeating on loop.

She did it.

Celine eyed the food on Laura's plate.

The knife in the drawer.

"Go on," she said. Laura hesitantly picked up the fork and dug into the food, tearing vegetables and dough. The same repugnant taste biting her tongue.

You'd be amazed what I have been up to since we last met.

Without saying a word, Celine snaked her hand under the table. Laura stopped chewing and her body froze. The sound of glasses clinking. Celine placed them onto the table, and then from somewhere unseen, a bottle of red wine. Laura's *favourite* red wine.

"What the hell is that?" Laura said, fighting back the tears. Her body felt hot. Woozy. She pushed the feeling away, blinking hard. Celine didn't answer. Instead, she unscrewed the cap. It sounded like a neck snapping and poured the gurgling dark red liquid into the glass. Laura eyed it, her body screaming for her to take it, to sink it, to make the pain in her mind go away. "What are you doing?" she said, her lips quivering. Her head began to pound. Sweat pouring from her underarms and from her face. Celine sat back, her face turning to stone.

"Just like old times," Celine said, lifting hr glass and taking a long drink.

"I'm sober…" Laura tried. She felt shit faced already. What was happening?

"You're sober?" Celine said, her arms folded over her chest, the spine of the glass nestled in her hand. "You're a lot of things, Laura Warburton, but sober isn't one of them. Go on. Drink it. I won't judge you. Just a sip. For me. You want my help? Show me how badly. Show me how far you will put your work in front of everything you love." Celine regarded the glass of wine. "Do it."

"Why do you have the knife?" Laura said, her mouth arid. Head spinning. Flattening her hands on the table.

"Come again?" Celine said.

"The knife," but it came out as '*naiyf*.' "Why do you have it?"

"You're questioning my cutlery now?" She said, laughing. "You need to chill out." Laura's face was flabbergasted. She needed to leave, right now. "Details, details," Celine continued. "You were always so precious on details."

"Tell me, Celine," Laura snapped. Celine shrugged.

"It doesn't matter," she said. "I'm enjoying this," she gestured to the two of them. "Me and you together, one last time."

"One last time?" Laura spat. The phrase cut Laura's rising anger in half, letting it writhe on the ground. "What do you mean?" Celine's smile grew and stretched from ear to ear. The faint tint of red wine on her teeth and lips.

"I just thought you could have one last drink before you die." On the death of the last syllable, Laura's face wrapped with confusion, and then with horror as she felt her stomach beginning to turn itself inside out. "Are you feeling okay?" Celine said, placing the bottle to her lips and taking a deep drink. Then Laura noticed. Her napkin. Filled with half-eaten pizza. Celine hadn't taken a bite, and Laura had consumed nearly her entire plate.

"I need to leave," Laura said, going to move, before stumbling, catching herself on the counter. The room was spinning. Celine stood up and moved to her, her body warping like she was made of elastic and being stretched and pulled by a giddy child. Morphing in

Laura's vision. She fell forward, and her stomach tied in knots, before erupting and exploding on the floor. "What have you done to me?" Laura said, her body flushing hot and cold, choking on her own bile. She took out her phone, fumbling it in her hand. Celine plucked it from her hand and tossed it onto the ground where it skidded and rattled, sliding under the large fridge. Laura tried to stand, but her legs gave way, sending her crashing to the floor. Grabbing out at the table, she knocked the pizza and plates onto the ground where they shattered in white, jagged shards.

"I don't need to test the fingerprints," Celine said. "Turns out I'm not as careful as I thought. That stupid photo frame. Slipped right from my hand. But thanks for bringing me the only piece of evidence that puts me there. Other than my diary, of course, but no one is looking at that." Celine crouched over her. Her voice hard. She plucked some of the green leaves from the pizza base, pinching one between her fingers. "Strychnine," she said. "Pretty, isn't it." She eyed Laura on the ground. "I'd say you have a few minutes before the effects really kick in." Laura's breath was sharp and shallow as her body began shutting down. Her heart and throat felt like they were on fire. Her eyes burning so badly she felt the urge to claw them out of her skull. "I just wanted to be alone. After you did what you did. Then Alex ... well he used me too. Then you came back. People just want to use me. No one ever stays. Just pick me up and throw me to the side when they're done with me. I do feel bad for Clara. But she had it all and didn't know how lucky she was. So, I'll take it all away. I'm happy she kept her mouth shut, though. I must have *really* scared her. That's the thing about fractured minds. They're easier to smash into pieces."

Laura struggled for breath on the ground, like someone had poured hungry fire ants down her throat. She wanted to slice through the meat and gristle to breathe. Her body began to shake, her mouth foaming thick and white. "I left you in my past, Laura, but you had to come crawling back into my world," Celine continued, tears brimming along her burning eyes. "You won't ever leave me alone." Her lips went tight. "This is the only way I'll be free from you. Now lie there and fucking die."

Chapter Thirty – One
Laura

Celine sat by the table, drinking wine with the same calmness as if it was a random Tuesday evening and there was nothing good to watch on TV. Laura had envisioned the way in which she would die. It was only natural working in the field she was in with danger at every turn. Maybe she lost control of a car during an emergency response call, or at the hands of some violent arsehole that decided he didn't want to come quietly.

But not like this. She thought of every possibility that she could have her life extinguished. Every eventuality, bar this one. The most obvious one. By someone who she knew. Someone she had trusted. Someone who was standing over her, as her insides were tearing themselves apart, staring down at her like a slug on the pavement baking in the hot sun. Someone that she had loved so fiercely. It made sense, in a sort of way. A full circle. From Ron to Celine. From addiction to relapse. From absolution to damnation. To be poisoned by the woman who knew how to make it. The woman she had reached out to for help. Celine was helping her out for sure. Helping her come to her way of thinking.

She tried to get up, tried to cry out. Tried to breathe, but she was losing that fight. She coughed onto the kitchen tiles. Thick clumps of flesh were being stripped from her stomach and insides, haemorrhaging through her mouth, matting between her teeth. Meat matter stuck in her throat. She was choking on her own blood.

"Help me…" Laura mouthed through the gore. Her

stomach twisted, bending her in half. Her irises shifted to the back of her head, eyes turning like cracked eggs oozing vermillion. Like the earth below Laura was quaking, Laura Warburton began to convulse.

"You know the worst part about you, Laura?" Celine said, sipping her wine. "You think that you are right, *all* the time. After you left me, my life was ruined. I got fired. I lost my home. Had to start again. Got myself back on my feet. Even met someone. Thought it was fate. But he had a wife. He was a user, just like you. So, for once, I took control." She sipped again. "I have everything packed. Alex is dead. His whore wife will take the fall. And you? Well, I know how to make this look like a suicide, and by the time they realise or give a shit to look into it further, I will be far, far away." She reached over and picked up the photo frame. "I'll make sure no one ever sees this." She tossed the frame onto the table where it rattled, and watched Laura choke on her own blood, small bubbles emerging from her lips as she writhed on the ground. Celine continued to drink. "And then, as if the stars aligned once more, you come back into my life. And here we are. The best part?" She leaned forward, like Laura was in the front row of a magic show. Celine was about to give the grand finale. "It was all your fault."

Celine crouched and retrieved Laura's phone from under the fridge. A standard iPhone. Easy enough to dissolve. The home screen littered with notifications from a 'Francis' and a 'BITCH.' She smirked, curiosity getting the better of her. Celine flicked through her contacts, typing in her number. The name 'Celine,' showed up. She was nothing special in Laura's world. No kiss. No love heart. No pet name. Just black and white. 'Celine.' With that, she took out a small pin from her kitchen drawer, took out the SIM card, and swallowed it. There would be no tracing her, and when she had got rid of the body and questions were asked about her phone hitting the cell site mass near Celine's home, she would tell the police that yes, she had seen her, and yes they had eaten and gone to bed together, before Laura left in the morning, saying that her mental health was bad and that she was going to take a long walk off a short bridge. Celine would make the call to the police in the morning. She would cry. Make it sound convincing. She would fill in the missing person's report and tell all about how Laura was struggling. Her mental health. Her addiction. The pressures of work. Tonight, however, she would get to work. She knew how forensic investigators worked, and how to fool them. She knew the chemical components of a body and how to dissolve bones and tendons correctly. How to clean up blood properly. Most people use bleach, but that activates the dogs and UV torches. Murder isn't hard when you know how to get away with it.

Chapter Thirty – Two
Francis

Laura's phone rang out. Burnell put her phone on her desk and stared at the cold McDonald's latte, picked it up, saw it to be empty, and placed it back down with a disgruntled sigh. Some damage had been caused at the crime scene. Not to the house itself, thank God, but the officers had spooked. She had sent another couple of patrols to help and to search the area. People loved causing trouble for the police when they were on sentry. The owners of the car had already rung in their complaint, and Burnell had dealt with it personally. She never tired of hearing the phrase "You're a public servant!" and "I pay your wages." The ingenuity was incredible. She wondered if the public were given a handbook of phrases to say to get their own way.

"We will look into it in the morning," she had told them, and then put the phone down. After working sixteen hours straight overseeing a domestic murder, someone smashing a window of a car was at the bottom of her shit pile.

Burnell checked her phone again. No call, but the message she had sent through to Laura showed *read*. She leant back in her seat, running her hands over her face, and stretching herself out. The case had gone to the CPS, and they were due to be looking over it soon for a charging decision. Then she would charge Clara personally, head home for a few hours' sleep. Then she would get Professional Standards involved to pull the thorn that was Laura Warburton out of her side for good. A bad apple can spoil a bunch, and Warburton was as rotten as they came. She tightened her lips and turned to Jeremy, who had his head in his hands. She cleared her throat. Jeremy shot up, his eyes closed, taking in a long breath.

"Focus," she bit. "Not much longer now," Burnell said. "In the meantime, I want you to start collecting the evidence for Sergeant Warburton's dismissal tomorrow." Jeremy felt the weight of guilt begin to crush him around his chest, like he was being ensnared by a giant serpent.

"I'll see what I can do," Jeremy said, lacklustre, pulling himself closer to his computer. Burnell studied him, her eyes burning from the lack of sleep.

"You know this is the right thing to do," Burnell said, her words like a cricket ball batted into an antique store. "When Laura is gone, you will be fully substantive. You only had the position because she was unwell. Now you are on the edge of charging a killer and ridding a problematic officer from our team. Your future is in your hands, Jeremy. I believe you will do what you know is right." With that, Burnell turned back to her computer and refreshed her emails again. Still nothing. She checked the clock, and they were way past burning the midnight oil. The sun will break along the horizon in soon, and with it came a new day, and a new beginning.

Francis walked into the room holding a radio. He was sweating. Burnell had had him completing enquires on the murder to make it airtight. He wasn't supposed to be in the office. She didn't want him anywhere near the main investigation. He couldn't be trusted.

"Did you hear that?" Francis said, pointing to the radio. "Laura's car has just been run through over the radio." Burnell scorned.

"Why are you in the office?" Burnell soured. "I told you explicitly to leave and complete what I told you." Francis batted the comment away, addressing Jeremy.

"The radio," Francis rebutted. "The vehicle that's just been ran through. It was Laura's car, but 'Celine Burrows' was driving it. That's not right." Jeremy's eyes widened. He went to speak, but Burnell cut in before he had a chance to take a breath.

"And?" Burnell bit. "It isn't illegal to drive around at night." Francis ignored her barking like a dog that wouldn't shut the fuck up, waiting for Jeremy to respond. Jeremy licked his lips, trapped between the Devil and the abyss.

"DCI is right, Francis," he said. "There's no significance to it." Francis felt the room's temperature begin to rise like he was sitting in an oven. His heart thumping in his head. His hand around the radio beginning to sweat. Francis' mind fractured.

Of all people, he thought. *You know exactly why this doesn't make sense.*

"Where is Laura?" Francis bit, waiting for a response. When none came, he followed up with, "I tried to call her, but she hasn't picked up." As soon as he said it, he knew he had crossed a line. Burnell's expression turned from stone to malice.

"Why are you speaking to her? You were told not to." Francis' mouth dried up, seeing his pension disappear before his eyes.

"Inspector Marriott," Francis said. "You know exactly what I am getting at. Laura was going to Celine's home, and she didn't want us to know. It was by accident that she got pulled over. We need to go to that address right now." Burnell stood and marched over to Francis. She wasn't a tall woman, maybe around five – five, but she made Francis shrivel into the ground.

"If you dare interfere with this investigation, then I will be sure to see you out the door with Laura personally." Francis felt the weight of the world crushing him. He had been a police officer for over twenty years. It was his life. He loved his job, but he loved it under Laura's guidance. She was chaotic, but she was a good leader. A maverick with a good heart. Dysfunctional as they come, but knew when something stinks, and she had been right this whole time. Burnell had it in for her, and she didn't want her on the case. The biggest reason was simply 'why?' He eyed Burnell, who glared at him behind her thick-rimmed glasses, so close that he could make out the fine hairs on her upper lip. Her lips were dry. The whites of her eyes flirting with bloodshot. She could crush him with an email, but he couldn't leave Laura to go at this alone anymore. She had been abandoned by all that she trusted. Everyone but him, and he had to do something. Francis looked over Burnell's shoulder. Jeremy was staring at the floor. A hopeless man in a hopeless situation.

"I'm going to that address," Francis said, moving into the MIU office and snatching a pair of keys from the board. "Something is wrong."

Francis ran across the car park, clutching the scrap piece of paper that he had used to write down Celine's address. He tried to call Laura again, pressing his ear to the phone, hoping to high heaven that she answered. Straight to voicemail.

"Answer the fucking phone, Laura!" He shouted to the robotic voice. He clicked the car key and saw amber lights flash in the dark. He marched to the vehicle, a small Peugeot. What the hell was he doing? He was throwing his career away. That was what. His wife was going to kill him. But he was a detective, and detectives search for answers, whatever the cost. Maybe Laura was right all along? He would have to buy her a drink after this. Non-alcoholic, of course. Maybe a new collar for her cat. Maybe some lube from how hard they were going to be fucked from Professional Standards.

He slipped into the car and fired up the ignition. He punched Celine's address into Google maps. It wasn't far. A few miles. This car didn't have blue lights and sirens, but he would fly through those red lights. Just like days in uniform, the motto of 'no lights on nights.' He put the car into first gear and set off. A hard slamming came on the bonnet. He looked up, his heart in his throat. Jeremy was standing there, his face aghast. Francis wound down the window as Jeremy moved to the passenger side door.

"If you think you can talk me out of it..." Francis began, his hands wrapped tightly around the steering wheel. Jeremy pulled the door open and lumbered his large frame inside.

"I'm not," he said. "I'm coming with you." Francis felt a wave of heat rush through him, banishing the cold air chill from his skin.

"What did you tell the DCI?" He said. Jeremy clipped his seat belt into place.

"I told her to shove her promotion up her arse." Both men smiled, sharing a moment of comradery. "Right," Jeremy said, pointing to the sat nav. "Let's get going." Francis released the handbrake.

"She's going to get us fucking sacked."

The two drove the car like they had stolen it. Jeremy tried Laura's phone again and left messages ranging from long apologies to calling her every name of under the sun. Francis thought it nice that he was showing her he still cared. They got onto a straight road, and Francis pressed his foot to the floor. The rev counter moving deeper into the red. The engine screaming at him to yield.

"Why do you think she's heading to Celine's address?" Jeremy said. "I thought they were done."

"The car that the traffic officer came back to. It was Laura's address, and then he passed Celine's details. She's heading to there."

"But why?" Jeremy said. "After everything that happened between them. You'd think she would stay a million miles away."

"Laura is an ex-alcoholic, right?" Francis said. "Addicts go to the thing that they aren't supposed to have in times of stress. It is like an old friend to them. A compulsion."

"So, you think she's getting drunk?" Francis shook his head, taking a hard right hard. Jeremy was pressing his foot into the floor, trying to find the brake that wasn't there.

"Other than alcohol, what else would a person go to when they're struggling with something?"

"I don't know," he said. "Friends, family?"

"And we know Laura doesn't really have any of those. But, an ex-lover? There's no way she could stay away from her when she's breaking into pieces." Like jigsaw pieces falling into place, Jeremy began to see the picture appear in his mind's eye. One of fear, desperation, and toxicity. It dawned on him. He had broken her when she was fragile to begin with. In the car park when she poured her heart out to him, he should have taken her inside. Spoken to her. But he didn't. And as much as he would deny it – call it unprofessional, his wife, or whatever. The reason he didn't was because he was too focused on his own career, rather than helping the woman who had saved his life.

"Where was the car ran through?" Jeremy said.

"Appleton." Jeremy's mouth ran dry.

"Near the murder scene. Didn't someone call in a damage job?"

"They did," Francis said, the streetlights blinking him in radiant light.

"She's been back to the house," Jeremy said, certainty in his voice. "Celine is ex-CSI. The DCI won't let her near the case. She's not only gone to her ex-lover, but she's also gone to someone who can help the case. She's found something, and we need to know what."

They arrived at the house. Both men stared out of the window into the darkness. The blinds were drawn, but they could see the golden light shining through. The walkway was lined with plants and shrubbery. A CCTV camera with an unblinking red eye perched above the brown door with the golden knocker.

"That Laura's car?" Francis said, pointing to the Audi on the curb. They stepped out into the dark, the moon dousing them in silver light. Francis moved to Laura's Audi and placed a hand on the bonnet. "Stone cold," he said. Jeremy eyed the house. It was tall and black. He felt a shiver run up his spine and eyed the black gate that stood in the way. When he crossed the threshold, there was no going back. Dante's Inferno running around his mind.

Abandon All Hope, Ye Who Enter Here.

"Let's go."

The gate was cold to the touch, and creaked as they moved through it, letting it fall shut with a loud rattle in silence that was so thick it could choke a man. The night air was still. Clouds glided lazily across the sky like ghost ships along black water.

"Call for some backup," Jeremy said, looking up at the monolith of the house. "If shit goes down, I want some uniform close by to help." Francis took out his phone and called the response Sergeant on duty. He didn't want to call up on the radio. The less Burnell knew, the better. If she noticed at all on her throne made of skulls, glued together by officer's tears and statistics. But then again, *fuck that wrinkly titty bitch* he thought. *Laura might need us.* He put in the call.

"They're on their way," Francis said. Then, "You sure about this? If she isn't here, or she's just having a good time, then you're up for the chopping block like me." Jeremy was trying to peer through the front window. He peeled himself away and turned to Francis, his eyes twinkling in the starlight.

"I'm sure. Now knock on." Francis stepped to the door and knocked loudly. A dog barked somewhere in the distance. They listened for movement. Nothing moved. Francis lifted the letter box flap and peered inside, but it was blocked by the black bushy hairs of a draft excluder. He put his fingers in, trying to part the fabric to get a better look.

"Celine!" Francis shouted. "Laura! It's Francis and Jeremy. Open the door!"

Chapter Thirty - Four
Laura

The sound of knocking. The fading of her heartbeat. Detective Sergeant Laura Warburton of the Wigtown Major Investigation Team stopped breathing.

Celine heard the loud banging on her front door. A jolt of fear cut through her. Quickly, she moved to the other side of the kitchen, stepping over Laura. She pressed the small monitor that was mounted to the wall and in hazy black and white, two men stood there in shirts and ties, holding up their warrant cards to the haze. The damn police were here. She turned to Laura and eyed her with venom.

"How the hell did you bring them here?" Did she put in a call before she got here? Was this all some set up to get her locked up? Celine thought Laura was coming for help with the case. But she knew all along it was her. Somehow. Somehow, Laura had pieced together the puzzle, and she had figured it all out. She was good. *Impossibly Good.* Even when Celine thought she had it all covered, all the bases loaded, and was on her way to a home run to 'unsolved murder' town, Laura Warburton was hot on her tail. *Fuck!* She thought, slamming her hands to her head. She had to think. Had to do something. They wouldn't go away. Wouldn't stop knocking. And if they couldn't get her to open the door, then they would break down the door and everything would be exposed. Even if she moved Laura, there was too much to clean up. It would take too much time. The room was heating up, like someone had lit a furnace underneath her. She had to do something. They knocked again.

Time's ticking.

She had to convince them that Laura wasn't here. Somehow. She would have to do everything she could to make sure that they didn't step into her house. If they got in, then the game was over. She went to the knife rack, took out a butcher's knife, and moved to the front door.

A few moments passed, and Francis was about to knock on the door again when it creaked open. Celine stood in front of her. Her eyes looked tired, but alert. She was trying to play it down, but Francis could see right through it. The over extension of her smile. The way her fingers were gripping the door handle. The faint smell of food in the air and the stain of red wine on her lips. But the tiredness went deeper. A kind of tired that isn't just physical, but one that goes all the way down to a person's soul.

"Can I help you?" Celine said.

"Sorry for knocking on so late at night," Francis said. "We're looking for Laura Warburton," Francis held eye contact and didn't say another word, letting the silence fill the space between them. People don't like eye contact, certainly not for any length of time. It was something passed down from the animal kingdom when eye contact meant a challenge. A threat. Maintaining eye contact, and not filling silence, were two powerful tactics to get people talking. It made the other party uncomfortable. It was very effective. And Celine was feeling the heat from Francis' gaze, and it was roasting her alive.

"I haven't seen her," Celine said meekly. Francis

furrowed his brow. He pointed to the Audi on the street.

"But that's her car, right there outside your house?" Jeremy was a step behind him, trying to peer past her into the house. The kitchen door was closed, a band of light cutting through the dark.

"Sorry," Celine said. She pinched the bridge of her nose and closed her eyes, shaking her head like she had forgotten what day it was. "I've been asleep. You woke me up. Still a little dazed. It's Laura's car. I haven't seen her properly in months. We were together. It didn't end well." Celine stopped talking, inviting Francis to fill the silence. A natural etiquette between people in a conversation, but Francis offered no such reprise to the quiet void that ensued. He didn't want to quell it. He wanted Celine to choke on it. Francis counted to nine in his head when Celine spoke again. "She was here earlier."

"And?"

"Yes. She came by, banging on the door. She was crying. Said that she needed to talk to me. She sounded drunk."

"Then what?"

"Nothing. I told her to go home and to leave her car here."

"She came to your house drunk and upset and you turned her away?" Jeremy chimed in from behind. Celine's gaze moved to his. Francis kept his eyes trained on Celine, and the sweat that was appearing on her forehead and the quickening of her breathing.

"Do you work with her?" Celine said.

"Yes," Jeremy answered.

"Then you'll know what she's like. She's done this before. She walks to the petrol garage that is open twenty-four hours, grabs a bottle of wine, and drinks it on the way home. She comes back in the morning to collect her car." Celine met Francis' gaze. "That's the last time I saw her." Francis nodded, pursing his lips.

"Laura came by, and you didn't answer, and she left to buy some wine?" Celine nodded.

"Correct." She fingered the door again. "Can I go now?"

"Not just yet," he said, putting his finger to his lip. "If you haven't seen her, then why can I smell food cooking, and why can I smell wine on your breath?" Celine's eyes widened.

"I had a drink myself, and I made some food. Is that a problem?"

"How long ago did she leave?"

"She didn't *leave*," Celine stressed. "She was never *here*. She knocked on, she left." She ran her hand along her scalp. A stress response. "Now, if there's nothing else?" Francis paused and looked Celine up and down. Maybe they had it wrong? They could go to the garage, check the CCTV, and then come back after if the story didn't check out.

"Thank you for your time," Francis said, stepping down from the step. The gravel crunching under his feet. Celine smiled, the door beginning to close.

"Have a nice night."

Francis lunged forward and pushed on the door, barging his way inside. The knife came down on his arm, cutting through his shirt, slicing through the flesh. He let out a fierce wail, grabbing out at the knife that came down at him like a pickaxe trying to smash rocks. Jeremy was there in a flash, slamming his frame into the door, his hand snapping through the gap to grab Celine. She brought the knife down again, slashing in a frenzy.

The glint of the blade flashing from the streetlights outside. It missed Francis' face, carving down the frame of the door. Jeremy grabbed a fist full of her hair, and Celine let out a loud shriek. Francis gritted his teeth, his body in overdrive, and pressed harder on the door, forcing it open where he stumbled and fell onto the ground. Jeremy kept hold of Celine's hair, his fingers locked into place like gripping a live electrical wire. He yanked Celine's head forward, slamming it against the corner of the door, her head splitting open. Celine stumbled back, allowing Jeremy inside. He rushed her, but Celine brought the knife up and slashed through the air, cutting through his jacket and shirt, carving a bloodied gash across his chest. Jeremy cried out in pain. Celine went at him again, the knife overhead like a guillotine about to drop. In a flash, Jeremy tore a picture from the wall, the blade scraping along the golden frame.

Francis pushed the red button on the radio, screaming for help.

Celine stabbed and thrashed, trying to get to Jeremy. The blade cutting through the air wildly like a violent wind made of razors. She sliced along Jeremy's knuckles. The picture crashed to the ground, the glass smashing, crunching under their wild feet like they were trying to crush flaming cockroaches. The blade buried into his shoulder, and Jeremy felt the knife's edge scrape against his bone, a stream of scarlet gushing from the wound. She pulled the knife out and plunged it into his thigh, where red exploded out of it like popping a blood blister. Jeremy crumpled to the ground, his arm, and leg pissing red. Celine rushed again, the knife jabbing towards his throat.

Francis slammed his fist into her jaw, sending a flash

of white lighting across Celine's fury, driving her head into the wall where it rattled. Jeremy tried to crawl away like a bloodied slug on the floor. A smear of crimson under his bulbous form. Celine straightened, bringing the knife in a deadly slash to Francis. He stepped back, then connected his fist to Celine's nose. It explodes in a grenade of blood and cartilage. He pushed Celine away, where she slipped and fumbled on the ice rink of red, slamming ribs into the wall mounted radiator. A cracking of bone. A splintering of ribs. The knife ejected from her hand. Francis pinned Celine against the wall, his hand wrapped around her face.

"Where the fuck is she? What have you done with her?" Celine coughed a thick clump of blood, her teeth cracked and seeped thick jam. Her face split into a smile.

"You're too late." Celine snatched the discarded knife from the floor and lunged forward. She sank her teeth into Francis' cheek so deep she felt her cracked teeth meet in the middle of his flesh. The scream was deafening. She unlatched like a fat leech. Francis rolled back, his hand pressed against the detached flesh, his back meeting the stairwell, and the knife plunging into his stomach.

Chapter Thirty – Five
Laura

The kitchen lights flickered as they came into focus. The stench of iron permeating her nostrils. Breath cracked her deflated lungs into life. Fingers twitched, and Laura Warburton rose back from the precipice of death.

Chapter Thirty - Six
Francis

Jeremy didn't know the human body held so much blood as he watched Celine remove the blade from Francis' stomach, before he fell to the ground, crumpling like a mannequin that had had its cord cut. He struggled to his feet, using his one working arm and leg, slipping, and stumbling with his bloodied hand on the doorframe. He couldn't die here. She moved to him, the knife in her hand. He was going to die. Lying on his back under the blackened sky, choking on his own blood while he gasped for air like a fish that had been left to suffocate on the deck of a fishing boat. Celine moved closer. Her face marred with crimson. Her feet slapping against the floor.

"You don't have to do this," Jeremy pleaded, fighting back the tears in his eyes. He never cried. Never. He had told mothers that their children won't be coming home. He has pulled dead bodies out of destroyed cars. He has watched colleagues die. Never a tear. But the tears didn't find him now because of his own impending annihilation. He was a religious man. Death was simply the next step in this journey. He was crying because the thought of never seeing his wife again crushed his heart like a crumpled crisp packet before it was discarded into the flames. His wife. His beautiful wife. She would get the knock at the door. The one knock everyone dreads may come one day. Two officers standing there with pain on their faces, as they removed their hats and asked to step inside. Celine didn't say anything, her eyes lifeless, void of any humanity. He was pleading with the Devil.

Where is the backup? His mind raced. *Where are the reinforcements?*

"You came to take me away," Celine croaked, resting her body on the banister of the stairs. "I didn't mean to kill him. I didn't mean for it to go this far." Jeremy's burning eyes went wide.

"It was you," he said. "You murdered Alex Weaver." Celine bit down on her lip and nodded slowly.

"You're not useless after all," she sneered.

"But why? Why would you do such a thing? Why would you let Clara be the prime suspect? She hasn't done anything wrong!" Celine said nothing, but lunged for Jeremy, the knife point aiming for his eyes. He released the door and slipped on his own blood, tumbling out into the night. Celine emerged from the black maw of the house. The moonlight dancing on the blade. Her face shrouded in shadow.

"Because I can," she said. "Because murder is easy when you know how to get away with it." Jeremy had a moment of clarity, like the shock of cold water in a black river filled with slippery dead fish. She ran her finger along the blade. "Alex. Laura. They got what they deserved. Users. Abusers. They have their own place in hell waiting for them. Clara was weak. She deserves to burn. As for you two?" Celine pointed the knife to Francis, who was slumped against the staircase, then back at Jeremy. "You two were just collateral. And when I'm done with you," Celine brought the knife to her throat. "I'll be leaving this place along with you." She stepped out into the cold.

"You're insane," Jeremy said, trying to crawl away along the gravel which matted into his open wounds.

"Funny," Celine said, stopping and thinking, like she

had just remembered something funny at a dinner party. "Laura used to call me that. I guess she was right after all." She raised the knife.

"Wait, Celine!" Jeremy called.

"Say goodbye to everything you ever knew."

Jeremy raised his hand, screamed for his God to save him, and slammed his eyes shut.

A sharp splatter of red exploded on his face. She had stabbed him. He knew it. Could feel it. Could feel the knife gouging against his insides. Feel the blade perforating his organs. The blood gushing out of him like a haemorrhaging a fountain of red.

But he continued to breathe. And through the beating of his heart inside his skull, he heard a guttural rattle. He opened his eyes. Celine was on her knees, her eyes wide as blood, thick and clotted. pushed past her lips. A knife blade jutting out from her throat like a shard of exposed bone. She began to shake, her body twitching violently before suddenly stopping and falling to the ground. Laura standing behind her.

"Goodbye…"

Laura released the knife which rattled on the paving. Celine's body swaying, before falling face first into the dirt. Jeremy dove to a knee, just in time to catch Laura as she crumbled, the last bit of her strength vanishing. Jeremy fumbled her with his hands, calling her name, touching the dried blood on her clothing. Her eyes were sunken into her head. Her face was ashen. He had stared into the eyes of the dying before. Had held those poor souls as they took their last breaths. The distance sound of ambulance sirens too far away. The reaper coming to claim them.

He had not cried then. A sort of discombobulation. A disconnect from the surrounding horror. That was what a cop had to do. They had to put on a mask. An act. To react to every terrible thing that they saw in a day's work would drive them mad, and their emotions and empathy drained from them like a vampire. But his eyes were burning now. His lip trembling, as he watched Detective Laura Warburton die in his arms.

"Stay with me," he said. He wondered if she could hear him. Her eyes staring through him, as if looking at something unseen to the rest of the world.

"Get Clara out," Laura croaked, her voice meek. Barely louder than a whisper in the dark. Jeremy absorbed the words, quite possibly the last words she would say. Always thinking about someone else. Dedicated till the last breath to bring justice to the world, and the quell the evil that wished to descend it into chaos.

Jeremy held her as sirens appeared in the distance. The dawn bled through the gloom of the house, but the room seemed much darker than it had been before. He whispered into Laura's deaf ears, willing her to hold on, but he knew that there was nothing he could do.

As the sirens drew closer, and the sun began to rise, Laura Warburton was dead.

Chapter Thirty - Seven
Clara

I remember it now.

She had been there. The other woman. Screaming that I was a whore. That she was the one he should love. She hit me to the head, and I crumpled onto the ground. I watched as she took a knife out of the rack and stab him. He collapsed onto the ground, and she stabbed and stabbed. Blood everywhere. The sharp hit of iron in my nostrils. The song Lavender Haze blaring on the Alexa, until she turned it off. She crouched next to me, her face an inch from mine. Her fingers bloody and dirty. The knife in her hand dripping with his insides. I thought I was next. But she brought her finger to her mouth.

"Shhh," she said, before slipping away, and leaving me in that cold.

I crawled away. Fumbling outside. I found the biscuits I threw away. So hungry. So terrified. And I found the locked gate hidden at the back of the garden. I forced my way out, and then I felt the cold of the pavement as I collapsed.

An eternity passed, and the morning light brought me back from the precipice of madness. I had been destroyed. Violated. Abused, and yet, a new day was on the horizon. The golden light casting away the darkness. Although its light yielded no warmth, I emerged from the shadows of the cell and I bathed in that cold radiance.

The sounds of the custody wing beginning to lessen, like someone turning down the heat of a boiling pan.

Snoring. Screaming. Crying. Turned down like the dial on a radio until it was mute. Like the song went, it's a new dawn. It's a new day. But as the serenity of the day touched me, the weight of it began to crush me. Today was the first day of the rest of my life, and I would spend it locked in a cage like an animal. Just like Alex had wanted. Even in death, he had controlled me until my last breath. Locked in chains like an animal. How much can you beat a dog before it finally bites back? I had bitten back. And now, I was going to be put down for it. I longed for death. Longed for a release from the prison I found myself in. A walled prison. A fleshy tomb. I could pull out my veins with my teeth and finally be free. It was now or never.

Through the sound of distant voices: the clinking of coffee cups. Laughter. Footsteps and heavy doors slamming closed. I heard it. Like a siren song coming through crashing waves on the shore. Like a lost key finally discovered to open the locked box. A familiar song. The melody plucking at my brain.

The song that had been playing. It had been on the tip of my tongue. The only words I could speak, like my voice, had been locked away. *Lavender.* I was hearing it again. But instead of feeling joyful and free, I felt terror. He played that song. He had found me, and he was drawing nearer to me. He had crawled out of the grave. His skin bloated. His eyes eaten by maggots.

The door opened, and blinding light befell me. A figure stood there. A woman. My bones felt like electricity was passing through them. Was it the detective from before? The red head? She would save me. I remembered now. Remembered everything.

But it wasn't her. It was another. Smaller. Thick-rimmed glasses and dark hair. Her eyes are unforgiving.

Her lips were tight. Cruel. She was coming to take me away. Regardless of my plea. Of what I said. It was too late. Alex had won.

"Clara," she said. "My name is DCI Burnell. Come with me," the woman said. Her tone firm, standing in the open doorway to the threshold to a live of the damned. I dared not move. Taking a single step would mean the floor would open up. Geysers of fire burst from the ground and devils with black horns and serrated teeth would drag me into the inferno. I shook my head, pressing my back into the wall. The golden light from the morning dawn protecting me. To move from it would be to allow myself to step into the world of shadow, where I would never see the sun again. Feel the touch of grass on my skin or wind through my hair. A world where the night is king, and we sleep on a bed of bones. "Come on," the woman said, stepping to the side. "I want to talk to you." She turned the song off, and the ensuing silence was deafening. "We have some new information about the case. I believe you have more to tell us." I stopped. My tongue moving. My lips trying to work. Then, a sound I had forgotten for so long slipped past my teeth. My own voice, finally ready to be heard.

"He hurt me," I said, and my legs shook. My eyes started to burn. Through the lump in my throat, I said the words I had always been too terrified to utter. "He hurt me so much."

DIARY

I knew you would come back, and I savoured the sound of your voice in my ear when you did. That you needed my help. After all this time, you still needed me. I put on my best dress. Did my makeup. Even wore the scent which you loved. I would die for you. You know that. I had told you before. My love for you held no boundaries. Transcended time and space. Us meeting was fate. Us reuniting was destiny. The day you left me was meant to be a kind of freedom, but I only felt hallow.

I tried to heal. Oh, how I tried to dig you out of my brain, but I couldn't. You festered and grew like a cancer in my mind. Like you told me that day at the station when I begged for you to talk to me. You called me a cancer, but you are the one that came back. I was in remission, and the more I dwelled on it the more I thought about it, the more I needed to get rid of you for good.

I didn't mean to kill Alex. That wasn't the plan. But as you have seen, things don't always work out the way they're supposed to. The wife was collateral damage. An unintended victim to our love, Laura. How many people are burned when the house sets ablaze? Simple bystanders in our union.

I picked you up, and I knew you wanted me. I would have let you take me there and then, but I had to be sure that this wasn't just a moment of lapse for you. That you wanted me just as much as I wanted you. I wanted to devour you, every piece of you. But you. As I soon found out, were here to use me again. You agreed to a date with me, only to appease me. And you let me sit there alone in that restaurant with a half drank glass of lemonade for two hours. I tried to call you. Tried to message you, but nothing went through. And then you have the audacity, the completely bad manners, to call me again and ask for help.

I decided right there and then. I had killed one person in the name of anger. I would extinguish you in the name of vengeance. In the name of love.

How many bodies would be left in your path before you were stopped? If people only knew who you really were. I would be hailed. Not villainised.

Strychnine is very easy to make if you know how. But I didn't want to make enough to kill you quickly. I wanted it to be drawn out. To make you suffer, so that I could sit there and watch you die.

When you're dead, I'll be sure to leave this place, and leave the sound of your voice to disappear in the wind.

See you soon.

With love.

C x

Chapter Thirty - Eight
Laura
January

Laura arrived back home from the intensive care unit. Her body filled with fresh blood and some stem cells to help repair the nerve damage that had been caused by the poison. She was tough. That's what the doctors had said. She had been minutes from death, and it was only through Jeremy giving her CPR that she managed to stay alive. She supposed that made them even.

They searched Celine's home, and found the diary of her and Alex, and more chillingly, her and Laura. It contained photos of them together, and plans of how to create a slow acting poison that incapacitates at first but kills slowly.

Celine would be cremated in a week. She still had Laura listed as her next of kin. Laura gave the instructions for her send off and then told the director to never contact her again. Clara told everything, and with the verification of her story, basic enquires that had been blocked by Burnell, she was placed into a psychological rehab unit for extreme trauma sufferers. Laura sent her a letter wishing her a fast recovery. She hadn't received one back. But there was time. There was always time.

Christmas came and went. The erected lights and songs on the radio had been stripped away, and a new year was upon the world. Back at the house, Bagpipe welcomed her with a string of meowing. Jeremy had popped in on him, and he was feeling plumper that usual. He had fed him well. Laura took in a sharp intake of breath as she crouched down, dropping her bag of clothes and belongings from the hospital on the ground.

"Hey buddy," she whispered, as his fur ran through her fingers. She fixed him up some tuna steak that she had in the fridge. She needed to go shopping. Laura put on some music and went and took a shower as hot as she could handle. Her body was broken. Her mind in tatters. But that was nothing compared to her heart. Celine. She had loved her deeply. And she had killed her. Self-defence. Justified. Whatever. All the phrases which the bosses had told her to justify not putting her in a custody cell. Jeremy had screamed her innocence. Even Francis, before he collapsed from blood loss and was driven away in an ambulance. Last Laura heard was he was doing okay, but he would walk with a limp for the rest of his life. Celine had done some damage with the knife. Of course, she did. She knew exactly where to cut.

The sun rose and fell, and Laura sat reading a book about a young woman in a futuristic world that was immortal. A glass of juice by her side. The call to get a bottle of wine was overpowering, but she gritted her teeth and took it a minute at a time. The Alexa was playing music softly. *Lavender Haze*, by Taylor Swift. She hated the song, but found it catchy, like almost all pop music. The doorbell went. Laura peered through her blinds. It was Burnell. Laura's stomach tightened. Why the hell was she here? She closed the book and, with great effort, moved to the front door.

"It's late," she said, eyeing her superior with disdain.

"I've come to talk."

"I'm resigning," Laura said. "I have my PSD meeting next week. Now, please." Laura went to close the door, but Burnell placed her hand on the door.

"I haven't come for that," Burnell said. Laura eyed her. Then, like someone welcoming a vampire into their home, held the door open and stood to the side.

"You have five minutes." Burnell stepped along the threshold and admired the décor. The grey walls. The flooring. Even stroked Bagpipe.

"Nice place," she said. Laura walked past her and took a seat at the kitchen bar. She went to the kitchen and pulled out a bottle of beer. The cap twisted with a hiss, and she took a thirsty gulp.

"I thought you were in recovery," Burnell said. Laura eyed her with venom.

"Bite me." She took another drink, sinking half the bottle of Heineken. "It's non-alcoholic."

"Should you even be drinking that?" She said, moving into the kitchen, standing opposite Laura who had her legs folded over and sitting back in her chair.

"What do you want? I'm tired and I want to go to bed." Burnell regarded the empty seat opposite Laura. Hearing no protestation, she pulled it out and parked her arse.

"I wanted to say that I am sorry for how I treated you," she said. "I wanted to tell you that you were right. I was wrong. We found the key to this whole thing, thanks to you. I don't agree with your methods, but they are right about you. You get the job done." Laura sat silently, sipping the beer. She didn't know whether to pour it over Burnell's head, or to wait until she was done, and smash it across her skull instead. "Clara told me everything. About Alex. About what he did to her. Unspeakable, really. How someone can treat another human being like that." She shook her head. "It's unthinkable."

"You'd be surprised," Laura said. "I know coercive control when I see it, and trauma manifests in a thousand different ways. I never got training on it. Not really. I had to learn from firsthand experience." Burnell let the words sink in. She felt like she was being scolded by a teacher at her old all girl high school.

"I know you thought I had an ulterior motive," Burnell said. Laura tightened her jaw.

"It had crossed my mind." Laura could feel the tears burning in her eyes. The lump forming in her throat. "I actually began to think that you had something to do with it. But now I realise you wanted the conviction to further your own career and were willing to do whatever you could to get there." Laura took another hefty swig. The burning of the bubbles was like acid on the ball of agony. "I killed the woman I loved," Laura bit, like a shotgun blast. "Do you know what that does to a person? I have literally given blood for this job. Given everything I have. So don't sit there and pretend that you know it all. What it takes to be a detective. And don't ever question my commitment to finding out the truth." A heavy silence fell between them then. Burnell's face was like stone. Until after a moment, Laura saw it begin to crack. Slowly at first, but then the pieces of the wall started to fall away, and crumbled into dust, revealing a face of pain that was hidden behind the facade.

"I had a daughter," Burnell whispered. Laura felt a stab through the heart, but she stayed silent. Burnell continued to speak meekly. Her eyes beginning to redden. Her hands beginning to tremble. "Hugo Black. I was the lead investigator on that case. One of his partners, the head of a pharmaceutical company, was named Francis Ward. Ward was responsible for strychnine contamination of a batch of cough medicine. My daughter drank that medicine, and she died in my arms. She was eleven." Laura felt the world crushing down onto her. All this time, Burnell had been in pain. It explained the arrogance. The determination. The failure. A pained mother trying to avenge her daughter by putting those responsible away. "Hugo Black and Francis Ward died in the fire at his home. Annabelle Jones was convicted but was murdered in prison. But I later found out there was another silent partner."

"Alex Weaver," Laura said, placing the beer on the bar with a slight tap. Burnell nodded, the pain leaking out of her.

"Alex Weaver was a silent partner in the business of Hugo Black. I didn't intend on being on the case. I was made aware and then I took it. And then I met you, and you know the rest. I got too involved. Too blindsided by my own grief. I caused more pain."

"Hurt people, hurt people." Laura said, barely louder than a whisper. Burnell nodded.

"So," she said, letting out a long breath. "I am going to take a step back. A new DCI will no doubt fill my spot while I get things in order. I'm close to retirement, anyway. One year, three months and fourteen days. Not like I'm counting." Both women shared a gallows laughter. "Which brings me to the next reason I am here." Burnell sat back in the chair, lacing her fingers together. "I don't believe Jeremy is cut out for the leader of the MIU. His leadership is sub-par, shall we say? So, I wanted to offer the position back to you." Laura felt her stomach both leap and churn at the same time. Could she step back up to the mark? Could she take the reins again? She had held it together with murders, CPTSD and alcoholism. But now she was better, wasn't she? Maybe her time to shine hadn't already passed. Maybe it was now? After everything she had been through, maybe it was all a test of her metal. A test of her strength. A baptism by fire.

"I'll let you know in the morning," Laura said, finishing off the beer, and then breaking a smile. "Thank you for being so honest. Thank you for coming by." Both shared a look between them. Nothing needn't more be said. They had said enough.

Burnell left a few minutes later. She had already told the PSD department that there would be no case to answer, and a little leaning on Bennett saw that to be cemented in stone. Laura would resume as the head of the MIU, and entering the new year, she would have full and final say over the way it was run. Jeremy, should he wish it, would resume as her Sergeant, and some new vacancies for DC's would be opened up. Francis would return when his wounds healed. Catherine may even get bored of breaking down doors and drug busts, and help the team once again bring killers to justice. *But that was just wishful thinking*, Laura thought as she went around the house, turning down the lights.

"Come on buddy," she said to Bagpipe, as he raced up the stairs to take his place at the bottom of her bed. Laura got three steps from the top, an agonising effort, and had to have a minute. She was going to hand in her resignation tomorrow. She didn't care what Burnell said. What PSD said. She had enough. The backstabbing and the betrayal. It was weighing on her heart too much and she was struggling to breathe. She needed a fresh start. To leave the police and to move away from the Wigtown for good. Maybe she could sell the house and head to France? Or even America?

Pursue her passion. Do something crazy like become a writer? She laughed. Who the hell would do that?

She tucked herself in bed. Bagpipe snuggling into her legs, and he curled up by her feet. His soft purring filtering through the silence. Laura tried to lay her head down and fall into a slumber, but sleep evaded her. She turned on the television at the end of the bed.

It was breaking news. Wigtown. They had discovered a body. An aerial view of the complex. Empty warehouses. Police tape. Laura hadn't even heard about this. No one had told her. She was so focused on Clara's case that she hadn't known.

She called Jeremy.

"What's going on?" She said. "I turned on the news. There's been a murder?" Jeremy let out a sigh.

"There's been a few Laura. CID have been looking into it whilst we were dealing with the Weaver case. Started finding them while you were in the hospital. But it doesn't matter to you anymore, remember? Enjoy your resignation. You're a great loss. Again, I'm sorry for everything." Laura felt herself torn between running to a new life and being dragged back into hell.

"I'll see you tomorrow," she said. "Tell Francis he still owes me a coffee. He'll know what I mean," then with a giddy tint, added, "and hold the vodka." She put down the phone. She looked at the newsreel. Bodies being pulled out of buildings. Officers and public speaking to the media. Even Bill Bennett made an appearance.

It was clear. Laura couldn't resign yet. She had one more case to solve. And judging by what was happening on the screen, she had her work cut out for her this time.

Will Laura catch this new foe? Or will it be the end of her?

Read book four 'DOWNWARD SPIRAL.'

Head to Amazon – Jay Darkmoore – 'Downward Spiral now!'

Don't want to miss the next exciting story from Jay Darkmoore?

Join his online community and world class newsletters.

It's much more than another boring newsletter.

It's an experience.

Scan below.

If you enjoyed this title, please leave a review. Reviews are how authors get more eyes on their work and helps them make a living out of this insane career choice.

Please. They're coming for my couch.

Jay Darkmoore lives in the Northwest of England. He has a background in crime and investigation and is a huge fan of all things dark and macabre. He enjoys putting his characters in terrifying situations, and then turning out all the lights.

He is the author of horror, thriller, and dark fantasy titles. His inspirations are Stephen King, Keith C Blackmore, and Nick Cutter.

When not at his desk, Jay creates YouTube content surrounding writing, narcissism and coercive control. You can find him in the gym, running through hills with his Springer Spaniel 'Miles,' or taking cold plunges and upsetting the local duck population. They are less than pleased with him.

He is the father to his son 'Joe,' who is his biggest fan.

Printed in Dunstable, United Kingdom